Totally Bound Publishing books by L.M. Brown:

To See the Sky

I0524371

MY BOYFRIEND'S AN ALIEN

L.M. BROWN

MY
BOYFRIEND'S
AN ALIEN

Chapter One

Zakrynious tapped his foot impatiently as he waited for his turn to appear before the elders of his people. The queue to the transformation chamber—the only one on the entire planet of Trimmeron—stretched as far as the eye could see. He'd been standing there for hours and he still couldn't see the doorway at the front of the queue. At least this would probably be the last time he'd have to go through the ritual of transformation. Then again, he'd thought that before.

"What are you hoping for, Zak?" Strathryn, the young Camyl'on directly ahead of him, asked. Zak hadn't met him before today, but they'd been waiting so long Zak felt as though they were old friends. "I want to see what life's like on Marinatia."

Zak laughed loudly, prompting a few glares and admonishments from the others in the queue. "Rather you than me."

"What's wrong with Marinatia?"

Zak shook his head. "Everyone who goes there comes back smelling of fish. Once you've turned mer, there's no way to ever get rid of the stink."

Strathryn snorted back his laughter as the line moved on a few more inches.

Zak had not expected this latest transformation. Already close to maturity when he'd last been brought before the elders, it had been something of a shock to find himself back here once again. He had frequently wondered during the last few days what he would end up as this time. He could discount his own race and those he had already changed into during his puberty, but there were still incalculable possibilities.

As one of a race of chameleon-like beings, each of their kind took on several new appearances during their years of puberty up until adulthood. They remained in their new guises until whatever powers causing the transformations determined them ready to change again.

Zak had spent his last transformation on the icy mountains of Gr'chn and although he had enjoyed his time amongst the hospitable mountain people, he had been eager to rid himself of the coarse, furry hide they had developed so as to more easily endure the harsh climate. He much preferred his own softer furred body.

When Zak had reverted back to his natural state on the previous world, he had expected to have full control over his body and the ability to change appearance at will. When he'd realized he didn't, he had rushed to catch the next spacecraft back to Trimmeron so he could take the potion the elders provided to trigger and ease the next transformation. Luckily Gr'chn was an Alliance world and the locals didn't think anything of the fact that he was suddenly a different species.

He had once asked his father why they had to go through with the transformations. His father had told him the story of one of their youths who had refused to drink the potion to trigger the change to a new form. The transition had come anyway, and had been extremely painful for the youth, so much so that he'd had to be cared for by their healers for several days afterwards. The healers were still working on a way for their healing waters to help anyone else who dug their heels in about taking the potion. Unfortunately, the transformation ritual was shrouded in secrecy and the elders refused to reveal the contents of the potion to anyone. Without the knowledge of the ingredients, the healers were working blindly as they searched for answers.

Finally, after another two hours of waiting, Zak reached the doorway. At least now he could watch those transforming before him, which would help to pass the time.

Zak could see his parents, Aristania and Cor'shi, sitting in the chamber along with family members of some of the other youngsters. He gave them a small wave and they looked back at him proudly. He had barely seen them for more than a few days together since his first transformation. Such was the way things had always been for those of his kind. To enable the youngsters to learn about each form they took, it was customary for each young man and woman to be fostered out to a family on the world native to their new body.

The line crept forward and Zak's turn to stand before the elders finally arrived. He didn't have a great deal to say. The elders had already received their report from his foster parents on Gr'chn, which told them all they needed to know. They had also extracted from him copies of his own memories of his time on

Gr'chn, adding his experiences and knowledge to their collective database.

All Zak had to do now was drink the vile concoction that would trigger his next transformation. He prayed it would be the last time he'd have to drink the revolting substance. When he reached maturity, around the age of forty, he would revert back to his natural form without being in control of the transformation for the last time. If he ever needed or wished to take on one of his other forms, that being any of those he had taken during the years of his puberty, he would be able to do so at will, and without the need of potions.

"Drink up, Zakrynious," the elder said as he passed him the heavy goblet. "Many others await their turn after you."

Zak gulped the lukewarm liquid down as fast as he could and waited for the potion to take effect.

The transformation never hurt, it simply happened. His first clue that the change had occurred was the realization that he stood shorter than he had been a few moments before. Not a great deal shorter, just enough for him to notice he no longer stood eye to eye with the elder before him.

He looked down at his hands and frowned as he observed their new and strange color. Pale ecru and smaller than he had been used to, they also had two more fingers on each hand than his natural form had. He wriggled the extra digits, already anticipating them being a nuisance until he became used to them.

"Well, this is quite unusual," the elder commented. He coughed nervously and looked behind him to the other elders. "I've never seen anything quite like this before."

Zak glanced toward his parents in the audience. They stared at him with expressions of surprise and perhaps a little curiosity. He turned back to the elder and waited for him to tell him where he would be living for the duration of his transformation. Until he knew which galaxy he would be residing in, he had no idea which spacecraft to go to.

One of the other elders stepped forward and peered at him closely. "Most irregular," he mumbled.

"What is it?" Zak asked. "What's the matter?"

"Why, we don't know what you are," the first elder replied. "I don't recall seeing one of those before."

"I thought we always took the forms of races who would play a large part in our lives." Zak looked from one elder to the other, waiting for one of them to explain what had happened.

The elder patted him on the arm kindly. "That's true. Now we just need to figure out what you are, so we can make arrangements for you to be fostered."

Zak nervously shifted on his feet.

"Perhaps we should deal with the remaining youngsters before we try to figure out what he is," one of the female elders suggested.

The elders readily agreed and Zak scurried over to sit beside his parents, where he could wait out of the way of the others.

Eventually the rest of the youngsters had taken their new forms and had left for the ships that would take them to their new, albeit temporary, homes. Many had cast him curious glances when passing him by. When the room had cleared except for his parents and the elders, Zak found himself the center of attention once more.

The very oldest of the elders, who was rumored to be nearly twelve thousand years old, stepped forward with a database access portal in his hands. "Let's see his teeth," he ordered.

Zak opened his mouth so they could look at them. He wondered what they expected to find.

"No fangs," the elder muttered. "We can discount several races with that bit of information."

Zak wondered how long this would take. Although he didn't feel as self-conscious as he had immediately after the transformation, he was far from comfortable being stared at by the half dozen elders as though he had become some sort of experiment.

They continued to poke and prod him for some time to come. Zak let his thoughts drift to more pleasant topics — like dinner — as he waited for them to figure out what in the world he had turned into.

"What's that?" one of the elders suddenly asked, pulling Zak from his wandering thoughts.

Zak looked at the elder who had spoken. He pointed toward Zak's abdomen. Zak glanced down at the front of his robes. The robes were designed to be loose fitting, just in case the wearer's new form was somewhat larger than expected. His robes now engulfed his smaller body, but there seemed to be something extra down below that hadn't been present before.

"Undo your robes," the elder with possession of the database ordered.

Zak, like most of his race, wasn't shy about being unclothed. He disrobed quickly and looked down at his new appendage. He had never seen anything like it before. No form he had ever taken had caused him to grow an extra part to his body just there.

One of the elders reached forward and poked the mysterious protrusion of flesh with a finger. Zak drew in a sharp breath and jumped backward. Never had a touch to his flesh felt like that. A shiver had gone through every part of his body and the rod between his legs seemed to stretch and extend even more.

"It can't be," the elder with the database said as he rapidly tapped the screen, searching for who knew what.

"Can't be what?" Zak asked, drawing his eyes away from the sensitive flesh for only a moment.

The elder ignored him for several minutes before finally giving him his attention. "I believe you may have turned *human*."

Zak had never heard the word 'human' before, but apparently several of the elders had and they gasped in astonishment. Or maybe horror? What was a human and how had this happened?

"Are you sure?" Gandr'ah asked.

"Not entirely. I'll have to check the records for the last time this occurred."

"The last time?" Gandr'ah pulled the elder aside though Zak could still hear their words. "You mean this has happened before?"

"Once, to my knowledge. It must have been around seven hundred years ago. Just can't quite recall the name of the boy who turned human. No one had any recollection of the world humans reside on and the youth was nearly fully mature before he even arrived on the planet. He seemed to enjoy life there. From what I remember, he returned to the place immediately after he reached maturity and hasn't been heard from since."

"Do you think he could still be there?"

"It's possible. Why? What are you thinking?"

Gandr'ah nodded toward Zak. "He needs to foster with someone and if the planet isn't part of the

Alliance, it would be better if he stays with one of his own kind, rather than the natives."

Zak waited as the elders nodded in turn. It seemed his fate had been decided for him, though he still had no idea of the name of the place he was destined to be traveling to.

After more discussions and looking up references, the elders decided Zak would leave for Earth—the rather boringly named planet of the humans—on the next available ship. Since Earth didn't form part of the Alliance, the elders explained that it might take a little while to find a craft going in the right direction.

They had eventually found the name of the only other man to have ever turned human buried in the archives. They'd sent a message to Darresh to let him know to expect Zak's arrival on the planet in the not too distant future.

In the meantime they would take the unusual step of implanting in him the knowledge Darresh had provided to their collective database to prepare him for life on Earth.

* * * *

Two weeks later, Zak said goodbye to his parents and stepped onto the spacecraft. The journey would take around sixteen hours and when he arrived he would be met by Darresh, the only other Camyl'on who had ever taken human form.

Zak watched the holographic entertainment display as the ship took him to Earth. He hoped the music would distract him from the images in his mind. After the elders had used their technology to implant in Zak all the knowledge Darresh had provided them with, Zak had reached the conclusion that humans were little more than animals. He had been far from impressed with what he had seen. Primitive and barbaric were two words that sprang to mind. The idea of turning round and fleeing back home seemed quite tempting. If only running away were one of his options.

Why ever had Darresh wanted to return to the place?

The elders had told Zak a message had been sent ahead of him to Earth, but from what he could see of the human race, it would be amazing if Darresh had survived to receive the news of his impending arrival.

He supposed he was lucky that Darresh had turned human before he himself had, because he didn't know if he could have handled traveling to such an inhospitable world on his own, with no friendly face to greet him.

Chapter Two

Sam Palmer gasped as he watched the bright lights skim slowly across the sky. Through his telescope he had the best view of anyone watching the skies in the local area tonight. Moving too slowly to be shooting stars, the purple blinking orbs were like no aircraft he had ever seen before. Perhaps it was just his inner geek egging him on, but he felt sure he was witnessing a genuine UFO. He slipped his phone from his pocket, and with one eye on the sky and the other on the screen, he phoned Lucy across the other side of town.

"You have the worst timing in the world, Sam," Lucy complained as soon as she answered the phone.

"You're watching them too," Sam guessed. "I've never seen anything like it before. What do you think they are?"

"What are you talking about?"

"The lights in the sky. Isn't that what you were watching when I interrupted you?"

"No. You interrupted me finally getting somewhere with Richard, everyone's favorite stud. Now he's gone wandering off to talk to Trudy."

"Sorry." Sam offered the apology even though he privately thought Lucy was far too good for a conceited arsehole like Richard.

Lucy huffed on the other end of the phone. "Yeah, yeah. So, what's this you've apparently seen?"

Sam's excitement, which had deflated slightly, built again as he described the mysterious phenomenon visible in the night sky. "They're in a perfect formation, going all over the place, kind of circling around the town, almost as though they're waiting for something."

"They're probably coming to take you away to perform all sorts of weird experiments on you," Lucy teased. "I can't believe you think I'd be watching the skies on a Saturday night."

"You used to like watching the stars with me."

"I used to like playing with Barbie dolls too."

Sam laughed. "It's hardly the same thing. This is science!"

"You're the science geek, not me," Lucy reminded him. "Why don't you put away the telescope and come down the pub with the rest of us. We're thinking of getting the late bus into the city and going to a club."

"I don't think so," Sam said.

"Why not?"

"I just don't feel like it."

"Maybe if you got out of your PJs and dressed up a bit you would."

"Who says I'm in my PJs?"

"No one, but I bet you are."

Sam looked down at his favorite T-shirt and ripped jeans. "Not tonight," he smugly replied.

"Then why not come and join us?"

"I don't feel up to it tonight."

Sam could hear the background noise around Lucy fading and he suspected she had gone somewhere quieter before continuing their conversation. "Are you okay?" she asked with concern.

"Just tired," Sam said. "It's been a long week and my mother's in one of her over-protective moods again."

"You can't really blame her."

"I know, but she's doing my head in with it."

"Then come out with us and get out of her way for a bit."

"Maybe next time," Sam suggested as he turned back to the telescope.

"Why not this time?" Lucy pressed on.

"I don't know any of your art crowd friends."

"If you took me up on my offers to come and join us, you could meet them. They're a great bunch."

"I'm sure they are."

"Then why not come with us?"

Sam sighed. Lucy didn't understand. It wasn't the same hanging out with her friends as with his own mates. Unfortunately, all his friends were long gone, moved on without him. "I wouldn't be very good company tonight," he finally admitted. "I should probably get some studying done while I can—else I'll no doubt flunk my exams all over again."

"It's not your fault you didn't get the grades you needed for the course you wanted."

"I was the one sitting the exams."

"Yeah, but you've had a lot to deal with the last few years. You shouldn't be so hard on yourself."

Sam sighed. "Just ignore me. I made the mistake of going on Facebook earlier and saw all my old friends were talking about how great university is, comparing notes on the different ones. It's frustrating seeing everyone getting on with their lives while I'm stuck at the local college and still living with my parents."

"Feeling left out?"

"A bit."

"It won't be long before you're there with them."

"I hope," Sam muttered. "I'm not banking on it."

Lucy's sigh on the other end of the phone echoed his own of a minute before. He should let her get back to her friends before he made her as depressed as himself.

Suddenly, something in the telescope's sights caught his attention. The lights had stopped somewhere over on the horizon. Several miles away and not particularly clear, they appeared to be much nearer the ground than they had been and were coming down even closer. If they really did belong to a spaceship, it had just come in to land. "Oh, my God."

"What is it?" Lucy asked. "Are you all right?"

"I'm fine, but I've gotta go," Sam replied before immediately cutting the call and tossing the phone to one side. His phone rang almost as soon as it hit the mattress and he didn't need to check to know it was Lucy demanding an explanation for his abrupt ending of their call. He ignored the ringing and concentrated on the mysterious activity on the distant hillside. Maybe this sleepy little hamlet was actually being visited by alien guests. Perhaps in the morning he'd wake up to find that the entire population had been replaced like a modern day *Invasion of the Body Snatchers*.

More likely his overactive imagination was supplying drama where there was none to be had.

Still, even after the lights had long gone, disappearing off to the west and out of sight, Sam couldn't seem to shake the feeling that he had witnessed something special.

* * * *

It was raining when Zak stepped out of the spacecraft onto the damp grass. He couldn't see any reason to have such weather here. There were no crops anywhere in sight and the only vegetation was clearly wild. He didn't understand why the humans were wasting their resources by making it rain here when the water could no doubt be put to much better use.

The drizzle also soaked into his scratchy woollen clothes that seemed to retain the water like some form of sponge.

Zak looked around for any sign of civilization. There was no one in sight as far as the eye could see. Cold, soaked to the skin and miserable, Zak felt sure he had been abandoned by the time Darresh arrived to meet him.

"Sorry I'm late," his foster father called as he hurried up the hill that had been the drop-off point. "The elders were rather vague about precisely where you would be dropped off and I was waiting on the other side of the town. When I saw the craft coming in to land, I hurried over here as fast as I could."

Zak shrugged and stomped down the grassy incline. The uncomfortable footwear had no form of grip on the soles and he slid down the damp slope, losing his balance twice during the short walk. "Can we just get out of here?"

Darresh halted his climb and waited for Zak to reach him. "I must say, the message from the elders came as something of a surprise. I've been here over seven hundred years and no one has turned human since I did."

"Lucky me," Zak muttered. "Let's just get this over with and I'll be gone before you know it."

"Hey!" Darresh caught hold of Zak's arm as he stalked past. "I never said I didn't want you here. Just that it's unexpected."

Zak looked at Darresh's hand in surprise and Darresh pulled it back. Apparently Darresh had picked up some strange human habits during his time here, such as touching other beings without their permission.

"Well, I don't want to be here. I don't know why the elders think being shipped off to this barbaric rock is necessary to my life, but I intend to get off of the planet as soon as I can."

Zak continued down the hill to what he assumed was Darresh's vehicle, though the contraption looked like nothing he had ever seen before.

"What's that awful smell?" Zak screwed up his nose as he drew near.

"Probably you can smell the petrol. Your senses are human now, but as you know, for a few weeks after transforming there'll be a residual trace of the powers you have in your own form and on our home world."

"Terrific. How fast does this thing fly?"

Darresh laughed. "It doesn't. This is a car and it travels along the ground on roads."

"You mean there aren't any flying transportation devices here?"

"Yes, but they're only used for long distances. We're not going very far. We'll be there in no time."

Darresh opened the door to the car and waved Zak inside. "Do you have a spare tunic in your pack?"

"Yes."

"You might want to change into it then," Darresh advised. "You'll catch your death of cold if you don't."

Zak took his advice and although it was a struggle to change into the unfamiliar clothing in such a confined space, he finally managed it.

"Just toss your things onto the back seat and we'll be on our way," Darresh said.

Zak did as he was told, then turned his attention to the interior of the vehicle. The dials and panels the other side of the car indicated where the driver sat. He hoped the journey didn't take too long.

Ten minutes into the drive Darresh finally broke the uncomfortable silence that had fallen. "I'm sure you know the natives of this world aren't aware of the existence of life on other worlds."

"The elders made me aware."

"So we thought it best that, while you're here, you pose as my real son. Eleanor—she's my partner—will act as your mother."

Zak turned to Darresh in surprise. "You have a human partner?"

"Yes, and before you jump to any conclusions, she's delighted to have you here too. She's quite looking forward to your stay, in fact."

Zak found that rather hard to believe. "You don't expect me to call you Father, do you?"

"In public and when we have company, it would be best if you did. Or another familial name if you prefer—Dad is commonly used these days. In private you may call me Darren, which is the Earth name I'm going by these days."

"Darren." Zak tested the name on his tongue. It sounded strange and he wasn't sure he had the pronunciation quite right.

"If you look in the glove compartment you'll find some documents you'll need in order to get by during your time here."

"What's a glove compartment?" Zak asked.

Darren took his hand off the wheel and pointed at the small compartment in front of Zak.

The papers inside were covered in gibberish. "I can't read these."

"Ah, yes. That's something I've been working on. You see, the written language here is different to any you've seen before."

"Why don't I have the knowledge from your earlier reports?"

"Because when I was fostered here I never had cause to read. I stayed with a poor family all of whom were completely illiterate. My lessons related to farming and how to survive in this world. Reading wasn't essential back in those days, not like it is today."

"How do you expect me to function on this planet if I can't read the language?"

"Like I said, I'm working on something to help with that. I'll show you when we arrive home."

"So what is this stuff?" Zak gestured to the papers on his lap.

"Mostly it's identification documents. I hope you don't mind, I've shortened your name to Zak."

"No, that's what most people call me anyway."

"Good. Your full name is Zak Johnson."

"What's that other part?"

"Johnson?"

"Yes."

"That's your surname. I know they aren't used on most worlds, but you'll need one here. It's a common enough name and won't draw suspicion."

Zak sighed and put the papers back into the compartment. They were no use to him until he could read the language.

They drove in silence for a few more minutes. Zak suspected neither of them was entirely comfortable with the situation they had found themselves in.

"So, tell me about Earth."

"What do you want to know?" Darren asked easily. "It's not a large planet compared to some of them out there, but there's still an awful lot to learn about the place."

"Do they really eat other living creatures here?" The reports of meat eating had been bothering him ever since the knowledge implant. He had heard there were still planets out there whose inhabitants ate other living creatures, but the civilized worlds had long since discontinued such barbarism. He'd never been fostered anywhere where he'd been expected to eat flesh and he hoped he wouldn't have to do so now.

"Some people do. There are others, vegetarians, who choose not to eat meat."

Zak contemplated Darren's reply for a moment. "Do you eat meat?"

"I used to, when I had no other option. Nowadays I don't, although my partner does."

"I can't believe you took one of the natives as your partner!"

"She's what humans call my soulmate." Darren said the words as though they explained everything. "We joined our life forces on Trimmeron. We're also what humans call married, which makes her my wife and me her husband. You won't know the terms, but they mean virtually the same thing as partner on our planet, just without the ritual of life sharing."

"You share your life with one of the natives?" Zak couldn't keep the shock from his voice. Everything from the knowledge implant indicated that humans were one of the most primitive races in the universe. How could Darren even consider spending his life with one of them?

"That's right."

"But why?"

"Because I didn't want to lose her. Human lives are far shorter than our own. Humans are lucky to live one hundred of their years."

"How long is a human year?"

"Three hundred and sixty-five revolutions of the Earth on its axis. Each revolution is called a day and takes twenty four hours to complete. Earth's days are shorter than ours by a few hours."

Zak nodded. "Three hundred and sixty-five days, got it."

"Well, except every four years when there's an extra day because it's a leap year," Darren amended.

"Huh?"

"Don't ask. I never really understood the calendar myself."

Zak sat quietly and did the calculations in his head. "Are you saying you joined with a native, knowing it would take thousands of years off your own life?"

"That's right."

"Why?"

Darren smiled as he faced the road ahead. "Simple really. I'd rather live five thousand years with my Eleanor than ten thousand years alone."

Zak shook his head. He'd never heard of anything so foolish. The sharing of lives might be a familiar concept—after all, his mother shared her life with a partner—but she didn't do so at the expense of thousands of years of her own existence.

"What else do I need to know to survive here?"

"Well, I suppose you should know about your human body."

"If you mean this annoying rod between my legs that seems to have a mind of its own, I've already noticed the wretched thing. It's rather hard to miss."

Darren laughed loudly. "Oh goodness, I'd forgotten what a shock it was when I first found myself with a cock."

"Is that what it's called?"

"It's one of the names humans have for it. I take it you've figured out what it is by now?"

Zak flushed and turned to look out of the window. Darren sounded amused at something and Zak had a horrible suspicion the joke might be on him. "Yes, I know it's for relieving myself. The elders gave me the knowledge you imparted to the collective database before I came here. I have your memories from your time on Earth before you reached maturity."

"They gave you my memories?" Darren appeared surprised, further confirming to Zak that this was not commonly done.

"Yes, not that there were many of them."

"That's because I was only here for a few weeks before the signs I was about to mature started to appear. At least you have some basic knowledge of this world." Darren turned to grin at him. "As for your cock, you'll no doubt discover it serves more than one purpose. I think you'll figure things out soon enough. Anyway, that wasn't what I was referring to. Your human body is frailer than what you're used to. Once your time here is up, you'll be able to revert back to your own form to destroy any illnesses you might contract, but until you reach maturity, you'll have to do what the humans do if you feel unwell and visit what they call a doctor."

"You mean they still have sicknesses on this world?" Zak couldn't believe they had sent him there if that was the case.

"Of course they do, as do most worlds," Darren pointed out. "Didn't you go to other worlds with sickness during the last few years?"

"Yes, but they made sure to decontaminate everyone I'd be coming in contact with before I arrived."

"You've only been fostered to Alliance worlds before now?"

"Yes."

"That explains it. However, since Earth isn't part of the Alliance, I'm afraid decontaminating the locals would be rather impractical, so you'll have to make do with the doctors if you become ill. You might also find yourself prone to injuries as well, especially until you're accustomed to your new body. The doctors on Earth aren't anywhere near as advanced in their methods as the healers on our world who tend to the injured, but I'm afraid you'll have to make do. Hopefully you won't end up with any broken bones during your stay here."

"This just gets worse and worse."

"You'll get used to your human body soon. You seem to have won the genetic lottery when you transformed."

"What do you mean?"

"You're pretty well built for your age, probably stronger than other teenagers and quite good-looking."

"Teenagers?"

"Those who are aged thirteen to nineteen on Earth are often referred to as teenagers. Teen age—get it?"

Zak felt rather dense as Darren explained the name to him. "But I'm forty."

"In our terms, yes. But you can't pass for human forty in your current body. To Earthlings you look about nineteen, maybe a little older, so that's what I've put on your papers."

"What else?" Zak asked, somewhat dreading the answer.

Darren paused a moment or two as he seemed to gather his thoughts. "I've stocked the bathroom at home with some basic medicines and a first aid kit for minor injuries. You'll find some other stuff in there too."

"Such as?"

"Just things you'll need. Toothpaste, razors, aftershave, stuff like that. I'm sure you'll figure out what's what soon enough."

"What do you do on Earth, or am I supposed to figure that out for myself too?"

"I normally teach history at a university in the south of England—that's the country we're living in. But for the next year I've relocated and will be teaching at the local college you'll be attending."

"What's a college?"

"It's kind of like a school, but the education offered is for older students and adults."

"School? You aren't serious? I finished that sort of education before my first transformation took place!"

"Well, I've news for you, Zak—you're going to college, at least for the duration of the courses of the subjects you're going to be studying."

"What could anyone on this primitive rock have to teach *me*?"

"I think they may surprise you," Darren replied.

"I thought I'd be learning how to ride horses or use the native weapons. That's what you put in your reports. Even fighting sounds better than this college."

Darren shot him a smug look and chuckled. "Fighting is one thing I hope you won't be doing. You'll find the locals view such activities as rather *primitive*."

Zak rolled his eyes as Darren turned his own words back on him. "The elders never said anything about this."

"That's because times have changed on this world. You won't need to learn the art of swordplay here. Things are much more civilized than they were back when I came here."

Zak groaned. He hadn't exactly relished the thought of learning about human weapons and how to fight, but the idea of sitting in some classroom was even less appealing. He couldn't believe he was being forced back into education. If humans, with their stupidly short lifespans, were still in education at nearly twenty, he didn't see much hope for the race at all.

* * * *

Darren passed Zak a strange piece of equipment that Zak looked at blankly.

"This is a translator to help you get accustomed to the language."

Zak pushed the device back across the table. "I already know the language, thanks. That's what the knowledge implant was for."

"The knowledge implant gives you all the information about Earth that was extracted from me seven hundred years ago shortly before I reached maturity. It's out of date now. It's a shame only those who haven't reached adulthood can have knowledge extracted and implanted. If it were possible, I'd try to update you. Unfortunately, this is the best option."

"Is it absolutely necessary?"

Darren gave him an annoyed look. "Okay, have it your way. You think you don't need this, so tell me, what would you do if I asked you to get the phone?"

Zak frowned as Darren switched from their native tongue to English. He could tell he had asked him to get something, but the word phone was entirely unfamiliar. He had no idea what Darren wanted him to do.

"See what I mean?" Darren said. "Seven hundred years ago phones hadn't been invented, so the knowledge implant can't tell you what it is I'm asking. Now put on the translator."

Darren helped him place the translator behind his right ear. "I've designed it to look like a hearing aid, a device used by the hard of hearing here on Earth. That way no one will notice it. Now I'll ask you again, can you get the phone?"

With the earpiece fitted Zak immediately noticed the difference. It didn't translate every word, but when Darren said phone, the translator told him it was a communication device.

"I've been adding to the translator's vocabulary as much as I can, but there are so many words, I'm sure I'll have missed a lot. I've added lots of words for modern items, many of which you'll find around the house, so we'll go through them to give you a visual."

"Okay," Zak agreed, wondering just how many things these primitive people could have invented in a mere seven hundred years.

Darren smiled at his compliance. "The other issue you're going to have, as you already realized in the car, is the written word."

"You said you had something to help with that."

"Yes." Darren passed him a second item, this one even stranger than the last. "These are glasses. Humans sometimes wear them to correct their vision if their eyes aren't working properly."

"My eyes work just fine."

"I know that, but these are special. Here, put them on like this."

Zak let Darren place the glasses on his face, balancing them on his nose and ears. "I don't see any difference."

Darren grabbed a book from the shelf behind him and opened it at a random page. "Okay, take a look at this and tell me what you see."

Zak looked at the page and frowned in confusion. "I just see the strange Earth language. Was something supposed to happen?"

Darren reached across the table and did something to the edge of the right lens and suddenly Zak could see writing in his own language hovering over the English version.

"You'll still have a lot to learn to bring your reading and writing up to speed, but these should help. I'd suggest working quickly over the next week."

"Because I've still got some residual abilities from my true form?" Zak guessed.

"Exactly. You can learn vast amounts of information in a short period of time and I'm hoping the lingering effects of that, as well as having recently been on Trimmeron, will help you learn the language nice and quickly."

Zak wasn't so sure and something about his expression must have given him away.

"You should find it pretty easy. English only has twenty-six letters in the alphabet. All words are made up of those."

"Only twenty-six?"

"Yes. Nothing like our own two hundred and fifty. You could probably learn English without any additional technology given a bit of time."

"Then why make these things?" Zak asked.

"Well, for one thing, we don't have much time before you have to be in college. You need to be fluent in English by next week or you'll really struggle. For another, this way will be easier for you."

"Is this how humans learn new languages?" Zak asked, impressed despite himself that the race had this sort of technical know-how.

"No, this is how they learn languages on Pry'nah."

"You were fostered there?"

"Yes. It came as a bit of a surprise to be sent to such an advanced world. I don't know who was more astonished, me or the elders. I often wondered why I'd been sent there, especially after I decided to settle here on Earth. Now I know why."

"Because you needed to know how to produce these for me," Zak concluded.

"Yes. I'm just glad I remember what they taught me there. It was so long ago I'm surprised I recall a thing."

Zak was quite relieved that Darren had remembered his Pry'nah lessons. Learning English would be a struggle, and without the devices Darren had just provided to him, Zak was pretty sure he'd never have been able to manage it in a week.

"Now, how about you come and meet Eleanor?" Darren suggested. "She's been eager to welcome you, but I wanted to set you up with these right away, to give you as much time as possible to get used to how they work. I think the best way for you to learn will be to just dive right in, so from now on we're only going to speak in English. You have enough from the implant to get by, so you should be fine."

Zak wasn't so sure. The translator speaking in his ear had been suspiciously quiet during most of Darren's speech, only occasionally giving him a little help.

* * * *

Eleanor was nothing like Zak had expected. Small and slim, the petite woman flew into the room like a hurricane and pulled Zak into a tight hug. Zak stood stiffly in her embrace, entirely unused to such exuberance. His own people never acted in such a manner, always politely reserved and aloof.

"I'm so happy to have you here," Eleanor gushed as Zak tried to draw in a breath. "Darren's told me all about you."

"What could he have said?" Zak asked suspiciously, his tongue tripping over the words as he struggled to speak in the strange language. "He's never met me before tonight."

"He's told me enough to know you're the first of your race to be fostered to Earth since he came here and made it his home. I hope you'll come to enjoy being here as much as Darren does."

Zak made a non-committal sound while privately doubting he'd ever return to Earth once his period of fostering ended.

Eleanor ushered Zak into the dining room where a feast of food had been spread out for him. He didn't recognize even half of the dishes.

"Darren told me you were likely to be a vegetarian like him, so I made all vegetarian dishes for your welcome dinner."

"Are you sure you cooked enough?" Darren teased. "You do realize not everyone has my healthy appetite."

Eleanor laughed and took a seat, patting the chair next to her for Zak to sit in. "We'll just have to live on the leftovers for the next week."

"Or three," Darren amended with a grin. "Come on, Zak, tuck in. I'm sure you're hungry after your trip. I doubt in-flight food has improved any in the last seven hundred years."

Zak wasn't sure where to start. He decided to play it safe by grabbing some of the fruit, which he at least recognized as having been common on Earth back when Darren had first arrived.

Eleanor nodded in approval and pointed at a dish down the far end of the table. "If you like apples, the crumble there is made of cooked ones."

Zak decided to try that next.

Eleanor and Darren chattered away as they enjoyed the meal. Zak remained mostly quiet, only answering direct questions. He felt self-conscious using this strange language, although neither Darren nor Eleanor made any comment on his fumbling attempts at English. He quickly found whilst it was one thing to have the knowledge, it was quite another matter to put it into practice. His brain knew what to say, but his tongue didn't seem to want to cooperate.

Outside, the sky began to lighten and the world's single sun rose for the day.

Eleanor followed his gaze to the window. "I should explain that most of this isn't what you'd call breakfast food, but since none of us went to bed last night, I guess it doesn't matter."

"Teaching Zak bad habits," Darren teased. "Not to mention making him think you do all the cooking round here."

Eleanor sniffed haughtily, though her eyes sparkled with mischief. "You're just jealous because I'm the one with the talent in the kitchen. It took you nearly a hundred years to figure out how to bake a simple loaf of bread."

Darren and Eleanor's banter was quite amusing to listen to, but after the long journey and barrage of information, tiredness had caught up with him and Zak couldn't quite stifle his yawns.

"I'll show you to your room," Eleanor said. "We're not quite moved in properly yet, but your bed has been set up. Tomorrow we'll go buy you some more clothes. The ones you're wearing are a little out of date. I'm sure I can adjust something of Darren's just for tomorrow, but I expect you'll want to pick your own clothes."

Zak looked down at the breeches and tunic the elders had given him to wear. The knowledge implant had told him they were similar to the ones Darren had worn during his fostering. He guessed he should be wearing something a little more like Darren's clothing. He readily agreed to the shopping trip Eleanor had suggested. He didn't want to stand out amongst the Earthlings any more than he had to.

"The elders didn't have any Earth currency for me to bring," Zak said as he followed Eleanor out of the room.

"Don't worry about money. Darren and I have it covered."

"Covered?" Zak frowned in confusion, his translator failing him as he tried to reconcile in his mind the words Eleanor had said with what she meant.

"We have plenty of money," Eleanor amended. "There'll be more than enough to buy you a suitable wardrobe."

Eleanor disappeared through the door, closing it behind her.

Zak found himself alone for the first time since Darren had picked him up on the hillside. The first thing he did was remove the glasses and the translator, tossing them carelessly onto the bedside table. How could the elders have sent him here with no thought of how he would struggle to learn the language?

Forgetting that Darren had arrived on Earth seven hundred years ago with no idea of the language at all, Zak huffed and complained to himself as he readied himself for bed.

Earth was strange and Zak had never felt more out of his element than he did right now.

Chapter Three

Zak had spent a week with the Johnsons, trying to figure out everything he needed to know to survive at college. The worst part was the language difficulties.

"How can a language have changed so much in seven hundred years?" he complained in his own tongue.

Darren shrugged. "I'm afraid it has and you'll have to learn it as best you can."

Zak fiddled with the translation device. "This thing is so uncomfortable."

Darren took the contraption off him, adjusted it slightly and passed it back. "Better?"

Zak placed it back behind his ear and nodded. "A bit. Is it really necessary?"

"I'm afraid so, at least for a little while. You won't have to wear it forever—just until you're caught up on the current English language."

"I still don't think I'm ready to interact with other humans yet," Zak said. "I can barely communicate with your wife."

Darren snorted. "You communicated with her just fine yesterday evening, though I'd appreciate it if you didn't speak to her in the tone you used or swear at her in our native tongue. What was that all about anyway?"

Zak cringed as he recalled the argument with Eleanor the night before. He didn't know what had gotten into him when she had asked him for the third time to do something the translator hadn't been able to help him with. His frustration had caused him to raise his voice in anger for the first time in his life.

"Well?" Darren prompted.

"Nothing."

"It didn't sound like nothing from where I was standing. In future, please remember for as long as you're here, Eleanor's your mother and if she asks you to do something, you will."

"I couldn't understand what she asked me."

"I know for a fact Eleanor is perfectly able to communicate any requests to you so you understand them. When I first arrived here on Earth it was Eleanor who helped me learn the language, and without the assistance of any off-world technology. She has vast amounts of patience and is quite remarkable when it comes to getting her point across. If you ask her nicely, instead of yelling, you'll find her most helpful."

Zak kept his opinion to himself, though he felt the unfamiliar urge to argue once again. Was it a human thing? He recalled that Darren's reports of his time on Earth had included lots of fighting and hoped it wasn't a sign of things to come. He pushed the unsettling thoughts from his mind and flicked through one of the books Darren had passed to him a short while ago. "Do I really have to go to college? I can't even speak the language yet."

"It might help if you tried to use English."

"It isn't my fault the knowledge implant's out of date."

"No, it's not, but that's what the translator is for. Now, get your things together or we're going to be late."

"You can't expect me to go to college if I can't understand the language."

Darren grinned. "Yes, I can. Now hustle."

Zak frowned as the translator buzzed in his ear, providing a translation for Darren's last word. "You switched to English?"

"Yes, now hurry up."

Darren seemed to have switched languages permanently. He strolled to the front door, gesturing for Zak to follow.

"I won't be able to drive you to college every day," Darren explained. "But for your first day I thought it best not to risk the bus."

"Where is this college?" asked Zak, having no recollection of having seen one in his brief explorations of the small village Darren and Eleanor lived in.

"It's in the nearby town, the same one where Eleanor took you shopping. It's not far, about half an hour's drive in rush hour traffic. The bus into town picks up at the end of the road and goes right past the college. I'll point out the stops on the way so you'll know where to get on and off tomorrow."

Zak climbed into the car and Darren passed him a sheet of paper. "What's this?"

"Your timetable."

"Great," Zak muttered, stuffing it into his backpack with barely a glance at the foreign script.

"Normally students choose their own A Levels, but in the circumstances I've picked them for you."

"And what exactly are A Levels?"

"They're a grade of lessons in this country. Most students take them when they're seventeen or eighteen years old and still in school. But many people choose to do them later in college and I think they'll be a good starting point for you. If anyone asks why you didn't take them last year just tell them you did different subjects, but you wanted to do some more before attending university. Maybe say you haven't made your mind up what you want to do at university yet and that you're furthering your education in the meantime."

"And what do I tell them if they ask about these subjects I already did?"

"Tell them you were concentrating on the science subjects. Our world is far more advanced in all forms of science than Earth is, so you should be able to put up a convincing performance if you're asked anything specific."

"I take it that means I'm not going to be studying Earth science?"

"No. You'll be doing History, which will give you a good idea of how this world has evolved over the years."

"And will give you the chance to keep an eye on me."

"Yes, there's that too. You're also doing English Language and Maths."

"I already know how to do mathematics."

"I know you do. Earthlings use base ten the same as us so you should find the subject easy enough to handle. I don't want to load you down with subjects you'll find difficult, but if you're here on Earth for any length of time you'll need to at least have some legitimate qualifications."

"How long is it until I get these qualifications?"

"You'll sit exams at the end of the course and if you pass them you'll have the A Level qualification for each subject."

"Exams too? Terrific! And I thought the translator was supposed to teach me English?"

"The lessons at college are different from what the translator does – you should find they help you catch up."

"Don't I get to do any fun classes?"

"I thought three A Levels would be enough for you, particularly as most of the subjects have entry requirements that I can't conjure up for you at a moment's notice."

"What do you mean?"

Darren stopped the car at the lights and leaned over to the glove compartment. He pulled out a booklet, which he passed to Zak. "This is the college prospectus. You'll see the subjects I've put you on have required GCSE grades, which you don't have, since you never sat those exams. I faked them for you, just like I did your identification papers. You have to remember I've had limited time to set things up, so I just gave you enough qualifications to do the subjects I've enrolled you on."

"Why not just let me hang around at the house for a few more weeks while you make up the other qualifications too?"

"Because not all of them are as easy as a bit of paper and ensuring if anyone checks up on you they find you on the national database. Some of the art courses, for example, require you to have a portfolio of your work. I can't put one of those together."

"Eleanor could," Zak pointed out. "She's an artist, isn't she?"

"Yes, but she isn't going to do that for you. It would be obvious as soon as you started the course that the work in the portfolio wasn't your own."

"So? I'm sure I'd catch up easily and my artistic skills aren't too bad."

"Zak, you have to understand, what I've done by faking your papers and grades is against the law. In the circumstances it's also rather necessary, but I'm not going to give you any qualification you ask for. If you want any more than the ones I've given you, you're going to have to work for them."

"I'm surprised you didn't just make me sit the earlier exams."

"I considered it, but this college only offers a limited number of GCSE courses and they're aimed at those who have already done the work in school and just didn't get the grade they wanted. You also have to be assessed for entry and I don't think you're ready for that yet."

"I don't think I'm ready to go to college at all," Zak grumbled under his breath. "Doesn't seem to stop you dragging me there."

"You're perfectly capable of keeping up with the subjects as long as you work hard and I'll do my best to help you as you learn the language."

Zak huffed and stared out of the car window.

Darren sighed and shook his head. "If you start out thinking you're going to hate it, you probably will. Why not look at it like an adventure?"

"That's easier said than done."

"Well, was there anything you were looking forward to when you received the implant about Earth?"

"The horses sounded interesting."

"Would you like to learn to ride one?"

Zak sat up straight. "Can I?"

"If you like."

"Today?"

Darren shook his head. "Sorry, there aren't any horses at the college. But if you concentrate on your lessons and keep up with the rest of the class, we'll see about introducing you to Eleanor's horses one weekend."

"Eleanor still has the horses?"

"They aren't the same ones you'd have seen in my memories, but yes, she still keeps some. She prefers to ride them around our estate down south, rather than drive one of the vehicles. In some ways she likes the old fashioned way of doing things, and far prefers horses to cars. We'll make sure you get to see her babies before you leave. She'll know doubt enjoy having someone to talk to about them. I've never had much fondness for the beasts after one of then kicked me where it hurts after it got spooked by a wild boar and bolted."

Zak wasn't sure he liked the idea of meeting Eleanor's horses after all.

"Come on, cheer up," Darren encouraged. "You might even enjoy college if you give it a chance."

Zak turned back to the window. His stomach felt as though it was tied in knots. He didn't recognize the feeling at all. Maybe he would enjoy college if he was more comfortable with the language everyone would be using. Instead he felt like he was in way over his head.

* * * *

Lucy slipped into her customary seat across from Sam. "Check out the stud over in the lunch queue," she whispered with a nod toward the young man in question.

Sam grinned as he took a bite of his sandwich. "Already seen him."

"What?"

"He's in my Maths class. Just started today actually."

Lucy looked at him expectantly. Sam knew what she was waiting for, yet he couldn't resist teasing her. "Sam!"

"Yes?"

"Well, who is he? Is he single?"

"How the hell would I know?"

"You could have asked him."

Sam snorted and shook his head. "I'm not going to go up to a new student on his first day and ask if he's single."

"Well, did you at least get his name?"

"Yes."

"Sam, stop teasing. What is it?"

"Why do you want to know?" Sam asked innocently. "Wanting to see if his surname sounds good after Lucy?"

"No."

Lucy sat back in her seat and folded her arms across her chest. Her glare had made lesser men quake in their boots. Sam, however, was made of sterner stuff and took a drink before he decided to put her out of her misery.

"His name's Zak Johnson."

"Johnson?"

"Yeah, what's the matter?"

"I had to go the admissions office this morning and overheard someone talking about a new History teacher starting today," Lucy explained. "Apparently Ms Foster was called out of town on some family emergency. The new teacher's a Mr Johnson. I wonder if they're related or something."

"Maybe. It's a bit of a coincidence for a new teacher and student to start here on the same day with the same name and there not be a connection."

Lucy nudged Sam with her shoe. "He's coming this way. Why don't you invite him to join us?"

"Why don't you?" Sam countered.

Lucy looked across at Zak and gave a dreamy sigh that turned into a disappointed one when he turned away from them and took a seat at a table near the entrance to the cafeteria. "Oh, isn't he gorgeous?" Lucy cooed. "He's to die for."

"Don't go all *Romeo and Juliet* on me. No one is worth dying for."

"Zak is. Just look at him."

"He doesn't look so special to me," Sam lied. With blond hair just a shade too long and a lean, fit body, he was certainly drawing stares from the other students. No one seemed to want to approach him, perhaps because of the scowl that seemed to be permanently etched on his face, marring his lovely features. Zak toyed with his food in between casting baleful glances around the room. Sam couldn't seem to stop himself gawking at him and when Zak caught him watching he still couldn't look away. The piercing blue eyes behind stylish metal-rimmed glasses seemed to sear right into his soul. He offered the new student a tentative smile. His heart rate sped up when Zak's frown vanished to be replaced with a small smile of his own.

Lucy didn't seem to notice Sam's preoccupation, but had spotted Zak looking in their direction. She gave a small wave and her hand in Sam's line of vision drew his attention away from the new student.

"When's your next Maths class?" Lucy asked after Zak had turned back to his lunch.

"Tomorrow afternoon," Sam replied. "Why?"

"Last period?"

"Yes."

"Perfect!"

"Why is it perfect?"

"You can ask him if he wants a ride home with us."

Sam laughed. "You do realize he might not live anywhere near either of us."

"I don't care. Just make sure you don't let him get away."

Sam groaned. "Oh, dear God, here we go again. Have you forgotten Richard already?"

Lucy couldn't seem to take her eyes off Zak. "Richard who?"

Lucy continued to rattle on about Zak though Sam was only half listening. He couldn't shake the feeling that maybe Lucy was going to find herself disappointed if she set her sights on Zak. The look on his face when their eyes had met had sent shivers down Sam's spine. He wasn't entirely sure, but he had a feeling that Zak's tastes didn't run toward females. He hoped for Lucy's sake he was wrong, even as he hoped for his own that his instincts were right.

* * * *

Zak had already suffered through his first two classes of the day. Actually he'd only attended half of the first lesson since Darren had taken him to the admissions office at the start of the day to get him a map of the college and fill in some paperwork. He'd eventually arrived at his first class when it was part way through and had endured the stares and snickers of the other students as he'd stumbled across the room, tripping over his own feet as he tried to navigate his way between the desks.

He had attempted to take notes, but had struggled to grasp the pen in his clumsy human hands. He cursed his own laziness since his arrival on Earth, wishing he had practiced his writing skills for more than a few minutes. He had foolishly thought that if he could hold the pen the right way that would be sufficient. He'd had no idea the classes would require him to take notes so fast. His frustration had increased as the morning had progressed.

Then he'd followed the crowd to the college cafeteria where he'd eaten some revolting slop they called a meal, at a table on his own.

Now he was trying to find his way to room fourteen, only all the corridors looked the same and he was completely lost. He had a feeling he'd left the map of the college in the cafeteria, but he had no idea how to find his way back there to check. He caught sight of a youth looking at him and decided the best way would be to ask someone directly.

"Hello," he said. "I'm new here. Can you show me to room fourteen please?"

"Are you yanking my chain?"

Zak looked at the young man in confusion. His knowledge implant told him what a chain was, but he couldn't see one hanging from the youth in front of him. "What chain are you talking about?"

"Maybe he's some sort of village idiot," one of the other boys suggested. "He can't even find what's right under his nose. Room fourteen is right behind you, you thick tosser."

Another boy, this one big and beefy, gave him a hard shove in the shoulder as he pushed his way past. "Watch out," he snarled at Zak.

"Loser," another boy snickered.

Zak wasn't an idiot, but he certainly felt like one today. He was vastly unprepared for this place. Everything seemed so strange and, well, alien. He had been to school on his own planet, but it was nothing like this. The Trimmeron establishment had been filled with students who wanted to learn the ways of the world, master practical tasks and go on in life with the knowledge they needed to survive. They helped each other and everyone felt welcome and happy to be there. Here, everyone seemed to know what they were doing already and no one seemed inclined to assist those who were in difficulty. Zak suspected it would be a miracle if he made it out of the college alive.

He decided to skip his next class and track down Darren in his office instead. Maybe he could convince him that college was a bad idea and they could find some other way for him to learn about the people of Earth.

* * * *

"This translator of yours is shit," Zak complained as soon as the door slammed behind him. "It doesn't tell me anything useful."

Darren waved him to a seat. "It's a work in progress. You have to remember I've been on this planet a long time now. I've learned the language as I've needed to. In fact I've learned a great number of the human languages. But I've only had a few weeks to work on putting the translator together for you. It's never been tested before since there's no one here I can test it on, not even myself."

"Well, it's crap."

"Clearly it's not doing too badly, since your language is getting much more colorful compared to the words I put into it."

"I didn't need the translator for that word. Someone at the table next to me at lunch used crap to describe the cafeteria meals, if that's what they're supposed to be. I didn't need a translator to tell me what it meant. It was clear from the moment I tasted the stew."

"You had stew?"

"Yeah, why?"

"Oh nothing, just that it contains meat."

Zak's stomach rolled. "You're joking?"

"No, I'm afraid not. But since you didn't come in here to talk about the food, can I ask what it is you're having difficulties with?"

Zak slumped back in his chair. "Where do I start? I can barely work my hands any more with all these extra fingers."

"You'll get used to them. It's just a matter of adjusting."

"I don't want to get used to them. They're a nuisance."

Darren sat back in his seat and smiled. "And what do you suggest I do about this problem? It's not like I can whip up a potion to transform you into something else. Only the elders have that technology. You have a human body and you're going to have to learn to cope with it."

"I hate it. It doesn't do what I want it to. My coordination has never been this bad."

"Surely you've taken other forms far more different from our own than this one is?"

"I'd rather my body was completely different. That'd be easier than this."

Darren appeared as confused as Zak felt. "What do you mean?"

Zak clutched his head as he tried to gather his thoughts. "It's like my balance is all shot to pieces. I can't get used to being without my tail."

"You don't need a tail to keep your balance."

"Then why do I keep banging into things and tripping over my own feet?"

"Because you haven't been doing much walking since you got here," Darren suggested calmly.

"When have I had time for going walking? I've spent most of the last week trying to get familiar with the language."

"I know you have." Darren looked thoughtful for a moment or two. "Maybe we should have left college for another week or two."

"Then you admit I was right?" Zak asked.

"I said maybe. The problem with putting it off for longer is that you'd have to catch up on even more work than you already do."

"Can I go home and come back in a week or two?" Zak asked.

Darren shook his head. "You're enrolled now and I think it best you get used to it. Since I've started work today I can't be at home with you to help you adjust to being human. At least while you're here at the college

I'm nearby. Besides, I'll bet in a few weeks you'll be running around like any other lad your age."

"What makes you so sure?"

"I remember my first days on Earth being filled with clumsy mishaps. I promise they won't last forever."

Zak couldn't tell if Darren was telling the truth or simply saying what Zak wanted to hear. "Can't you make me some Earth medicine to help?"

Darren quickly covered up his chuckle. "I wish it were that simple. Only time will help you get used to your human body. Now, shouldn't you be in class somewhere?"

"I couldn't find the room," Zak muttered, without bothering to mention that someone had pointed the room out to him and if he had looked a little harder he'd have found it himself.

"I gave you a map this morning — all the classrooms are clearly marked on it."

"I lost it."

Darren pulled open a drawer and pulled out his own copy of the map. "Here, take mine. I'll get another from the office."

"Thanks," Zak said as he stuffed it into his backpack.

"Anything else?" Darren asked. "Only you're already late for your lesson and you don't need to fall any further behind than you already are."

Zak wondered whether he should say anything about the other thing that was troubling him to Darren or not. His foster father seemed to like the people of Earth.

"Zak?"

"Is everyone here on Earth rude and unpleasant?" he finally asked.

"Of course not. Has someone been rude to you?"

"Just a few students who I asked for help finding a room."

Darren smiled and shook his head. "I'm sure they're the exception and not the rule. You'll find most people are quite helpful, if you give them a chance."

While Zak wasn't sure if he believed him, he didn't feel like arguing with him. He'd find out soon enough whether all students were like the ones he'd met so far. He stood up to leave the room when he remembered he had one more question. "What does yanking a chain mean?"

Darren, who had already turned back to his paperwork, looked up to answer. "Oh, that's a way of asking if someone is joking. Are you kidding me? Are you yanking my chain? And a whole load of others. They all mean pretty much the same thing."

"Thanks," Zak muttered as he let himself out of the room. So many words for the same thing. This was going to take quite some time to get used to, if he ever did.

* * * *

Sam sat on the wall outside the college, waiting for Lucy to drive round from the student car park and pick him up. Across to his left, Zak Johnson headed in his direction. Maybe Lucy wouldn't have to wait until tomorrow to offer Zak a ride home.

Zak was, undeniably, the best-looking boy Sam had ever laid eyes on. His loose shirt didn't hide his fine body and Sam wondered if the student had been on any of the athletic teams in school. He certainly had the physique for sports.

Sam kept one eye on Zak as he approached, trying to watch without being obvious in his staring.

"Hey, Zak," Sam called as he approached. "How was your first day?"

Zak looked at him in surprise before he walked over to him and gave him a hesitant smile.

"I'm Sam," Sam said as he held out his hand for Zak to shake. When the other boy didn't take it he drew back awkwardly.

"You were staring at me in the lunch room," Zak said.

Sam blushed. "Sorry."

Zak shrugged and started looking around him as though searching for someone.

"Well, see you in Maths tomorrow," Sam said as he prayed for Lucy to hurry up and save him from dying of embarrassment.

Zak turned back to him. "You're in one of my classes?" he asked.

"Yeah. Maths with Miss Randall."

Zak nodded and sat down on the wall beside Sam, still gazing around the bustling hordes as they scrambled for their cars and the buses.

"Looking for someone?" Sam asked.

"My dad," Zak said. "He's supposed to be meeting me after classes to take me home."

Sam pointed over to the lay-by. "Rides and taxis usually pick up over there."

"My dad's inside," Zak explained. "He teaches History here, and is making me take the subject."

"You're in your dad's class?" Sam cringed at the thought of being in a class taught by one of his parents. As over-protective as his mother was, at least he could escape when he came to college for the day.

"Yeah."

"That must suck."

Zak frowned in confusion. "Suck?"

Before Sam could reply, Lucy was pulling up and pipping at him. "Come on, Zak, let me introduce you to my friend Lucy. She's going to give me a ride home. I'm sure she won't mind dropping you off as well. You can send your dad a text to let him know."

Zak looked a bit confused, but he followed after Sam.

Sam, with his typical clumsiness, tripped over the edge of the curb and Zak grabbed his arm to steady him. Sam's heart rate increased at the touch. This was not good. Zak wasn't necessarily gay and Lucy had already declared her crush on the new student. What sort of a mate would he be if he were to hit on the object of his best friend's affection?

Zak climbed into the back of the car with Sam and pulled out his mobile phone. How did this thing work again?

"What's the matter?" Sam asked. "Will your dad mind you not waiting for him?"

"No. I just can't remember how to send a text message."

"How can you have forgotten how to send one?" Lucy asked with a laugh. "I must text at least a hundred times a day."

"When she should be listening in class," Sam added. "Is it a new phone?"

"Yeah," Zak replied.

Sam chuckled. "I remember when I upgraded my phone last year. It took me forever to figure it out. Want me to send the text for you?"

Zak breathed a sigh of relief and passed him the phone. "Go ahead."

Sam grinned. "Wow, you've got the latest model. I've got the same make but mine is an older version."

"Can you work it?" Zak asked.

"Piece of cake," Sam said as he navigated the phone. "You only have two people listed in your phone," he said. "Darren and Eleanor."

"Yeah, they're my mum and dad."

"You have your parents listed in your phone by their first names?"

"Yes." Zak had the feeling this was wrong, but he wasn't the one who had put the numbers in there, Darren had done that for him.

"Geez, Sam," Lucy interrupted. "Just send the damn text and stop grilling the poor bloke."

Sam quickly tapped in a message to Darren and sent it. A moment later the phone rang causing everyone to jump.

Sam passed the mobile back to Zak who fumbled to answer the call.

"Hello?"

"What's this about a ride home?" Darren asked without introduction. "And don't pretend you sent that message yourself as I know you didn't."

"Sam sent it."

"Who's Sam?"

"He's in my Maths class. He said Lucy would give me a ride home."

"And who's Lucy?"

"Sam's friend."

"Is she driving right now? Is the vehicle moving?"

"No, we're still in the car park."

"Put her on the phone. Now."

Zak handed the phone to Lucy. "My dad wants to talk to you," he explained.

Lucy looked nervous as she took the phone from Zak and held it up to her ear.

"Yes, I have a clean license… I'll tell him… No, I've not been drinking… Yes, I know where that is, Sam's on the same street… No, I'll go straight there… Yes, I'll do that."

When Lucy finally finished the call she handed the phone back to Zak. "Geez, Sam, I think we've just found a parent even more protective than your mother. Anyone would think Zak had never been allowed out on his own before. Zak, Darren said to remind you to put your seatbelt on."

Zak buckled up and sighed. "Do you know where you're going?" he asked. He hoped so as he had no idea how to get home from the college if she asked him for directions.

"Yep," Lucy replied as she pulled out of the car park. "According to your dad, you just moved in down the road from Sam."

"Really?" Sam asked, apparently quite pleased with this bit of knowledge.

"So, what subjects are you doing at college?" Lucy asked.

"A Levels in English, Maths and History," Zak said.

"Oh, you're in Sam's Maths class. In case he hasn't told you, Sam's a science nerd."

"What's a nerd?" Zak asked.

Lucy looked at him through the rear-view mirror. "You know, a geek."

"What's a geek?"

"Is English your second language or something?" Lucy asked.

Zak did a quick calculation in his head. "It's my ninth language."

Sam's jaw dropped. "Ninth?"

"Yes. I'm still learning a lot of the local terms."

Suddenly another vehicle cut in front of Lucy. She hit the horn and yelled out of the window, "You stupid fucker!"

"What's a fucker?" Zak asked, though he had a fair idea it wasn't anything pleasant simply from her tone.

Sam covered his mouth to hide his amusement at Lucy's astonished expression. He had a feeling that being friends with Zak would be an interesting experience.

Chapter Four

Darren and Eleanor were laughing about the 'typical English weather' when Zak wandered into the dining room. Darren sat at one end of the long table working on marking homework assignments while Eleanor sketched him from the other end. Zak was bored and the rain they were joking about had put a damper on his plans to go exploring. It hadn't seemed to do anything other than pour with rain since he had arrived on Earth. The few days there had been decent weather, he had been stuck in college.

"Hey, Zak," Eleanor said when she looked up and saw him hovering in the doorway. "You want me to draw you?"

Darren didn't give him time to answer. "Have you done your homework?"

"Yes," Zak replied.

"With the workings out of the maths problems written down?"

Zak ground his teeth in frustration. He had already had this lecture from Miss Randall, earlier in the week.

"Yes, though I still don't see why I have to when I do them in my head."

"Because you earn part of your exam marks by showing how you worked out the solution. You need to learn how to do this the Earth way."

Zak thought the Earth way was frustrating and longwinded, but this time he kept his opinion to himself. Darren's usual response to such complaints was to repeat some silly Earth saying about 'when in Rome...' Consequently Zak was learning to hold his tongue.

"Why have you stayed here on Earth for so long?" Zak asked as he sat down at the table. "When you know what wonderful worlds are out there, why stay on this one?"

"I stay here because I love this world, as does Eleanor." Eleanor nodded and smiled from her end of the table.

"Well, of course *she* does, it's her planet."

"It's mine too now. I've not taken another form since my last transformation into that of a human."

"What? Never?"

Darren smiled. "Well, just once, when I returned to report to the elders. After that I reverted back to human and have stayed this way ever since."

Zak cast a glance toward Eleanor and lowered his voice. "Does Eleanor know what you look like in your natural form?"

"This is my natural form now, or at least it feels so to me. Though to answer the question you meant, yes, she does. She came with me when I went to complete my report, didn't you, darling?"

Eleanor nodded, though it was clear to Zak that she was only half listening now and concentrating more on her sketchbook than on the two of them.

"She's in her own little world now," Darren whispered. "I hope one day you find someone like her. Have you made any more friends here yet?"

"Um."

Darren turned a piercing gaze onto him. "What happened to Sam and Lucy?"

"Nothing, why?"

"Well, it's the weekend and normally lads your age are out with their friends."

"Sam and Lucy have been friends for years."

"You can never have too many friends," Eleanor suddenly piped up, letting them know she wasn't as oblivious to the conversation as they'd thought. "Why don't you go over to Sam's and see what they're up to today?"

"Are you trying to get rid of me?" Zak asked. He had meant the question to be teasing, but a small stab in his chest betrayed his hurt at the feeling that he might no longer be welcome.

"Of course not," Eleanor replied. "But why hang around with us old fogies when you could be out having fun with people your own age?"

"Fogies?" Zak frowned at the unfamiliar word. Although the translator was getting better, every now and then someone said a word it simply couldn't handle.

"People," Darren provided. "And Eleanor's right. Sam's only up the road. It wouldn't hurt to go see what he's up to."

"But it's pouring with rain."

"It's stopped, in case you hadn't noticed," Eleanor said.

Zak looked over at the window and sure enough the clouds were dispersing and there was a teasing hint of sunshine in the west.

"Go on, get out of here," Darren said. "Just be back for tea."

Zak stood up and left the room. His feelings of hurt at being shunted out of the house intensified, even though he was sure they weren't justified in the slightest. He pushed his conflicted emotions aside, grabbed his coat and slipped out of the front door.

He knew the way to Sam's house, but decided to go in the other direction. He didn't want to intrude on his weekend, not without an invitation. To do so would be rude and the last thing he wanted was to be considered such. He shoved aside the unsettling thought that he might be hurt if Sam didn't want to hang out with him today. His people didn't get hurt over silly things like feelings. Their emotions were always completely under control. At least they had been until he'd turned human. Now he felt like a stranger both inside and out.

In such a tiny village, there wasn't much to explore and Zak quickly grew bored with wandering around looking at the buildings. He reached the edge of the residential area, where the landscape turned rural. He was about to turn back when he saw something at the far side of a field. Drawing closer, he wasn't sure at first if it was one of the horses he had been eager to see since before his arrival, but after climbing over the fence and walking halfway across the field he realized it was.

What with one thing and another, Darren and Eleanor had not had time to take Zak to see Eleanor's horses. She apparently kept a stable full of the animals at their home in the south of England. Had Zak known there were some of the creatures so close he would have visited them ages ago.

Quickening his pace, he hurried over the muddy field, nearly losing his shoes in the process.

The horse, who didn't seem particularly bothered about the rain, ignored Zak until he was practically upon him.

Zak raised his hand cautiously to the animal. The beast was much larger than he'd expected after seeing them in the knowledge implant. Then Zak remembered he was shorter than he was used to being, while Darren was a huge bear of a man. To Darren, the horse would probably be quite small, while to Zak it was a mountain.

Searching his knowledge, Zak recalled how Darren would climb onto the back of the horse and ride it to where he needed to go. Without cars and other modern modes of transportation, the horse had been Darren's only way to travel, other than using his own two feet. The horse stood placidly as Zak patted its neck and let him stroke the coat.

"Will you let me ride you?" Zak asked quietly.

The horse, not surprisingly, didn't reply. Zak took that as a good sign and swung himself up onto the animal's back. He wasn't sure what he had done wrong, but the moment he took his seat the creature seemed to take offense to his presence and charged down the field. Zak managed to hold on for only a few seconds. The sudden movement took him completely by surprise and before he knew it he was flat on his back in the middle of what seemed to be the muddiest patch of the field.

Moving his limbs cautiously, he determined that nothing was damaged except for his pride. Though when Eleanor saw what a mess he had made of himself, he might have to reassess that.

Deciding that horses were perhaps best left alone for the time being, Zak left the field the way he had entered it. A crack of thunder overhead signaled the weather was changing yet again and by the time he reached the houses, the rain had returned, even heavier than before. At a loss for what to do next, Zak was considering returning home when he spotted Sam and Lucy entering a small café on the corner of the main street. Maybe he should approach them and see if they wanted to spend some time with him.

His decision made, Zak followed after them.

Lucy spotted him first and waved him over to where they stood queuing at the counter.

"Hey, what brings you out in this miserable weather?" she asked.

"And why are you covered in mud?" Sam added.

"My parents seemed to want me out from under their feet," Zak replied. "And I fell off a horse."

"You know how to ride?" Lucy asked. "I used to take lessons before my parents divorced."

Zak gestured to his wet and muddy clothing. "As evidenced by my appearance, no I don't have a clue how to ride. I was just trying to find something to do to pass the time."

"Join the club," Sam said. "There's nothing to do round here when the weather's bad."

Lucy laughed. "Except chores. My dad wanted me to mow the lawn this weekend, but thankfully the rain put paid to that idea. I crept out of the house before he found me something else to do instead."

"Your dad makes you do manual labor?" Zak was appalled. What sort of world was this, where the older generation forced the youngsters to do their work for them?

Lucy stepped back a step at Zak's vehemence and exchanged an odd look with Sam. "It's not like that. I just have chores to do and that's one I don't really like. Thankfully the weather's turning colder and it won't need doing again until next year."

"I'm sure your dad will find you plenty of other things to do during the winter," Sam teased.

"Don't remind me," Lucy complained. "But I don't have chores today, at least not yet, which means I can come out here to the sticks and visit you."

"Do your parents make you do manual labor?" Zak asked Sam.

"No, I'm lucky," Sam said. "My parents don't make me do too much round the house."

"Well, that's different," Lucy pointed out.

Sam elbowed Lucy in the ribs. Zak felt certain Lucy had intended to say more before Sam had nudged her, but he couldn't imagine what. At least it seemed as though Sam's parents weren't the slave-drivers Lucy's dad was.

"So," Lucy said brightly after they had purchased their food and sat down at one of the tables. "How are you enjoying being at the tech?"

"Tech?" Zak asked.

"College," Lucy amended. "I keep forgetting English isn't your first language."

"It's okay, I guess," Zak replied.

"What did Miss Randall call you back for earlier in the week?" Sam asked.

"She was complaining I hadn't done the work properly."

"How come?"

"I didn't include the workings out. It just seems like a total waste of time to do that."

"I can't even figure her problems out without scribbling down my notes," Sam said. "Even if you're some kind of genius, you'd better do things properly, though. You don't want to have to repeat the course like me."

"They made you do the course all over again?" Zak had thought things couldn't get any worse than enforced education at his age. He couldn't imagine how awful it must be to be made to stay, and do things over again had to be even worse.

Sam sighed. "I missed too many days of school and when I sat my A Levels I didn't get all the grades I needed for the course I want to do at university, which is why I'm now stuck at the local college instead of being in university with everyone else."

Lucy gave him a pat on the arm. "You'll make it to university, just you see."

"If I get the grades," Sam reminded her. "My marks last time round were even lower than I anticipated, and I wasn't exactly expecting a lot."

"You had a lot to deal with last year," Lucy pointed out. "You're doing much better this time around."

"You had a lot to deal with too," Sam pointed out. "Helping your dad raise your younger brothers can't have been easy, but you got the grades you wanted for your art course."

"The entry requirements for my course weren't anywhere near as high as a university, though. Stop worrying so much. You'll do fine this time."

"We're only two months into the term," Sam said. "A lot can happen between now and the exams."

"You'll make it," Lucy insisted.

Zak suspected from her tone that this was a conversation the two of them had had several times before. "I'm sure you will too," Zak agreed. Even though he didn't know the full story behind Sam's repeating the course, it seemed like the right thing to say.

Sam smiled at him and Zak felt his heart rate quicken for no reason at all. He grinned back and for a moment or two Lucy was completely forgotten.

Lucy looked from Sam to Zak and back again. "Oh great," she muttered. "What is it with the men around here?"

"Huh?" Sam turned to Lucy questioningly.

"You get ones like Richard, who are gorgeous, but know it, and the nice guys are all gay. How is this fair?"

"Are you saying I'm ugly?" Sam teased.

"With your jet black hair and green eyes a cat would envy?" Lucy snorted and rolled her eyes.

"What's gay?" Zak asked without thinking.

Before Sam or Lucy could respond to his question, Sam suddenly keeled forward.

"Sam!" Lucy rushed to stop Sam from falling into his food. "Are you okay?"

Sam nodded slowly. "Just came over a bit dizzy."

"Your nose is bleeding," Lucy said as she handed him a tissue from her purse.

Sam took the tissue and used it to stem the blood.

"Is it...?" Lucy began.

Sam quickly shushed her. "I'm probably just coming down with something."

Lucy didn't look as though she believed him. "Do you want me to drive you home?" She was already rummaging through her purse for her keys.

"Would you mind?" Sam asked.

Lucy was already on her feet. "I wouldn't have offered if I did."

Zak watched as Lucy helped Sam out of his seat. Yesterday Sam had been healthy and well—now all of a sudden he was ill. How did these humans survive when they were constantly being afflicted with disease?

"Do you want a lift home?" Lucy asked Zak. "I can drop you off on the way."

"I'm okay," Zak replied. "I'm just going to stay here for a bit."

"Are you sure?" Lucy asked. "It's no trouble."

Zak nodded and waved them away. If Sam was ill and Zak caught whatever it was he had, he'd fall behind in his classes all over again. The last thing he needed was to be inflicted with some awful human disease while he was stuck here. Still, he felt a twinge of guilt at the disappointment he saw in Sam's eyes. He hoped he soon recovered from whatever ailed him.

Chapter Five

Life on Earth still wasn't ideal, but with Sam and Lucy at his side, Zak found it wasn't quite as bad as it had been when he'd first arrived.

A favorite place to hang out was the quaint woodland park and lake a few miles out of town. It was a popular tourist spot, with visitors coming from miles around to view the ruins of the old abbey. Zak had to stop himself from telling Sam and Lucy the story Darren had shared with him about staying there himself one particularly stormy night many centuries before.

According to Sam and Lucy, the day was unseasonably hot for the time of year, so they intended to make the most of the sunshine while they could. Considering how much rain he had seen since his arrival on Earth, Zak didn't blame them in the slightest.

They relaxed on the grass with a picnic lunch, tossed a strange plastic disc called a Frisbee to each other and snacked on lollies and ice cream cones bought from the ice cream van. For the first time in a long time, Zak was actually having fun.

Of course, things weren't perfect. Zak still struggled somewhat with the English language and every now and then he said something that caused the people around him to stare at him as though he was some sort of idiot. Yet he found hanging out with Sam and Lucy—being with real friends—made life on Earth much more bearable.

"Hottie at two o'clock," Lucy said as she tossed the Frisbee to Zak.

Zak looked at his watch—causing him to miss the catch entirely—and saw that it was nearly five. "It's well after two," he said.

Lucy laughed at him, something she did rather frequently. She pointed straight ahead. "Twelve o'clock is that way." Then she moved her arm to her side. "Three is over there."

Zak quickly caught on and looked in the direction of two o'clock. Hanging out with Lucy had quickly clued him in on what exactly constituted a hottie, and the man playing with his dog across the grass lawn was definitely that.

The man was tossing a ball for the dog to run after and bring back to him, making the animal—in Zak's opinion—one of the dumbest creatures on Earth.

As the dog brought back the ball for the umpteenth time, Zak concentrated on watching the owner. The longer he stared at the man, the stranger he started to feel. His breath quickened and he felt a stirring in his groin like nothing he had experienced before.

"Are you okay?" Lucy asked. "You're looking kind of flushed."

Zak nodded mutely and dropped down onto the grass. "Just feeling a bit funny," he replied.

Sam chuckled and looked away, though Lucy continued to fuss over him. "Are you going to be okay for the club tonight?"

"Maybe we should reschedule?" Sam suggested. "If Zak's not well, we can always go next Saturday. I still have a Chemistry paper to write anyway."

Lucy rounded on Sam with a glare. "You're just looking for an excuse to back out. Even if Zak can't make it, you're having a night out, like it or not. Your paper isn't due until Wednesday and you need to have a bit of fun."

"I've been having fun all day," Sam replied.

"And you're going to have more fun tonight," Lucy declared before turning to Zak. "What about you? Are you still up for clubbing?"

"Yes, definitely." Zak had no idea what this club Lucy kept talking about was, but it sure sounded better than sitting at home with his foster parents.

Sam started to gather their things together. "We should probably head back if we're going to get something to eat before going into town."

They packed up the rest of their picnic and went back to Lucy's car, Lucy casting a last longing glance back at the dog owner, who had now been joined by his girlfriend.

* * * *

The club was noisier than anywhere Zak had ever been in his life. He could hardly hear himself think. Thankfully, his translator masquerading as a hearing aid provided something of an excuse for why everyone had to constantly repeat things for him.

"What do you want to drink?" Lucy yelled in his ear as they pushed through the crowd at the bar.

"Um, a Coke?"

Lucy rolled her eyes. "Don't tell me you don't drink alcohol."

"What's alcohol?" Zak asked.

Lucy clearly thought he was joking and laughed loudly. "You're nineteen years old, so don't expect me to believe you don't drink."

"Lucy, not everyone goes out with the sole intention of getting plastered," Sam said. "If Zak wants a soft drink, then let him have one. I'm going to stick to Coke myself."

Lucy snorted. "You have an excuse," she said. "But I'm not drinking alone on the one night of the week my dad's not working and can look after the brats."

"You pick a drink for me," Zak said.

"Don't give her free rein," Sam warned. "She'll have you passed out before ten o'clock if you do."

"I wouldn't do that," Lucy argued.

"Just get him a beer," Sam said.

Zak had never heard of beer, but he guessed it was alcohol because Lucy didn't argue with Sam about his choice.

"What are you drinking, Sam?" Lucy asked.

Sam gave her an amused look. "Why do you always ask me that? You should know what I like by now."

"You know the one time I don't ask, I'll get it wrong," she replied before she took their money and shoved her way to the bar, returning a few minutes later with their drinks.

"These better not be spiked," Sam warned her before he took a drink.

"I wouldn't do that to you," Lucy replied, clearly hurt at the suggestion.

"And Zak's?" Sam asked.

"I promise it's just beer. You can check it if you like."

"You know I can't."

"One little sip won't do anything if you're that worried for him."

Zak took a quick drink of the beer and was far from impressed. The bitter taste was like nothing he had ever had before, or ever wanted again.

"Do you dance?" Lucy shouted with a nod toward the dance floor where people were gyrating to the music. The dancing was unorganized and chaotic, nothing like the graceful movements of his own people. There was also far more touching involved with human dancing. It didn't look very difficult, though, and he let Sam take his drink so Lucy could drag him onto the dance floor.

He stumbled over his feet a little as they found a place where they could just about move.

Lucy pressed against him and Zak tried to mimic her moves, watching the others around him as he attempted to figure out whether he was doing this right.

They carried on this way for several songs, some upbeat and others slower. Eventually Lucy seemed to run out of steam and pulled him back over in the direction of where Sam sat in one of the booths chatting to someone Zak vaguely recognized from college. He had a feeling he might have been in one of Sam's science classes, though he wasn't sure which one and had no idea what his name might be.

One thing he did know was that he didn't like the way he appeared to be leaning into Sam. He liked Sam's laughter at whatever he was saying even less.

"Let's get another drink from the bar," Lucy said, pulling a reluctant Zak back toward the bar.

"I didn't finish my last one," Zak shouted.

"It'll be warm now. Besides, I could tell from your face you didn't like the beer. I'll get you something else instead."

Zak let Lucy do as she pleased and took the fruity drink from her hand when she returned. He didn't know what the drink contained, but it was a vast improvement on the beer and he downed it in three gulps.

"Whoa," Lucy said as she stared at him. "Take it easy. That's vodka, not orange juice."

"It's better than the beer," Zak replied. "I'm going to get another one. Will Sam want another drink?"

"Get him another Coke," Lucy said as she waved him to the bar and made her way over to Sam.

Sam looked up as Lucy appeared at the table. "Having fun?" he asked.

"Loads! Are you?"

"Sure," Sam said. "Where's Zak?"

"At the bar getting you both a drink."

Sam smiled and strained to see Zak through the crowd. "Are you getting anywhere with him?" he asked.

"No."

"It looked like you were having fun out there," Sam said with a grin.

"I was, but he wasn't having that much fun, if you know what I mean."

Sam knew exactly what she meant, but had no intention of rising to the bait. Unfortunately, Gary from his Chemistry class didn't know Lucy as well as he did.

"What do you mean?" Gary asked curiously. "He seemed to be having a good time from what I could see."

Sam groaned, knowing Lucy was about to say something completely inappropriate.

"He wasn't getting hard when I rubbed up against him," Lucy replied.

Sam would have liked to blame Lucy's runaway mouth on the alcohol, but since she was exactly the same stone-cold sober, he couldn't.

"With a gorgeous bird like you?" Gary gave her a skeptical look. "Do you think he might be a pouf?"

"The word is gay," Lucy hissed.

Sam rested a hand on her arm, hoping to calm her down before she did something stupid, like punch Gary. If she did, *that* would be because of the alcohol, but if he could keep her out of trouble, he would. He and Gary weren't close friends, so he wasn't aware Sam was gay. Sam didn't hide his sexuality, but nor did he broadcast it to all and sundry.

Zak appeared at the table with what looked to be a Coke for Sam and some sort of alcopop for himself. Sam took the Coke from him and sipped it.

"You aren't drinking?" Gary asked.

"Not tonight," Sam said.

"Paul's our designated driver tonight," Gary said with a nod across the room.

Sam wasn't driving, but he let Gary think that was the reason for his choice of beverage. Only Lucy knew the real reason he wasn't allowed to drink, and he intended to keep it that way.

"Do you want to dance?" Zak asked Sam.

Gary, who was halfway through taking a drink, nearly choked as he looked from Zak to Sam.

Lucy nodded eagerly. "Come on, drink up and let's all get back out there."

Gary appeared a little uncomfortable around them and quickly made his excuses to return to the rest of his friends.

Sam wished, not for the first time, that he could persuade Lucy to come with him to the town's solitary gay bar. As supportive as she was of him, he had a feeling he might be pushing his luck if he suggested it to her.

Zak pulled the two of them onto the dance floor and Sam's pulse raced. Maybe if Lucy was right about Zak, he might be persuaded to go with him.

On the other hand, Sam considered as Zak's arms flew in all directions, not even close to being in time with the music, if all gay men were supposed to be graceful on the dance floor, Zak must be as straight as an arrow.

His lack of knowledge about Zak's orientation did nothing to stop his body reacting to the heat of the other man pressing against him as the floor became crowded and they were pushed closer and closer together.

He pushed his contemplative thoughts aside. Tonight it didn't matter whether Zak was gay or straight. They were just a group of friends out on the town having a good time. He found he was glad that Lucy had pushed him into coming out with her.

Chapter Six

"Would you care to explain?" Darren asked as soon as Zak entered the kitchen the next morning.

"Not really," Zak muttered as he rested his head on the cool surface of the table. Why was everything so loud this morning?

"What time did you get in last night?"

"About three," Zak replied.

"And didn't it occur to you to phone and let us know you were going to be out past your curfew, which, I might remind you, happens to be midnight?"

"I forgot."

"You were drunk. What were you thinking getting into such a state?"

Zak glared at Darren through one eye. "I didn't know this stupid human body wouldn't be able to handle a bit of alcohol."

"Go easy on him," Eleanor said as she put a glass of water and two white tablets in front of him. "It's probably his first hangover."

"And his last," Darren snapped.

Although he resented the idea of agreeing with Darren, Zak found himself slowly nodding. The movement made his head spin and he bolted for the sink, making it just in time.

Even more worrying than the way he felt this morning was the disturbing fact that he couldn't remember a lot of what had happened the night before, including how he had gotten home. He suspected Sam had made sure he got safely back to the cottage and knew he owed him a big thank you the next time he saw him.

Darren on the other hand didn't seem to think Sam deserved his thanks. "Clearly Sam and Lucy are a bad influence," he said. "Maybe you should try to find some other friends to hang out with, ones who don't go out drinking at the weekends when they should be studying."

"Sam does study," he argued. "So does Lucy. Lucy practically brings up her younger siblings too, while her dad works nights."

"That's beside the point," Darren replied loudly with a distinct lack of sympathy for Zak's pounding head. "They should be focusing on their college work at such a crucial time in their lives. You said Sam failed some of his exams last year?"

"Yes."

"Maybe if he'd spent less time down the pub and more time with his nose in his books he wouldn't be repeating the year now."

"You don't know why he failed them. He just said he'd missed too many days at school."

"Probably from lazing in bed at home, nursing a hangover. From now on I don't want you going out getting drunk or hanging round with Sam and Lucy.

You're here to study human culture and that's what you'll be concentrating on from now on."

"From what I've seen, going out on a Saturday night and getting drunk *is* part of human culture."

Darren banged his fist on the table, causing Zak to cringe as his head spun once more. He glared back at Darren. He recognized the stubborn set of his jaw. His foster father was about to lay down the law and Zak could only dig his heels in so far. He guessed Sam and Lucy wouldn't be welcome round here for a while.

* * * *

On Monday morning, Zak left for college early, intending to catch the bus rather than head to Sam's house to wait for Lucy to pick them up.

Darren had ranted about bad influences all through Sunday until Zak had taken refuge in his room. All of Darren's lecturing couldn't take his mind off the upcoming conversation he would have to have with Sam and Lucy.

His first class was English, so he knew he could put off the inevitable a little longer. Unfortunately he had Maths straight after and by the time the lesson arrived, he had decided avoidance was the best course of action. Rather than face Sam, he walked straight out of the main doors and wandered over the road to the nearby park.

The place was quiet on the chilly autumn day. A few people came through the grounds, mothers with pushchairs and owners walking their dogs. Zak sat down on one of the benches and watched the people passing him by.

He liked Sam and Lucy and he knew he'd miss them if he did as Darren said and went out of his way to make other friends. His phone rang and Zak saw Sam was trying to contact him. He hit decline and turned the ringer onto silent. The phone vibrated a few moments later as a new message arrived. Zak ignored it.

Lunchtime came and went and although Zak felt his phone vibrate to signal several more new messages had arrived, he didn't bother to check what they were until the sky began to darken.

The first message was from Sam asking why he wasn't in class.

The second was from Darren with the same question.

Lucy's message told him she had waited for as long as she could after college, but since he hadn't shown he would have to make his own way home instead of getting a lift from her.

There was another message from Darren asking if he was with Sam or Lucy and warning him about bad influences. Zak sent a quick text back to Darren telling him he was on his own.

Darren immediately called him back.

"Where are you?"

"Out."

"Out where?"

"Just out. I'll be back later."

"Zak, you aren't used to Earth and you've never been out on your own this late before. It's not safe."

"I'm perfectly all right."

"I want you to get the bus or a taxi home right now."

"I'll come home when I'm ready to," Zak argued, ending the call before Darren could say anything else.

The air became chilly as the sun disappeared below the horizon. When it started to spit with rain, Zak finally decided to make a move.

He walked to the bus stop, taking shelter just before the heavens opened. He grumbled to himself about the uncontrollable Earth weather as he waited for the bus to arrive.

He climbed aboard and saw that the vehicle was almost empty. He paid his fare and took a seat near the back. He didn't want to go home yet, but he wasn't stupid enough to risk ill health by staying out in the rain.

As the bus approached his stop, he made the decision to go and visit Sam instead of returning home straight away.

Sam's mother answered the door. She appeared surprised to see him there, but let him in, shouting upstairs to Sam.

Sam appeared at the top of the stairs. "Where were you today?" he asked. "I told Miss Randall you were ill, but I don't think she believed me."

"I didn't feel like going to class," Zak said as Sam came down the stairs and waved him into the empty lounge.

"I often don't feel like going to class," Sam said. "I don't just bunk off, though."

Zak laughed bitterly. "And he thinks you're a bad influence."

"What? Who thinks that?"

"My dad. He wasn't too happy with me after our night out."

"Neither was Lucy's dad. She was in an even worse state than you."

"I don't remember."

"Neither does she. We dropped her off first and then the taxi brought us back here. You could barely walk from the taxi to your front door."

"My dad wants me to find other friends instead of you two," Zak said.

"Oh."

"It's stupid. You weren't even drinking *and* I'll bet you're the only reason I made it home unharmed."

"Maybe it would be better if we didn't hang out together for a while," Sam suggested. "Just until your dad calms down."

"What?"

"It'll only antagonize him if he thinks you're disobeying him. Give it a week or two and he'll probably change his mind."

"You're taking *his* side?"

"It's not about taking sides. But when you live with your parents you have to live by their rules. It won't be forever, and we'll still see each other at college."

In his head Zak was aware that Sam's words were perfectly reasonable. Darren would calm down. Time would move on and everything would go back to normal, or at least as normal as anything on Earth was. He knew he should tell Sam he agreed and make his way home. Common sense dictated that was the correct course of action.

Yet Zak struggled to find the right words. He stared at Sam as a new and strange sensation came over him. There was a tight feeling in his chest and a stinging in his eyes. He quelled the instinct to shout at Sam and vent his frustration.

Sam looked at him. Zak could tell he was waiting for him to say something in response.

Zak shook his head and turned to face the window.

"It'll only make your father angrier if you disobey him," Sam said.

Zak's vision blurred. Even though his human sight wasn't anywhere near as sharp as his natural vision, it had never done this before. Occasionally, usually first thing in the morning when he had just woken up, or later at night when he was tired, his focus was slightly off, but never like this.

"Are you okay?" Sam asked.

Zak rubbed at his eyes. He was shocked to feel dampness on his cheek. He swiped his hand across his face as he bolted for the door.

"Zak?"

He didn't stop to answer Sam. He had to get out of here until he figured out what was happening to him.

Zak arrived home at a dead sprint. He didn't stop to greet either Darren or Eleanor. Instead he raced up the stairs and sought the privacy of his bedroom. He locked the door behind him and hoped his foster parents hadn't seen him come in.

Water still leaked from his eyes and no matter how hard he rubbed them, it wouldn't stop. He looked into the mirror and saw that his face had turned a blotchy red color. His eyes appeared sore and his nose had started to run along with his eyes.

He looked absolutely awful.

"Zak?" Eleanor's soft voice came from the other side of his door. "Are you okay?"

"I'm fine," Zak lied, although he didn't even sound like himself. His voice cracked and another sharp pain hit him in the chest. There was also a small ache starting in his head, which only added to his miserable state.

"Are you sure?" Eleanor called. "Have you had anything to eat?"

"I'm not hungry," replied Zak. Even though he hadn't eaten, he had no appetite at all.

Eleanor continued to call to him through the door until he swore at her in his own language and told her to go away and leave him alone.

Things had been going so well. He had actually started to believe he was settling in on Earth, and now everything had fallen apart. Curling up on his bed, Zak tried to bring his body back under his control. No matter what he tried, he couldn't seem to pull himself together. He closed his eyes and tried to will his body to go to sleep. Finally, in the early hours of the morning, he at last fell into an exhausted and fitful slumber.

* * * *

"You're home early today," Eleanor said as Zak threw his backpack onto the sofa a few days later. Eleanor sat in the window seat, drawing in her sketchbook.

"Not much else to do round here," Zak complained. "Why couldn't we live in one of the cities?"

"We thought it would be easier for you to get used to our human ways if you weren't being bombarded at every turn."

"I already feel like I'm getting stuff thrown at me from all angles."

"It'd be worse if we were in a city," Eleanor told him as she set aside her pad and pencil and gave him her full attention. "Now, I doubt boredom is your problem today. You're upset about Darren's decision regarding your friends, aren't you?"

"It doesn't matter."

"They're your first friends on this world, of course it matters."

"No, it doesn't."

Eleanor smiled at him. "You know, if you gave me a chance, you might find I understand better than you think."

"There's nothing to understand. Darren doesn't want me to be friends with Sam and Lucy, and Sam agrees with him!"

"Oh."

"What's that supposed to mean?"

"You're upset because Sam has said something to convince you he doesn't want to be friends."

"I don't care if he doesn't want to be my friend anymore."

"What did he say to you?"

"It's none of your business," Zak snapped. "You're not my mother! Just because you haven't got children of your own, it doesn't mean you get to boss me around instead."

Eleanor recoiled as though he had slapped her.

"Zakrynious, that's enough!" Darren suddenly shouted from the doorway. "My study, immediately."

Zak was tempted to refuse, but he knew an order when he heard one, and Darren was angrier than he had ever seen him. Zak realized in that moment that Darren had once been a powerful warrior, one capable of putting him in his place if he chose to do so.

Once inside the study, Darren shut the door and pointed at one of the chairs. "Sit down."

"I'd rather stand."

"Sit down!" Darren roared.

Zak dropped into the seat like a stone.

"I will not tolerate you speaking to your mother that way."

"Eleanor isn't my mother."

"While you're here on Earth, she is. All she was trying to do was help. There was no need at all for the way you reacted. If you didn't want to confide in her, all you had to do was say so."

Zak sulked as Darren lectured him.

"You will go through there and apologize immediately."

"I have nothing to apologize for."

"Oh yes you do. Eleanor is a good mother and she didn't deserve to be spoken to like that."

"She knows nothing about being a mother."

"Of course she does. Eleanor has raised many children of her own."

"What?"

"You heard me."

"Where are all these children then?"

"They are long since dead, as are their own children. Unfortunately, as Eleanor is essentially human, so are all the children she gives birth to. They have a human lifespan, which you'll recall is much shorter than our own. Since it was too upsetting for her to continually outlive her children we decided not to have any more for a while."

"Oh."

"She has dealt with difficult children in the past and she is more than capable of dealing with you. Until now she has been going easy on you at my request."

"I'm not a child and I don't need dealing with."

"Then stop acting like a child, and a spoiled one at that. If you want to be treated like an adult, then you need to start behaving like one."

Zak nodded and stood up to leave.

"Hold on a second. I've not finished yet."

Zak turned back to Darren. "What else is there to say?"

"I've been reading through the reports the elders sent me on you."

"What reports?"

"The ones from your previous placements. I have to say, they took me by surprise."

Zak waited for Darren to continue. He had not seen the contents of the previous reports and had no idea what they had to say about him.

"It's like they're about a different person," Darren said. "They refer to a mature young man who's helpful and friendly, pitches in whenever it's needed, usually without even being asked, takes instruction without question and is an asset to every community he joins. What happened to him, because this doesn't sound like you at all?"

"I'm the same person," Zak muttered. A feeling of shame washed over him as Darren gazed steadily at him, waiting for an explanation he couldn't give.

"Is it me you take offense to?" Darren asked. "Would you perhaps be happier with an Earth family?"

"No!"

"Then what is it?"

"I don't know," Zak said. "I've never felt like this before."

"Like what?"

"I can't explain it." Zak ran his hands through his hair, tugging at the strands with frustration. "It's as though everything I feel is amplified. When I was learning to navigate the spacecrafts, I didn't like taking orders any more than I do here, but I could control my temper and resentment. Now I can't."

"Ah." Darren nodded in understanding and flicked through the reports the elders had sent him again. "It looks like you've never been in a form where emotions are quite so strong. The races you have fostered with are similar to those of Camyl'ons—not showing their feelings and burying them instead."

"Is there anything I can do about it?" Zak asked.

"Not really. You'll get used to them eventually."

"How do you manage it?"

Darren chuckled. "Until you arrived, I thought I was doing quite well, but as you've seen, I'm not perfect, just like humans aren't. I haven't lost my temper like I did today in several hundred years. I remember when I first arrived here I was a menace, losing my temper every time someone laughed at me, which was rather a lot. I got into a lot of fights those first few years."

"I want these feelings to stop," Zak said. "I hate being so out of control."

"All you can do is take some time to become accustomed to them. If you think you're going to lose your temper, count to ten before you speak. If you feel resentful of something you've been asked to do, remember you've been asked to do a lot worse on other worlds before you were sent here. Cleaning your room or doing your homework properly are hardly strenuous tasks compared to some of your previous chores."

"I know."

"Can you at least try to settle in while you're here?"

Zak ducked his head and avoided Darren's gaze. The feeling of shame intensified with every passing minute. He had done very little to get used to his new home and he knew it. "I suppose."

"You don't sound very enthusiastic about it," Darren said. "I take it whatever has happened between you and Sam has something to do with that?"

Zak shrugged and remained silent.

"Would you like to talk to me about your argument with Sam?" Darren asked when a couple of minutes of awkward silence had passed.

"Not really."

"You can confide in me, you know."

"Sam doesn't want to be friends with me anymore. What more can I say?" Zak forced a smile. "At least you won't have to worry about me sneaking out to visit him."

"Maybe I was a little hasty in my decision, but I was rather angry with you after you came home drunk at the weekend."

"Well, like I said to Eleanor, Sam agrees with you. He doesn't want to hang out with me anymore so you have exactly what you wanted."

"I don't want you to be miserable while you're here. Did you know there's an Earth phrase that says time flies when you're having fun?"

Zak stared at Darren in confusion. "I don't understand. I was having fun at the club and I lost my memory of some of the time there. Is that what you're referring to?"

"No. What I mean is if you try to settle in here and enjoy learning about Earth and what it has to offer, you'll find your time here passes much quicker than you'd expect."

Zak wasn't sure he believed Darren. No one, certainly not his own people, had the power to speed up or slow time down. Did humans possess such a power? Or was it just one of those ridiculous sayings Earthlings had that didn't mean what you thought it did? He suspected that was probably the case.

"I am trying to settle in and I thought I was doing better."

"You're doing what you're told, I agree with that," Darren said. "But you're doing it mostly with very bad grace. Humans may not be as advanced scientifically as our people, but they are far from primitive and you won't learn anything of value about them if you continue to look down your nose at their way of doing things."

Zak cringed. "I guess I owe Eleanor an apology."

"You do indeed."

"I really don't know what came over me. I've never spoken to my real parents like that."

Darren snorted. "Unless things have changed considerably on Trimmeron in the last few hundred years, I doubt you've spoken to your parents much at all since your first transformation."

"I suppose not."

"Human parents take a much more active role in raising their teenage children than our people do."

"So I've seen."

"Eleanor only wants what's best for you, just like any human parent would."

"I know."

"No, you don't, because you're not used to being human or dealing with our emotions. One day you will understand, but until then I'm going to request you show her the respect she deserves."

"I'll go and apologize to her."

Darren nodded approvingly.

Zak left the room and went to find his foster mother, but she was nowhere in the house. Guilt washed over him as he realized his unruly temper had probably really hurt her. He hoped she would give him a chance to set things right.

* * * *

Sam stared at the ceiling of his bedroom, idly tossing a ball into the air and catching it. Lucy sat at his desk skimming through the essay she had just finished writing for her History of Art class.

"Where's your telescope?" Lucy asked.

"In the other room," Sam replied.

"What's it doing in there? I thought you liked to watch the stars from in here."

"I do."

Lucy chuckled. "Have you been using it to spy on Zak?"

"No."

"Sam..."

"Fine, yes. I couldn't help myself. I miss him."

"You could do something really wild and just give him a call."

"His dad wants him to stay away from me."

Lucy got up from the seat and moved to the bed. She nudged Sam's legs aside and settled herself down. "You aren't going to let that stop you being friends, are you?"

"I don't want to get Zak into trouble."

"I think Zak might like the idea of getting into trouble with you," Lucy teased.

"What do you mean?"

"Oh come on, I've seen the way he looks at you. No straight guy would look at another man the way he gazes at you."

"You think Zak's gay?"

"Definitely."

"Does it bother you?"

"Why would it?"

"I thought you liked Zak."

"I do like him."

"You know what I meant. You fancied him from the moment you saw him."

"Yeah, what of it? I fancy several hot film stars as well, but it doesn't exactly bother me that they're out of my reach."

"Says the girl who put on mourning when Jared Padalecki got married."

"That was years ago and you're deliberately missing my point. Zak clearly has the hots for you."

"You think so?"

"Yes, I do. You should ask him out or something."

"Have you forgotten that his father wants us to stay away from him?"

"No, but I don't see why that should make any difference. Just pick up the phone and call him."

Lucy didn't wait for him to reach for the phone. She snatched the ball he was tossing out of the air and replaced it with Sam's mobile. "Call him and ask him out."

"What should I say?"

"You could suggest he goes with you to see that action flick you've been trying to talk me into watching for the last week."

"But how do I make him realize I want it to be a date and not just as friends?"

Lucy rolled her eyes. "Men are so useless."

Sam ignored her insult and called Zak. Even if he couldn't pluck up the courage to make it a proper date, at least it would hopefully get their friendship back on track.

* * * *

Zak still hadn't tracked down Eleanor when his mobile phone rang. He looked at the screen and saw

Sam's name there. They hadn't spoken since Zak had run out of Sam's house. He tried not to get his hopes up as he answered the call. Sam might just want to ask what homework they'd been set this week.

"Hi," Sam said. He sounded a little unsure.

"Hi."

"How are you doing?"

Zak's curiosity was piqued and his hopes shot up a notch. "What are you calling me for?"

"I'm sorry I said we shouldn't hang out together."

"You are?"

"Yes. I'm sorry if it sounded like I was taking your dad's side. I didn't mean to."

"It doesn't matter. My dad's calmed down now."

"Does that mean he's changed his mind?"

"We talked earlier and he said it was just his anger talking."

"Why didn't you phone me?"

"You said you didn't want to hang out with me anymore."

"Only because I didn't want to get you in trouble."

Zak could hear Lucy in the background saying something he couldn't quite make out.

"I'm just getting to it," Sam said.

"What?" Zak asked.

"Nothing, I was just talking to Lucy."

"Say hello to her for me."

"Zak says hello," Sam dutifully repeated. "Er…"

"What is it?"

"I was wondering if you'd like to go to the cinema this Saturday. There's a new film showing I'd like to see and I thought you might enjoy it. Or we can go and see something else, if you don't like the sound of this one."

Zak didn't care what they went to see. As long as Sam was his friend again, he'd be happy to watch anything.

Chapter Seven

Zak raced down the stairs, eager to meet Sam at the end of the street and catch the bus to the cinema.

"Don't run down the stairs," Eleanor called from the living room.

"Sorry," Zak shouted back, glancing in the room as he passed. When had Eleanor come back home?

"What did you say?" Eleanor asked, turning to him in surprise.

"I said sorry," Zak replied, thinking she hadn't quite heard him.

Eleanor's expression of surprise remained on her face and Zak felt another wave of shame at how he had dismissed her. He glanced at his watch and saw he had a few minutes to spare before the bus arrived. Time enough for what he had to do.

He joined Eleanor in the living room and sat down across from her. "I've not been very fair to you, have I?"

"You've needed time to get used to Earth ways, I understand that."

"There's no need to be nice about it. I know I've been—what's the word Darren uses?—a brat?"

Eleanor smiled. "Just a little."

"I'm sorry, I really am. I didn't mean to lose my temper."

"I know. You're still getting used to human emotions."

"That's no excuse."

"No, and it won't work the next time, but for now we'll let it go. Let's start afresh."

Zak nodded his agreement.

"So, you seem to be happier now. Where were you rushing off to?"

"Sam and I are going to see a movie."

"I take it that means you and Sam are speaking again?"

"Yes. He phoned me earlier." Suddenly he remembered that Eleanor might not realize Darren had given the okay for him to be friends with Sam and Lucy again. "Darren has changed his mind about them."

"I know. I spoke to him a little while ago," Eleanor looked at the clock. "You'd better run then. The bus to town will be here any minute. Maybe you'd like to bring Sam back here afterwards?"

Zak saw she was right about the time and stood up to leave. "Maybe I will," he said. "See you later, Mum." The new word didn't feel quite as strange on his lips as he would have expected it to.

Sam stood waiting for him at the bus stop. Zak arrived at his side just as the bus turned the corner at the end of the lane. "Just made it," Sam said.

"Where are we meeting Lucy?" Zak asked.

"Lucy doesn't really like action movies," Sam explained. "It's just you and me, if that's okay?"

"No problem," Zak said as the bus pulled up and they climbed on board.

They chatted away on the journey, talking about anything and everything. As they walked from the bus stop to the cinema, the topic turned to favorite films. Sam had seen a lot of films in his life, more than Zak even knew were in existence.

"The last time I went to a movie with Lucy it was awful," Sam said. "The only films she can stay quiet through are chick flicks."

"What's a chick flick?"

Sam gave him an odd look. "I keep forgetting English isn't your first language. Chick flicks are girlie films about love and romance and all that mushy stuff."

"Don't you like love and romance?"

"Not really. I prefer films with a bit more action, but Lucy doesn't care for them. You'd think having a hunk like Christian Bale in the film would shut her up, but not even that helps. She talked all through *The Dark Knight Rises* and I ended up going to see it again on my own the following week. I've been trying to talk her into coming to this film showing today for the last week, but she says I bitched about her yapping so much last time, this time she'll make me go on my own."

"So I'm the last resort, huh?"

Sam stumbled to a halt and his face turned pale. "No! I wanted to come see this with you."

Zak had a feeling his attempt at teasing Sam had fallen flat and he diverted the subject back to Sam's favorite films.

"Probably the *Batman* films," Sam said after a few moments of contemplation. "Though I did enjoy the new *Superman* flick that came out last year. Still can't beat Christopher Reeve for the man of steel, though, right?"

"Er."

Sam turned to face him. "Oh no, please tell me it isn't so."

"What isn't so?"

"You haven't seen any of the *Superman* movies, have you?"

"No."

"What about the *Batman* ones?"

"Sorry."

"But they're classics! How can you not have seen any of them?"

"They don't show them where I come from."

Sam looked at him askance. "So, what are your favorite films?" he asked.

"I quite liked that *Supernatural* film Lucy had on her television that time." Zak recalled she had talked through most of the episode and suddenly understood why Sam might have wanted to go to the cinema with him instead.

"*Supernatural* isn't a film, it's a TV series. Films are longer and mostly tie up everything at the end of it. Though there are a few exceptions like the *Lord of the Rings* trilogy."

Zak could tell his confusion was showing on his face by Sam's next words.

"You've no idea what I'm talking about, have you?"

"Sorry."

"You really haven't seen any movies at all?"

"I don't think so."

"Damn," Sam muttered. "We'll have to fix that and soon."

"Aren't we going to see a movie right now?" Zak asked.

"Yeah, and after today we're going to get you caught up on the classics."

Zak liked the sound of that, even though he felt like a freak for his lack of knowledge about the human custom of watching movies. But, with Darren restricting his television viewing to the education channels for the moment, Zak had a way to go to catch up.

Thankfully they soon arrived at the cinema and Sam changed the subject to what flavor popcorn to buy. Zak had no idea what popcorn was and shrugged, telling Sam to pick whatever he liked. They ended up spending so much time choosing they almost missed the start of the film.

The lights were already down when they made their way to a pair of seats near the back of the room. Sam sat down first and Zak took the seat near the aisle.

"You'll really enjoy this," Sam whispered as the big screen in front of them played a commercial for some kind of vehicle.

Zak whispered back to Sam that he was sure he would.

As the film played on the screen, Zak began to feel rather strange. There was something happening *down there* and it was totally out of his control. He shifted in his seat and tried to change his position so it wasn't as obvious.

Sam laughed at something happening up on the big screen in front of them. The sound sent a zing right through Zak's body, culminating in an uncomfortable tightening of his jeans. This had been happening to him quite a lot recently, but not to this extent.

Zak tried to concentrate on the movie, but it wasn't holding his attention as it had before. His awareness of Sam heightened with every minute.

"Are you okay?" Sam whispered.

Zak groaned as Sam's warm breath against his ear added to the problem down below.

"Fine," Zak hissed.

Sam took him at his word and dipped his hand into the big tub of popcorn. At the touch of Sam's fingers brushing against his own, hidden in the confectionary, Zak sank even lower into his seat as he tried to figure out what was happening to him.

Sam put a handful of popcorn into his mouth and started to chew. When Sam placed a hand on Zak's thigh the pain in his groin became unbearable and he shot up from his seat. "I've got to go," he said, causing several other people in the cinema to shush at him.

He didn't wait for Sam to reply. He grabbed his jacket and bolted for the exit.

Glancing over his shoulder, Zak could see Sam hurrying after him, but he ducked round the corner and into a nearby shop, hiding behind a display stand until he was sure the coast was clear.

The tightness in his jeans was like nothing he'd ever felt before. The pain of the swelling hadn't subsided after he'd fled the cinema. In fact it had even gotten worse the moment Sam had passed him by.

What new torture was this? He'd thought he was finally starting to get used to having a human body. He could handle a pen as well as his classmates. He no longer tripped over his own feet, or at least not as frequently as he had on his arrival on Earth. Just when he'd thought he had it all figured out, something new had happened to throw him off course.

Hidden from view, he pressed the heel of his palm into his groin, hoping the pressure would ease the swelling. It didn't help much.

What must Sam have thought about him running out of the cinema like that?

Zak had a feeling he had screwed things up once again and he didn't know what made him feel worse, the painful swelling at his groin or the thought of Sam being angry at him for leaving in such a way.

* * * *

Darren wasn't home when Zak charged into the house. Eleanor was in her studio, but Zak had no intention of asking her about his current problem. She was a human and a female one at that. He'd learned enough from his time on Earth to figure out that Earth women didn't have what he had hanging between his legs.

Zak hurried into the bathroom and closed the door. It seemed as though he was better now anyway. Certainly he wasn't as uncomfortable as he had been back in the cinema. The swelling appeared to have gone down a lot. Perhaps he was simply contracting one of those strange Earth illnesses. He hoped it was nothing serious. It was bad enough he had this extra appendage getting in the way all time—the last thing he needed was for the wretched thing to swell up again and become even more cumbersome than it already was.

By the time Darren came home, Zak was convinced he had overreacted. The swelling had gone down and the bulge had returned to normal. He was glad he'd not told Eleanor or even Sam about it. With a bit of luck it wouldn't happen again and he could forget about the incident entirely.

In the meantime he had to go and see Sam and make sure things were still all right between the two of them. What must he have thought of him, running off the way he had?

* * * *

After Zak had disappeared on him, Sam had searched for him for some time. Eventually he'd had to give up and return home. His parents would be worried about him if he stayed out later than he'd told them he would.

He tried calling Zak, but his phone went to voicemail.

Lucy answered her phone on the first ring. "How'd it go, stud?"

"Crap."

"What happened?"

"I don't know. One minute we were watching the film and the next he was running out of the cinema like the hounds of hell were after him."

"Was it a horror film?"

"No, and I doubt a horror flick would scare him into running off."

"Then what happened?"

"I think maybe he freaked out when I touched him on the leg."

"You finally made a move and he freaked. What happened exactly?"

"He ran out of the cinema and disappeared. I couldn't find him anywhere and had to come home."

The doorbell rang downstairs and Sam let his mother answer the door.

"Sam, you have a visitor."

Sam went to the top of the stairs and saw Zak standing at the bottom of them. "He's here. I've got to go, Lucy, bye."

Zak stood at the foot of the stairs with a nervous expression on his face.

"I'll be in the kitchen if you want anything," Sam's mother said and she disappeared toward the back of the house.

"Why did you run off?" Sam asked.

"I'm sorry."

"Were you ill?"

"I'm not sure," Zak replied.

"What's that supposed to mean? You went running off like a crazy person. I was scared something had happened to you."

"I'm sorry."

"Stop saying you're sorry! Just tell me what's going on."

"Can we just forget about what happened?"

Sam could tell Zak was avoiding his questions, but he couldn't bring himself to ask the one he really wanted to know the answer to. Had Zak freaked out because of Sam touching his leg the way he had?

Lucy thought Zak was gay, but maybe he hadn't come to terms with his sexuality yet. If this was all new to him, then he'd need time to get used to the idea. Sam knew when to back off.

"Okay," he agreed. "Do you want to come upstairs?"

Zak nodded and ran up the stairs to join Sam.

At least Zak wasn't avoiding him completely after his clumsy and apparently unwanted pass.

* * * *

"This is intolerable," Zak muttered as he hurried down the corridor and into Darren's office without knocking. How many times was this going to happen to him? First at the cinema, then in Lucy's car as she'd driven him and Sam to college and now here in class as well. This was the third time this week and he'd had enough. It looked like he would have to ask Darren about the strange affliction after all. From Darren's memories he had a vague recollection of him suffering in a similar manner, though nothing in his knowledge told him Darren had understood what was happening to him. He hoped that some time during the last few centuries Darren had figured it out.

"Zak, what is it?" Darren asked with concern on his face.

"This." Zak pointed down at his crotch. "How the hell do you make it stop doing this?"

Darren looked down and a red flush covered his face. Zak could tell he'd embarrassed the older man, but right now he didn't care. He was in pain and leaking some sort of vital fluids and he had no idea what was happening to him.

"Well, don't just stand there looking!" Zak shouted. "Tell me what's wrong with me."

Darren seemed to realize Zak was genuinely worried and waved him toward a seat.

"I don't want to sit down, that only makes it worse."

Darren sighed. "I never thought I'd have to have this conversation. All my other sons managed to figure things out just fine on their own."

"Well, I'm sorry your other sons were so much smarter than me. But I'm just a stupid alien who doesn't know what's wrong with me."

"There's nothing wrong with you at all. Now calm down and take a seat."

Zak ignored the latest request to sit down. "If there's nothing wrong with me, why does it keep swelling up like this? And it's bleeding some white stuff. I thought human blood was red?"

"Human blood is red. The white stuff, as you call it, is semen."

"What the hell is semen and why is it leaking out of me all of a sudden?"

"Take a seat."

"Why do you keep telling me to sit down? That won't make it stop."

"Because you're wearing a groove in my carpet with all your pacing," Darren snapped back. "Now, sit down."

Zak threw himself into one of the chairs and folded his arms sulkily. "Fine, I'm sitting down. Now tell me what this semen stuff is and how I can make it stop."

Darren sat behind his desk and started tapping away at his laptop. "Here we are, the definition of semen..." He twisted the computer round so Zak could read the entry in the online medical dictionary.

"I don't understand even half of those words. Your stupid translator is failing on me again. It's like there isn't a word in our language for this. I just want to know why my cock keeps swelling and leaking and how to stop it."

"Are you doing anything specific when it starts doing these things?" Darren asked. "Or are you with someone in particular?"

"I wasn't touching it, if that's what you're asking. The first couple of times it happened I was just talking to Sam. This last time I was on my way to class."

"Maths?"

"Yes."

"The class you share with Sam."

"You know it is. Just tell me what's happening to me."

"Let me get this straight," Darren said. "You've been getting erections while you're talking to Sam?"

"Is that what you call it? An erection?"

"Well, yes. That's one term for it. Though there are other names for it as well."

"There seems to be a dozen names for everything on this bloody planet, if you ask me."

"Yes, I know it seems so at times. Anyway, back to the point. It sounds to me as though you being with Sam and thinking about him is what triggers these. Am I right?"

Zak thought back to each time the swelling—no, the erection—had occurred. "Yes, I think so. Is that important? Oh, crap, I'm not allergic to Sam, am I?"

Darren smothered a chuckle that caused Zak to glare at him again. "No, I promise erections aren't caused by any form of allergy. Do you like Sam?"

"Of course I do. He's my best friend."

"I'm glad you and Sam have patched things up. I admit I was wrong about him being a bad influence, though I'm still not so sure about Lucy. Sam appears to be a nice young man. All his teachers speak highly of him."

"I'm so glad you approve," Zak muttered sarcastically. "Now, how about you tell me how to get rid of the problem?"

Darren blushed again and turned the computer back around. This time he typed in the word *masturbation* and turned the results round to show Zak.

Zak wasn't sure what all the words in the description meant, but the images on the screen left nothing to his imagination. He clicked on one of the pictures and a video began to play. It looked a simple enough process to get rid of the problem.

"Just try to do this in the shower if you can," Darren muttered. "It'll save Eleanor on washing the sheets if you do this in your bed."

Zak practically ran from the office, the swelling in his trousers even more painful than it had been before he'd gone into the room.

He dug the map of the college out of his backpack and looked for the showers. He knew they were there somewhere.

"Where are you?" he muttered to himself as he searched the map, finally locating them on the ground floor near the sports complex. "Yes!"

He hurried down the corridor and raced down the stairs. Most of the students from the last sports class were getting changed back into their clothes. A few still lingered in the showers, washing off the grime and sweat of their lesson. Zak stripped off his clothes and hopped into the showers, determined to get rid of this problem once and for all.

Out of the corner of his eye Zak could see a few of the other young men looking in his direction. He ignored them and leaned forward, bracing one hand against the wet tiles. He gripped his penis with his other hand and stroked up and down the length in the same way that the man on the computer screen had done. It was too dry so Zak reached across and turned on the shower. The water made it a little smoother going, but he wasn't entirely sure he was doing it properly.

Zak tried to recall what he had seen on the monitor and remembered that one of the images was of a man using both hands, one to touch his length and the other to cup his testicles. Since he needed one hand to brace himself against the wall, he let go of his dick and directed his attention toward his balls, squeezing them and learning to his surprise that it felt pretty good.

He shivered as he found a particularly sensitive spot. Damn, this human body was like nothing he had ever had before. It was so responsive to his touch. Why hadn't he tried a little exploration before now?

Of course the answer was simple—until now he had not been interested in the body he was stuck in. It had been merely a vessel and something he had to endure.

Now he saw things differently. He needed to touch every single spot and discover all of its secrets.

Suddenly the image popped into his head of Sam being the one doing the touching. Sam's fingers ghosting over his cock and touching him intimately. Sam stroking his back and arse and all those places Zak couldn't quite get to. Were there any more spots just out of his reach that he and Sam could discover together?

He returned his attention back to his erection, stroking the length more rapidly as he strained to reach some pinnacle he didn't completely understand. He felt out of control, his body no longer entirely his own.

"Sam," he groaned as he touched himself. "Oh, God, Sam!"

His legs buckled and he braced himself to stop from falling to the ground. His vision blurred as he lost what little control he had left and semen shot from the end of his penis, hitting the tiles opposite him.

When he had recovered himself a little, Zak became aware of the sound of clapping and laughter behind him. He turned to see a crowd of students in various stages of undress watching him with wide eyes and open mouths. He had a feeling he had done something wrong again, even though all he'd done was follow

Darren's advice. He shifted uncomfortably and the crowd eventually began to disperse, leaving him to clean up before drying off with a towel someone had left behind, retrieve his clothes and get dressed.

A few other students lingered nearby. None of them spoke to him although a few were clearly whispering about him, pointing in his direction and snickering openly. He thought he heard one of them use the word 'queer' and although Darren's translator told him it meant odd or strange, Zak had a feeling that wasn't what they meant.

* * * *

Sam sat on his usual spot on the wall, waiting for Lucy to drive round and pick him up. It was spitting with rain and he hoped she turned up before it started to throw it down.

Thankfully Lucy arrived before the downpour, and he practically ran to the car.

"You'll never guess what I heard today," Lucy announced as soon as he had gotten into the passenger seat.

"Probably not," Sam muttered. He hoped Lucy didn't make him try to guess her gossip. It seemed his luck was in and Lucy was too eager to divulge what she had heard to make him play twenty questions.

"I heard Zak was caught tossing off in the college showers today."

"Zak doesn't do any sports classes."

"I never said he did."

"Then why would he be in the showers?"

"I don't know. I heard he ran in there between classes, stripped off his clothes and just started wanking right there in front of everyone."

"I don't believe it. Why would Zak do something so stupid? Why would any bloke, for that matter?"

"Swear to God. I heard it from Tanya, who heard it from Trudy and Amy."

"Oh, then it *must* be true." Sam had no idea who Tanya or Amy were, but Trudy had been at his school and was hardly the most reliable source of information.

"There's no need to be sarcastic."

"You're telling me gossip about something that happened in the boys' changing rooms and your three sources are all girls. Forgive me for being a little skeptical."

Lucy waved away his skepticism. "You haven't heard the best bit yet."

"I'm not sure I want to."

"Oh, you'll want to hear *this*."

Sam knew there would be no putting her off telling him the apparent highlight of her gossip. "Okay, what's this so-called best bit?"

Lucy grinned widely and waited for several seconds before continuing. "Zak apparently cried out for you when he was coming."

"Don't start that again. I told you what happened on the date that never was. I thought we were in agreement that Zak's not gay."

"I never agreed to anything of the sort. He's definitely batting for your team."

"What makes you so sure? He had plenty of opportunity to make his feelings known at the cinema. I made it pretty clear I was interested in him and he ran out on me."

"He's probably scared of how intense his feelings are for you," Lucy said with a knowing nod.

"I think you're barking up the wrong tree here. Zak doesn't fancy me. Maybe he knows someone called Samantha." Even as he said the words, Sam doubted they were true. But if Zak really did like him, why had he run off?

"Rubbish. He was talking about you."

"And what are you expecting me to do about it?"

"Well, you could ask him out on a date."

"We went to the cinema last weekend, remember?"

"You need to make it clear that you're attracted to him. Throw yourself at him if you have to."

"I'm not going to make a fool of myself again."

"Do you want to be a virgin all your life?"

"Shut up."

Lucy grinned. "I think you and Zak look pretty good together. You're the guy Zak fantasizes about and I bet you've had a few wet dreams about him as well."

"Even if I had, I wouldn't tell you."

"So you have..."

"No," Sam lied. Zak had been the star of his sexual fantasies from the day they had met. He hoped that Lucy was just guessing and that his crush wasn't quite as obvious as it appeared.

Lucy shook her head. "I don't believe you. You're both hot for each other, I can tell."

Sam thought back to their trip to the cinema. Zak had bolted the moment Sam had touched his leg. What had been the reason for his rapid departure from the cinema? Was he freaked out by another guy touching him, or did his own feelings have him running scared?

Zak, whose final class of the day was English on the top floor of the building, finally appeared and dashed for the car. He wasn't so lucky in avoiding the rain.

"Have a good day?" Lucy asked with a grin.

"Not bad," Zak replied as he climbed in the back seat.

"Anything interesting to tell us?" she pressed.

"Like what?"

Sam shifted in his seat, hoping Lucy was too engrossed in teasing Zak to notice his fidgeting. He had a feeling he would need a certain type of shower himself this evening, one with Zak making a special guest appearance of his own. It wasn't just his hopes that had been raised with the latest bit of gossip to do the rounds.

* * * *

"Zak, come down here right away. I want to talk to you."

Zak looked up from the textbook at the sound of Darren's voice calling him from downstairs.

"Zakrynious, now!"

Zak tossed the book aside and slowly responded to the shout. He found Darren in the living room, pacing the carpet. Eleanor sat on the sofa, anxiously watching her husband.

"What's the problem?" Zak asked.

"What the hell did you think you were doing?" Darren shouted.

"Darren, darling, you don't have to shout," Eleanor interrupted before Zak could respond to the question. Not that he had an answer anyway. He didn't understand. Had he done something wrong?

"The showers," Darren prompted impatiently. "Wanking in the college showers, what the hell were you thinking?"

Zak was none the wiser, though from the look of mild embarrassment on Eleanor's face, she knew what Darren was talking about. "What's wanking?"

Darren opened his mouth to speak, but instead let out a loud sigh. "Oh, Zak."

"I don't understand," Zak said.

Darren sat down in one of the wingback chairs and gestured for Zak to take a seat as well. "Wanking is another name for masturbation."

"It is?"

Darren ran a hand through his hair and groaned. "Yes, so do you want to explain why the hell you were masturbating in the public showers?"

"Because you told me to."

"I did nothing of the sort."

"You said to do it in the shower to save Eleanor on cleaning the sheets of my bed," Zak argued vehemently. He glanced at Eleanor as he spoke and her blush turned an even deeper shade of red.

"I meant the shower at home, on your own, not in the ones at the college where anyone can see you."

Zak folded his arms over his chest and huffed. "Then you should have been more specific. There are humans doing it on the Internet for everyone to see. How was I supposed to know you meant for me to go sort it out in private?"

"I didn't imagine for a minute you'd do something so stupid," Darren shouted.

Eleanor tutted loudly. "Darren, yelling isn't going to help."

"What was I supposed to do?" Zak snapped back. "My next class was with Sam and I couldn't go there with my penis practically poking through my trousers, could I?"

"Yes, that is *exactly* what you should have done. Every man in the world gets erections at inconvenient times. It's something you learn to deal with."

"You told me to deal with it by masturbating in the shower!"

"I didn't mean right then!"

Zak stood up and began to pace the floor. "You know I'm still struggling with this stupid language. You'll just have to be clearer about what you tell me in future."

Darren glared at him. "You can't blame all of this on me. Part of it is just plain common sense. If you were on any other world, would you have considered having sex in public?"

"I wasn't having sex! That's something animals do."

Darren took a deep breath, clearly trying to rein in his temper. "And humans."

"What?"

"Humans reproduce by having sex."

"They do?"

"Yes."

"Why wasn't that bit of information included in the knowledge extracted from you after you were fostered here?"

"I'm sure it must have been," Darren said. "You just seem to recollect what you like and disregard the rest."

"Actually," Eleanor interrupted again, "maybe it wasn't in the knowledge they took from you."

Darren looked at Eleanor. "It must have been."

Eleanor shook her head, a tiny smile playing on her lips. "Have you forgotten our wedding night so soon?"

Zak had no idea what she was talking about, but her words made sense to Darren and he groaned and put his head in his hands.

Zak looked at Eleanor for an explanation.

"Darren's time here before he reached maturity was rather short, not even a month, although it was long enough for him to decide he wanted to spend his life with me. However, it wasn't long enough for a proper courtship to take place, at least not one that would satisfy my father. We were married after our return here."

"At the point of your father's sword," Darren muttered.

Eleanor chuckled and nodded. "Well, what did you expect after taking me away for so long without a chaperone?"

"It wasn't like anything happened while we were on my home world."

"No, but I seem to recall that was because you didn't know what we could have been doing. It was only on our wedding night, after our return to Earth, that you learned about the delights of the bedchamber. My mother was rather impressed I'd married a virgin."

"You told your mother about our wedding night?"

"Yes, she wanted to know I was okay."

"Did you have to tell her *everything*?"

Eleanor laughed. "I promise I gave her an edited version. But you do see the point I'm trying to make?"

Darren seemed to realize where Eleanor was going with this and turned to Zak with an apologetic smile. "I'm sorry. I'd completely forgotten when I learned about human sex. You're quite right. You wouldn't have the knowledge from the implant."

Zak accepted his apology with a curt nod.

"I'd also managed to forget you aren't a typical teenage boy."

"What do you mean? Am I not like other humans?"

"Yes, except most teenage boys seem to think about sex the majority of the time. I suspect we'll need to further your education in that regard before much longer. In the meantime, and for future reference, masturbation is a very sexual activity."

Zak's mouth opened in a small 'o' and he gulped nervously. When he found his voice it was hoarse and croaky. "But I was on my own."

"Ignoring for the moment the fact that you actually weren't alone, masturbation is a very private thing, done either alone or in the company of a lover."

"Are you telling me I just had sex with myself in public?" Zak yelled, his voice sounding more like a screech than anything else.

"Essentially, yes."

"Oh, shit."

Zak paced across the floor again. "How much trouble am I in?"

"Not as much as you could be. I told the principal you were doing it on a dare and it won't happen again. It won't happen again, right?"

Zak nodded. "Right. Never again."

"I guess I'd better go brush up on sex education to make sure we cover the right topics," Darren said. He sighed and closed his eyes. "There's a conversation I never imagined I'd be having."

Eleanor chuckled, earning herself a sharp look from Darren.

"What do you mean?" Zak asked.

"It means we'll have to have a talk about sex between two men, since from our discussion in my office and your subsequent shower, it would appear you're homosexual."

Zak's translator finally came through with an explanation for homosexual and he frowned thoughtfully. "I wanted Sam to touch me in that way, so I guess I am."

"Perhaps this discussion can wait for another day?" Eleanor suggested. "Dinner will be ready soon and I've invited a couple of guests from the gallery who are interested in displaying some of my landscapes. I don't think this subject is really an appropriate topic for the dinner table."

Darren looked as relieved as Zak felt at the idea of putting off what would almost certainly be an embarrassing discussion.

Zak didn't want to think about human sex at all. He knew humans were essentially animals, just like most beings were, including his own species. He just hadn't realized until now that they still reproduced like animals too. Sexual reproduction had been phased out on Trimmeron thousands of years ago. Instead the scientists of their world created new life in their laboratories, ensuring the best possible matches between the donors. Over the centuries their people had evolved not through nature, but through science. Zak wondered briefly what his natural form would be like now if their scientists had left well enough alone.

Sex, meanwhile, when it had no longer become necessary for the survival of their species, had become a rarity, just like hugs, touches and anything else that invaded another's personal space.

Zak recalled the touch of Sam's hand on his thigh in the dark cinema and his cock reacted instantly. When had he become so comfortable with the idea of being touched?

"Homosexual," he whispered, trying the word out on his tongue.

"Are you okay with this?" Eleanor asked.

Zak jumped, having forgotten she was there. "I never thought of myself as a sexual creature," he admitted.

"Neither did Darren," Eleanor replied. "That isn't what I meant, though. Are you comfortable with being attracted to other men?"

Something in her tone of voice worried him. "Is there something wrong with attraction to men?" he asked.

"No, but not everyone on Earth feels that way. In some countries, it's illegal."

"Is it illegal here?"

"No, England decriminalized homosexual behavior last century. But there are still some people, even here, who might take offense to you if they find out you like men."

Zak wasn't sure he liked the sound of that. Then again, Sam had been the one to touch him first and if Sam was okay with it, and he suspected he was, Zak could learn to live with any critics the two of them had to face.

Chapter Eight

Sam didn't want to get his hopes up, but the more time he spent with Zak, the harder it was to stop himself from wanting more than friendship with him.

He decided against asking Zak about the shower incident, even though he was dying of curiosity to know if it had really happened. Sam would take things at a slow pace and see how things went. With a bit of luck he wouldn't expire from excessive horniness while waiting.

"Are you okay?" Zak asked as they worked on their final Maths assignment for the year.

"Yes."

"You're pretty quiet."

"Just thinking."

"About anything in particular?"

"Not really. Just about Christmas and stuff."

"Does your family celebrate the holidays?"

"Yeah. We have a huge family dinner with all the relatives each year. What about you?"

"We're going away for New Year," Zak said. "My parents have a house in the south where they hold an annual party each New Year's Eve."

"That sounds nice."

"They said I can invite a friend if I want."

Sam drew in a sharp breath.

"Only if you don't have any other prior engagements," Zak hurried to assure him.

"I'd like to come to your house very much," Sam said. "I'm sure my parents would agree to me going."

He suspected his mother might not be too happy about him going away for a few days, but provided his health didn't deteriorate, he figured he could talk her round.

Zak's face lit up as they talked about their plans. Sam's own excitement grew at the realization that he would be spending at least part of the holiday period with Zak and maybe he could tell him how he felt while they were away.

* * * *

The Johnson house was not what Sam had expected. With a gatehouse, stables and its own private chapel, it was an honest to goodness mansion with grounds sprawling out in all directions.

"I can't believe you didn't tell me about this place," Sam said.

"Um," Zak faltered. "Not much to tell really."

"Is everything okay with you boys?" Zak's father asked from the front of the car as he navigated it around the back of the house toward the barn, which appeared to have been converted into a garage.

"Fine, Mr Johnson," Sam replied. "Just admiring your house."

"I've told you before, please, call me Darren. I take it this isn't what you expected, huh?"

"Not exactly. I thought all teachers were poor."

Darren laughed loudly. "The wages aren't what you'd call great, but I love teaching. This place is inherited, though. It's been in my family for generations."

"It looks amazing."

"I'm sure Eleanor would love to give you a tour of the place. She knows the history as well as I do, but unlike me, she also remembers all the interesting bits of gossip."

Eleanor twisted round in her seat. "Don't believe a word he says."

"You mean you don't know the gossip?" Sam asked.

"Yes, I know it, but so does he."

They all laughed while Darren vehemently denied the accusation.

Once they were settled into the guest rooms, Eleanor took them on a tour of the house, telling them story after story about the inhabitants who had lived there.

There were many family portraits in the gallery and Sam could see the resemblance between many of the men and Darren. There were also similarities between Eleanor and some of the females in the paintings. In fact, when Sam looked closely, he could swear they were all the same person, just with vastly different styles of clothes and hair. When he commented on his observation, Eleanor simply smiled and moved on to the next picture and story.

Sam could tell Zak was equally interested in the history of the place and the people who had lived there. He asked a lot of questions, even more than Sam, and Eleanor had an answer for every single one. Sam wondered why he showed such an avid interest, when surely he must have heard all these stories many times before.

"Have you ever been a teacher?" Sam asked.

"No, I've always been an artist," Eleanor replied. "I just enjoy remembering the past."

"Are any of your paintings on display here?" Zak asked.

"Yes, a few of them."

"Can we see them?" Sam asked.

Eleanor nodded and led them into the study. "This is one of mine," she said, pointing to a landscape of mountains set against a sky with three moons.

"Is this—?" Zak didn't finish his question before Eleanor nodded.

"Yes, these are the mountains you grew up near."

Sam looked closely at the painting, not recognizing the mountains as well as wondering why there were three moons.

"It's not an exact representation of them," Eleanor continued hurriedly. "I took a few liberties, as you can see. I was going for a fantasy look."

"Which mountains are these?" Sam asked. He was sure they weren't in England and he wondered where Zak had grown up. Zak had told him he knew many other languages, yet Sam was ignorant as to much of his youth.

Zak looked like he might be about to reply, but Eleanor deftly cut him off. "How about some lunch?"

Sam and Zak voiced their enthusiasm for the idea and they all made their way back downstairs. Sam hoped he could remember his way around this place. With so many rooms and corridors, it would be remarkably easy to get lost.

"You like it here?" Zak asked.

"Very much."

"Me too."

"Who wouldn't like it?" Sam said with a grin. "I can't wait to see this place full of guests for the party."

New Year's Eve was the following evening and Eleanor and Darren had a lot of work to do. Sam and Zak offered to help, but with the staff they had hired for cleaning, catering and valeting, they weren't needed and had nothing to do except explore the house and hang out together.

For Sam, the time alone presented the perfect opportunity to test the waters with Zak. Casual touches, lasting just a little longer than usual, were not rejected by the young man he was rapidly falling for and it gave him the encouragement he needed to press on with his advances.

Sam promised himself that before the New Year rolled in, he would tell Zak exactly how he felt.

* * * *

The fireworks were spectacular. At least a hundred people had joined the Johnsons to ring in the New Year. The balcony in Zak's room looked out over the wide expanse of lawn toward the stand Darren had erected away from the house. Darren and two of his staff members were taking it in turns to set off sequences of rockets every five minutes from eleven o'clock onwards.

"Look at that one," Sam said as he pointed toward a particularly large explosion of green and silver.

Zak gasped in delight. He would never have believed Earthlings could make such spectacular fireworks.

"You look like you've never seen fireworks before," Sam teased.

Zak blushed. "I have, but they weren't as good as these."

"You should see the ones in London. They light up the whole sky."

A triple explosion of red and gold accompanied by some of the loudest bangs yet nearly drowned out Zak's response. "Maybe next year we could go and see them."

Sam's delighted grin in response almost made Zak forget he probably wasn't going to be on this planet when the next New Year rolled in.

"My dad says they didn't used to do fireworks at New Year until the millennium, then suddenly it became something of a tradition."

"The millennium?" Zak asked.

"The year two thousand, dork," Sam answered with a nudge to Zak's shoulder. "Do you want to hear about some of the other New Year traditions we have?"

"Sure."

"Well, there's a song we all sing called *Auld Lang Syne* when midnight comes."

Zak looked back into the bedroom at the clock on the wall. "It's almost midnight now."

Sam smiled and even in the dim light, mischief was visible in his eyes. "So it is."

"What other traditions do you have?"

Sam glanced into the empty room before turning to look back out toward the village. "Well, there's one more tradition you might enjoy."

"What's that?"

Sam leaned on the metal railing but didn't answer.

Everything quietened momentarily as the fireworks halted. Downstairs people counted down the last seconds of the year in loud unison.

Zak leaned on the railing beside Sam, trying to see his face in the darkness. "What's the other tradition?" he asked again.

Sam turned to face him. He mumbled something under his breath and stepped right up to Zak. "This," he whispered right before he pressed his lips to Zak's.

For several seconds, Zak had no idea what Sam was doing. He had seen a few other people doing this, mostly at the club they had gone to — what was this touching of mouths called again? — but he'd not taken a great deal of notice.

Before he could recall the word, he felt Sam's tongue coaxing his mouth open and pushing its way inside. Zak panicked as soon as he felt the invasion in his mouth and he pushed Sam away with far more force than necessary.

"What are you doing?" he asked as he wiped his hand across his mouth.

"It's a New Year tradition," Sam replied. "We do this at the stroke of midnight."

Zak decided immediately he didn't like this tradition as much as the fireworks and the party. "You put your tongue in my mouth," he said. "That's disgusting."

Sam stepped back slowly. "Shit," he whispered.

Zak picked up his glass of punch from the table and took a long swallow. When he turned back to Sam the other man had disappeared from the balcony. The bedroom was empty and the door leading to the hallway stood open.

The sounds of singing drifted up from downstairs. The New Year had begun, but Zak no longer felt like celebrating. He wasn't sure exactly what had happened, but he had a feeling he might have made a mistake that couldn't be passed off as simply because he came from somewhere different.

* * * *

Sam locked the door to the guestroom and threw himself onto the bed. His mobile phone, abandoned on the bedside table, bleeped with the alert for a new message. He grabbed the phone and saw Lucy had messaged him wishing him a Happy New Year. The temptation to throw the phone across the room was almost overwhelming. So far it seemed as though this year was going to suck as badly as the previous one.

A knock on the door and Zak's concerned voice asking if he was in there did nothing to improve his temper.

"Piss off," he called without moving from the bed.

"Sam, are you all right?"

"I'm fine. Piss off."

"Are you sure?"

"That I want you to go away? Yeah, I'm sure."

"I meant are you sure you're okay?"

"I'm perfectly fine. It's the middle of the night and I want to go to sleep."

"But I thought you said the party would go on for a few hours after midnight?"

"It is. You should go downstairs and join the others. I'm going to sleep."

Sam didn't wait for Zak to say anything else. He grabbed the ear buds for his iPod and turned on his music. Tomorrow he would go home and try to forget he had ever met Zak Johnson.

* * * *

Zak woke up irritated and tired. He hated his human body when it felt like this. None of his other bodies had ever had this problem with lack of energy.

The previous night he had spent nearly an hour trying to talk to Sam, only to be ignored almost completely. Eventually he had given up and gone back to his own room. The last thing he'd felt like doing was re-joining the partygoers.

He wandered downstairs and found Eleanor in the kitchen, cleaning up some of the debris from the festivities.

"Morning, sleepyhead," she said as Zak stumbled to the fridge and looked for something to help cure his headache.

Zak grabbed a carton of juice and took a long swallow.

"Glasses are in the cupboard," Eleanor reminded him. "Is Sam up yet?"

"Don't know."

"I guess everyone's a little late getting started today," Eleanor said. "I've only been up ten minutes or so myself."

Zak glanced at the clock and saw that it was almost noon.

"Did you have a good time last night?" Eleanor asked. "We didn't see much of you and Sam after supper."

"We went upstairs to watch the fireworks from my balcony," Zak said.

Eleanor gave him a bright smile. "They were good, weren't they? Much better than last year, though I suspect the weather ruined most of the displays then. At least it stayed dry last night, though the wind was bitterly cold."

Eleanor continued to chatter away while Zak sat on one of the stools gazing out of the window. Darren was outside on the lawn picking up rubbish. From the large bulging bag he had with him, Zak guessed he had been working out there for a while. Zak wondered whether he should speak to him about what had happened the night before.

"I'm going to help Darren," Zak said, only realizing after he had spoken that he had apparently cut Eleanor off mid-sentence. She didn't call him on his rudeness, merely waving him toward the door.

Outside it was nearly as cold as it had been the night before. He missed his insulating fur more than ever.

"Hey," Darren said as he picked up a brightly colored piece of rubbish. "Have you come to give me a hand collecting the fireworks?"

"Sure."

Darren smiled and pointed toward the border of flowers. "There are a few rockets in the flowerbeds if you want to get them."

Zak dutifully went to collect the rubbish. They worked in silence for nearly fifteen minutes while Zak tried to work up the courage to ask his question.

"What's bothering you?" Darren asked.

"Can I ask you something?"

"That's what I'm here for. What's the matter?"

"Er..."

"Does it have anything to do with Sam leaving at first light?"

"What?" Zak dropped the rocket as Darren's question registered in his mind. "Sam's gone?"

"Yeah. He called a taxi to take him home. I told him to wait until tomorrow, if only to save on the price of fares today, but he insisted on going. He wouldn't let me pay for the trip either. He's as stubborn as you."

"I'm not stubborn."

"You're worse than a mule. What happened to send Sam running home?" Darren asked.

"I don't know. I didn't even know he'd gone."

"He didn't tell you he was leaving?"

"No."

"What did you do?"

Zak turned his back on Darren. "I love how you automatically assume it's something *I've* done. It couldn't possibly be something Sam did."

Darren stepped around so he was in front of Zak. "I'm sorry. I didn't mean it to sound like that. It's just that when I first arrived on Earth and people were pissed off at me, well, it was usually because I had said or done something that isn't normally done on this planet."

"Like wanking in the public showers?" Zak said with a small, embarrassed smile.

"Yeah, like that. Now, are you going to carry on stalling or are you going to tell me what happened after the two of you left the main party last night?"

"We went upstairs to watch the fireworks from my balcony."

"And?"

"And we talked about New Year traditions."

Darren waited patiently, not pushing or prompting Zak until he was ready to open up.

"He shoved his tongue in my mouth," Zak finally blurted out.

"Ah. He kissed you."

"*That's* what it's called!" Zak exclaimed. "I've been trying to remember the word all night."

"Well, as long as your vocabulary issue is sorted, how about we get back to the question of why Sam left."

"I don't know why he left."

"You can't fool me," Darren replied with a knowing expression on his face. "You and Sam have been getting pretty close the last few weeks. Last night he kissed you and this morning he ran back home. It doesn't take a genius to figure out this isn't the full picture. What else happened between the kiss and this morning?"

"He went to his room and locked the door on me."

"Zak!" Darren's patience was clearly reaching its end. "Did you kiss him back?"

Zak kicked at the grass with the toe of his shoe. "No, of course not. I didn't even realize what he was doing at first."

"Ah."

"Will you stop saying 'ah' like it explains everything?"

"But it does. You've never kissed anyone before, just like I never had before I came to Earth. I remember my first reaction when a rather forward young lady decided she wanted to get to know me better and gave me my first kiss." Darren shuddered visibly. "It was quite a traumatic experience."

"Is that any way to talk about your wife?" Zak teased, knowing he was stalling again.

"It wasn't Eleanor who kissed me—it was her younger sister, Mary. Goodness, I've not thought about her in years."

"What happened to her?"

"She eloped with a French merchant, much to the horror of her parents. Now, back to your kiss with Sam. What exactly happened when he kissed you? What did you say and do?"

"He shoved his tongue in my mouth!" Zak pulled a face. "It's a disgusting thing to do."

"You didn't say that to Sam, did you?" Darren cringed at Zak's nod. "So, let me get this straight. Sam kissed you and you told him it was disgusting. Anything else?"

"I might have pushed him away from me to make him stop. Then he went and locked himself in his room and wouldn't talk to me except to tell me to piss off."

"No wonder he ran off."

"Surely he knew it was a revolting thing to do?" Zak said.

"Humans don't think so, at least not when they're kissing someone they have feelings for. They often find it most enjoyable."

"They do?"

"Yes. I have to admit I'm not too fond of it myself, but Eleanor enjoys it."

"I've never seen the two of you kiss."

"That's because we don't do it very often, and when we do, it's usually behind the closed door of the bedroom. Eleanor knows I don't really enjoy kissing so we don't bother very often."

"You actually let her put her tongue in your mouth?"

"Yes. You have to remember that human sex is very much about putting parts of your body into your lover's or the other way around. Humans have very physical relationships."

Zak blushed. "I can see that from the way they keep throwing themselves at each other."

Darren sighed. "We really are going to have to sit down and have a chat about the birds and the bees when we get home."

"Huh?"

"It's just an expression," Darren explained. "Humans use it to describe talking about sex."

"Oh."

"Remind me when we get back to have a chat."

Zak nodded although he had no intention of doing anything of the sort. He had managed to avoid that particular discussion so far, largely because he suspected Darren was doing just as much to avoid it. Despite being on Earth for so long, Darren still wasn't very comfortable discussing certain things, sex being one of them.

"You're going to have to talk things over with Sam," Darren continued.

"Maybe it would be best to leave things as they are."

Darren gave him an appalled look. "Why would you want to do that? Sam's your friend and it's pretty obviously he wants to be even more. If you don't talk to him, you'll lose him entirely."

"I'll lose him anyway once I leave Earth."

"You could always stay here longer. Remember, human lives are very short compared to ours. You could live here with Sam for the rest of his life and still have thousands of years left to explore the rest of the universe."

"I don't want to stay here any longer than I have to."

Darren gave him a small smile. "You know, this place isn't so bad when you get used to it. And I think you're already starting to like it."

"No, I'm not. I hate being back in education, I hate having a human body and I hate feeling so dumb all the time."

"You're not stupid. You'd pick things up quickly enough if you just gave it a try."

"I don't want to give it a try. I want to finish my exile here and go home."

"I thought you were starting to settle in a little."

"I'm making the best of a bad situation, that's it. I hate Earth and everything about it."

"Does that include me and Eleanor?" Darren asked.

Zak flushed at his inadvertent insult of his foster parents. "No, of course not."

"Or Sam?" Darren pressed on. "Do you hate him?"

"Only a complete arsehole could hate Sam."

"You have to sort things out with him. Even if you can't love him in the way he wants, you have to at least clear the air."

"But—"

"You need to talk to him and explain things."

"Explain what? It's not as though I can tell him the truth."

"Why not?"

"I thought I was supposed to keep my alien origins a secret from the locals."

"Well, I wouldn't recommend putting an ad in the paper or telling everyone you meet you're from another planet. But telling a close friend is different. You should consider it."

"When did you tell Eleanor?"

"I didn't. She saw the craft drop me off and knew from the start I wasn't from this world."

"She did?"

"She thought I was some sort of god come down to Earth. Eventually she accepted I was just a mortal, although not a human one. When my time being fostered here came to an end, I took her with me and she understood better."

"That doesn't mean Sam will believe me if I tell him."

"Sam's a smart young man, and people in this day and age at least consider the possibility of life on other planets. Sam's into astronomy as well, isn't he?"

"So?"

"He's been studying the stars and the sky for a long time. He might believe you if you tell him the truth."

"And if he doesn't?"

"Then you cross that bridge when you come to it. But you at least need to consider giving him a chance."

Zak wasn't so sure. Darren had come to Earth in a different age. At the moment, Zak was just scraping by with only a couple of friends. If he told Sam the truth and he didn't believe him, what would stop him telling everyone that Zak was a lunatic who thought he came from another planet?

The one thing he did agree with was that he needed to try to patch up his friendship with Sam, though, without resorting to telling him the truth, he had no idea how he was going to do it.

Chapter Nine

Lucy barged into Sam's room before he had even gotten out of bed.

"Go away," Sam muttered from under the duvet.

"Not going to happen," Lucy replied as she bounced on the edge of the bed. "What are you doing back here so soon?"

"I wasn't feeling well."

"Since when have you let that stop you doing something you want to?"

"Since now."

"Why aren't you at Zak's house in the country?"

"It's a mansion."

"Really?"

"Yeah."

"Wow. So, why aren't you at Zak's *mansion*?" Lucy poked him through the duvet and Sam batted her hand away before burrowing farther under the covers.

"Going there was a mistake."

"Why?"

"I don't want to talk about it."

"Did something happen between you and Zak?"

Sam groaned. Lucy knew him way too well and unfortunately he knew her well enough to realize she wasn't going to go away until he had answered all her questions. "No."

"Oh, God, you had sex with him, didn't you? Was it good? Who was on top?" Lucy was way too perky for this time in the morning.

"Shut up."

"So you *did* have sex with him."

"No, I didn't. Go away."

Lucy jabbed him in the ribs again. "I thought you were going to make your move while you were staying with him."

"I did."

"Oh."

"Yeah, oh."

"What happened?"

Sam crawled out from under the covers and sat up. "It turns out he's not gay after all."

"Of course he is. Why else would he have called out your name when he was tossing off in the showers?"

"A dare or a bet? Just to play with my feelings for kicks? Take your pick of reasons. Or maybe it never actually happened?"

"Of course it happened. Everyone was talking about it."

"Neither of us was actually there, though. You know how rumors start. Or maybe he was thinking about another Sam, one who is really called Samantha."

Lucy looked thoughtful for several long moments before shaking her head. "He's gay, I know it."

"What makes you so sure?"

"Because my gaydar is better than yours."

"There's no such thing as gaydar."

"Sure there is, and mine is telling me Zak is a guy who likes cock."

Sam sighed. "If he does, he doesn't want mine."

"You could have fooled me."

"He pushed me away when I kissed him, okay? I kissed him at midnight on New Year's Eve and he pushed me away and said I was disgusting."

"Are you sure?"

"Of course, I'm sure."

"What had you been eating that day?"

"What?"

"Maybe you had bad breath. Was it definitely *you* he thought was disgusting or was it the kiss?"

Sam racked his brain to remember. "Maybe he did mean the kiss."

"See, I'm right, as usual. You'd probably been eating garlic or something. Next time you kiss him, take a breath mint first."

"There won't be a next time."

Lucy wouldn't take a hint. She was determined to see him and Zak in some romanticized version of domestic bliss, whether they wanted it or not. "Of course there will. He likes you and you like him."

"And apparently I'm a crap kisser. I'd not eaten anything he hadn't that night."

"I'm sure you're a great kisser. How many boys have you kissed?"

"Just Zak."

"Oh. So this was your very first kiss."

"Yeah. Sucks, huh? I finally meet a guy I really like and when I get up the nerve to kiss him, he thinks it's disgusting."

Sam waited for Lucy to say something else. He was mildly surprised when nothing was forthcoming. Eventually he sighed and nudged her with his foot.

"Let's just forget about it. Zak's clearly not interested in me and there's no point in whining about it. I'll finally get to university next year and I'll be able to meet guys there."

"You think you can forget about Zak so easily?"

"Yes."

"Rubbish. You've been mooning over him since his first day."

"Guys don't moon. That's a girl thing."

Lucy gave him an offended look. "You could have fooled me. 'Oh, Lucy, you wouldn't believe how smart Zak is'. 'Lucy, Zak said the funniest thing today'. 'Don't you think Zak looks really good in blue? It matches his eyes so well'. 'Isn't Zak the sweetest guy you've ever met?'"

Sam gave Lucy a kick to stop her reminding him of all the things he had come to like about Zak during the last few months. "Okay, maybe I've been mooning a little. But it stops right now."

"We'll see."

Sam nodded. "Yes, you will. From now on if anyone asks me about Zak, my answer is 'Zak who?'"

* * * *

"Go away," Sam said for the third time.

"I'm really starting to hate those words," Zak complained. "Can we at least talk about what happened?"

"What for?" Sam replied. "You made it perfectly clear you aren't interested in me."

"But I *am* interested in you."

Sam turned his back on Zak and addressed Lucy. "Did you see the hot new bartender at the pub last night?"

Lucy, bless her, knew exactly what he was doing and played along as he'd suspected she would. "Oh yeah, and he was definitely checking you out. We should go back there on Saturday night and see if he's working again."

"Sam, we have to talk," Zak insisted.

"I'm talking to Lucy right now."

Zak tugged on his arm until Sam had no choice except to face him.

"What?" he snapped a little more harshly than necessary.

"I need to explain what happened on New Year's Eve."

"I made a pass at you and you knocked me back," Sam said. "What's to explain?"

"You have to understand why."

"No, I don't. I'm fine with what happened. You aren't interested in me, so I've set my sights on someone else."

"I already told you I'm interested in you." Zak's voice was getting louder and drawing unwanted attention from students at the nearby tables.

Sam could tell Zak wasn't going to be put off for long. "Fine, come round to mine after dinner, say at seven o'clock, and we'll talk."

"Great!"

Zak's grin was contagious and Sam had to bite the inside of his cheek to avoid smiling back at him. He wasn't going to fall for Zak's quirky charm a second time. He would listen to whatever Zak had to say and then it'd be over and he'd forget about him.

* * * *

Zak arrived on Sam's doorstep right on time. Sam hadn't expected otherwise.

"Can we talk now?" Zak asked.

Sam didn't know if it was the best idea to hear Zak out right now, when he was still hurt and angry about what had happened, but Zak had made it clear he was determined to tell Sam the truth, whatever the truth happened to be.

Sam led them through to the kitchen and poured them each a glass of Coke. "You've got ten minutes to say your piece and get out of here."

"I'm not sure where to start."

"How about you start by telling me why you thought it would be funny to screw with my head the way you did?"

"What do you mean?"

Sam took a deep breath to calm his already rising temper. The humiliation he had felt on New Year's Eve crashed over him again. "If you aren't into guys, all you had to do was say so."

"I am into guys."

"You could have fooled me. How can you be into blokes when you think it's disgusting to kiss another guy?"

Zak looked kind of sheepish. "We don't have kissing where I come from."

"And where would that be?"

"Trimmeron."

"Where's that? I've never heard of the place."

"That's because it's another planet."

Sam thought he'd misheard. Surely Zak hadn't said what he thought he'd said. "Did you just say you're from another planet?"

"Yeah, that's right. I'm what you'd call an alien."

Sam slammed his glass down on the counter. "You're a dick."

"You don't believe me."

"Of course I don't. Why did you think I would? Because I'm into astronomy? I'm studying the stars and the planets, not looking for little green men."

"I'm not green. In my true form I'm sort of a pale blue."

"Of course you are." Sam's response was sarcastic, yet Zak seemed to be nodding as though he were being serious.

"I'm more furry as well," Zak continued. "Our bodies are pretty different to human ones."

Sam folded his arms across his chest and gave Zak a smug smile. "All right then, let's see this other form of yours."

"Er…"

"I'm not going to scream or run away or anything," Sam said. "I want to see this for myself."

"I can't."

"Why not?"

"Because during our puberty we take the forms of other beings and get fostered out to other worlds to learn about new cultures and people. Until I reach maturity I've no control over my body. I'm human until the next transition."

"That's awfully convenient."

"Hardly," Zak muttered. "I'm stuck as a human in a body I don't understand and it's about as inconvenient as you can imagine."

Sam didn't believe a word of Zak's explanation, but he had a sneaking suspicion he knew where this was going. "I suppose you're going to tell me you don't have mouths, right?"

"No. We just don't use them like humans do."

"Well, I guess that's that then."

Zak looked confused. "What do you mean?"

"I think we should just forget about what happened at New Year and maybe spend a bit of time apart."

"Why? I thought we were friends."

"We are, but I like you as more than a friend and I need to move on from that. I can't if we're hanging out together all the time."

Zak shook his head. "But I feel the same way."

"It won't work," Sam replied.

"Why not?"

"Because either you're a liar who thinks I'm an idiot or you're an alien who doesn't want the same things I do."

"You don't believe me, do you?"

"No, I guess I don't."

Zak took off his glasses and rubbed his eyes. As Sam took in Zak's dejected expression he realized he *wanted* to believe Zak's outrageous story. He stared into Zak's eyes, admiring the rich shade of blue that made him think of exotic oceans. Sam was so busy gawking he didn't realize that Zak was holding his glasses out to him.

"Here," Zak said. "Take a look through these."

"I don't need glasses."

"Neither do I, except for reading. Take a look through them."

Sam put the glasses on though he couldn't spot any difference in his vision. "What am I supposed to be seeing?"

Zak picked up a discarded newspaper from the other end of the counter and passed it to Sam. "Tell me what you see."

Sam looked at the paper, wondering if there was a story in it about an alien invasion or something.

Instead the page was the entertainments section, where his parents had circled a couple of films and shows they were perhaps planning on going to see.

"I see the cinema listings," Sam said. "Is there a point to this?"

Zak reached across and did something to the right arm of the spectacles that caused them to give a tiny click. Sam blinked several times as the glasses blurred and strange symbols appeared in his line of vision.

"What do you see now?" Zak asked.

"There are some weird symbols floating above the paper." Sam looked over the top rim of the glasses and saw everything was entirely normal. Only through the lenses could he see the strange symbols.

"That's a translation into my language," Zak explained. "Darren, who's also from my world, made them to help me learn English."

"I suppose it makes sense that your parents are aliens as well." Sam could barely keep the sarcasm from his voice.

"Only Darren is. He's not my real father, he's my foster father. Eleanor, his wife, is human. He was fostered here when he was my age and decided to stay."

"With a whole universe out there he decided to settle on Earth?"

"Yes."

"Guess your world must be pretty crap."

Zak bristled with indignation. "It's a beautiful world. You've seen it yourself in Eleanor's painting of the mountains."

"She said that was a fantasy painting."

"Because Earth only has one moon and no one would accept it was a landscape true to life."

Sam didn't believe a word of it. He held out the glasses for Zak. "Here, you can have these back."

"Do you believe me?"

"No."

"But what about the glasses? You saw my language through them."

"Or they could just be a novelty item you found in a joke shop."

Zak took the glasses back and put them on. "What you think is a hearing aid is actually a device to translate spoken words for me."

"I suppose you want me to try that out as well."

Zak shook his head. "No. It wouldn't work with you, because you already know English. It's tuned to my brain, translating words I don't know for me. Besides..."

Sam frowned as Zak's voice trailed off. "What?"

"I'd just rather you believe me on my word."

Sam wished he could say he did, but how could he?

"Even if I do say I believe you, I think it'd be better if we go our separate ways."

"Why? If we enjoy each other's company, why should we spend time apart?"

"Because I want a guy who wants the same things I do."

"How do you know that's not me?"

"Because the man I spend my life with will actually enjoy kissing me," Sam snapped. "He won't think it's disgusting and push me away."

"I spoke to Darren about it and he says he can put up with being kissed by Eleanor. I can do the same."

"Put up with it!" Sam snarled. "I don't want you to put up with it. How do you expect to have a relationship with another guy if you can't even stand the thought of having his tongue in your mouth? Do you have any idea what two men do together?"

"Not really." Zak flushed as he looked away. Sam had a feeling it had taken a lot for Zak to admit his ignorance.

"Well, let me enlighten you," Sam said. "They kiss each other, and they suck each other's cocks."

Zak looked at him aghast. "They what? You mean you've actually put another man's penis in your mouth?"

"No," Sam admitted. "But I'd like to and I can tell you don't. You know what else gay men like to do with each other?"

Zak shook his head.

"They like to rim each other."

"Rim?"

Sam nodded. "That's right. You'd hate it, though."

"You don't know that."

"Sure I do. You can't stand the idea of sticking your tongue in my mouth. Do you expect me to believe you'd jump at the chance of shoving it up my arse?"

Zak's eyes nearly bugged out of his head. "You just made that up."

"No, I didn't. Don't you know anything about gay sex?"

"I've looked up sex, but what's gay sex? Is it when people are really happy about it?"

"Are you serious?" Sam couldn't believe anyone had led such a sheltered life that they had to actually look up what sex was and didn't even know what gay meant. "How can you not know what gay means?"

Zak ran his hands through his hair in frustration. "I know what it means, or I thought I did. But you're using the word in a context that doesn't make sense to me."

Sam recalled once again that English wasn't Zak's first language and he decided to give him the benefit of the doubt. "Gay is another word for homosexual."

"Why does English have so many words for the same bloody thing?"

"I don't know. So, what do you know about gay sex?"

"Darren explained to me about using condoms, if that's what you mean."

"No, it wasn't."

"Why don't you tell me about it, if you're such an expert?"

Sam pinched the bridge of his nose with his thumb and forefinger. "I'm not an expert, Zak. I'm a nineteen-year-old virgin. Most of what I know about gay sex is from watching online porn. Maybe you should do the same."

Zak seemed to be waiting for him to say something else. Sam didn't know what to tell him. The guy he'd thought of as a potential boyfriend wanted him to believe he came from another planet. Boy, did he know how to pick them.

"Just get out of here," he said.

"Sam, I..." Zak's voice trailed off as Sam glared at him. "Can I call you later?" he asked in a small voice.

"I don't think that'd be a good idea."

Zak didn't argue with him.

Sam shut himself up in his bedroom for the rest of the evening. Lucy tried calling him, but he sent her to voicemail and switched off his phone.

He didn't understand how a nineteen-year-old could expect someone to believe he had never heard of kissing. Kissing was a custom all over the world and Zak would have to have been living under a rock not to know what a kiss entailed.

Or on another planet, a small voice whispered in his mind. He shut the voice of insanity down immediately.

He knew there were people out there who lived very sheltered lives, but Darren and Eleanor seemed perfectly normal people. He wondered whether they knew their son was deluded. He wondered briefly whether he should speak to them about Zak's declaration of alien origin. He quickly dismissed the idea as visions of Zak being carted off in a straightjacket popped into his mind. Zak might be crazy, but Sam was sure he wouldn't hurt anyone.

Of course, the only problem with that argument was that Zak already had. Sam's heart had been well and truly stomped by the first guy he had ever truly fallen for.

Chapter Ten

Zak had messed things up completely and he knew it. Sam was barely speaking to him after their chat at his house and he had no idea how to fix things.

For two weeks Sam avoided him, ducking into classrooms when he saw him coming and racing from the college at the end of the day before Zak could catch him up. In Maths Sam arrived at the very last minute and made sure to take a seat as far away from Zak as he could. Some days he wasn't there at all.

Lucy, Zak's only other friend, appeared torn between her loyalty to Sam and her sympathy for Zak. She regretfully told him she couldn't give him a ride to and from college for a while and seemed to be genuinely sorry about it.

"You need to figure out what you want," she told Zak when he approached her to ask how Sam was doing.

"I want Sam," Zak replied.

"As a friend or a boyfriend?"

"What's the difference?"

"Sometimes I do wonder about you," Lucy said. "Sam likes you, I mean he *really* likes you, and you rejected him."

"I told him I'm sorry about that."

"I know, he told me, but sometimes that isn't enough. Sam can't just turn off his feelings for you."

"I don't want him to."

"What do you want?"

"I want to be with Sam, but I don't know what he wants from me. I don't know what I'm supposed to do."

Lucy gave him a sympathetic smile. "How much do you like Sam?"

"More than anyone else here."

"Did you really call out his name while wanking in the college showers?"

Zak's face heated with embarrassment. "I thought everyone had forgotten about that by now."

"So you did?"

"Yes."

"Then you *are* gay?"

Zak nodded, knowing now, after his talk with Sam, what she meant by this. "I think I am. I'm not sure. This is all really new to me."

"Do you want to have sex with him?"

"I don't know."

"Well, maybe by the time you figure out what you want he'll be ready to listen to you."

Lucy gathered her things together and left Zak to his thoughts. Did he want sex with Sam? He had no idea. He wasn't even sure what it meant to have sex with another man. He guessed it was long past time he found out.

* * * *

Research—that was the answer. If the Internet had the answers to every other question out there, surely it could help him with this one.

Sam had suggested that Zak look for gay porn, so that's what he started with. The number of results the search brought back was high and Zak felt sure he'd find the answers he needed within them.

Darren popped his head round the door about half an hour into Zak's search. "You're awfully quiet in here. Is everything okay?"

"Sure."

"Anything I can help with?"

"No, I'm just looking for gay porn."

Darren coughed and backed up. "Um, okay... Just...um... I'll be downstairs in my study if you need me. Not that I think you'd need my help with...er...that."

Zak chuckled as Darren rapidly hurried from the room, closing the door behind him.

After spending several more hours doing research, Zak was horny as well as confused about what he wanted. He had watched numerous videos of men doing various things to each other and he now had a much better understanding about what two gay men did together. What he didn't know was what he wanted to do with Sam.

His people were not very affectionate at all. They didn't hug or kiss and they didn't have sex. Physical relationships weren't something they engaged in. Then again, he considered as he looked down at his human body, his people didn't even have the same physiology as he had now. They didn't have a penis with what seemed to be a mind of its own. They didn't wake up each morning hard and aching for something they didn't even fully understand.

Sam understood, though. Sam was human, just like Zak now was.

Zak looked at the computer monitor where two men were sucking each other's cocks at the same time. Could he do that? Would Sam like to do that with him? Zak licked his lips as he imagined taking Sam's hard flesh into his mouth. What would he taste like?

The video finished and Zak closed down the web browser.

He had watched men fuck, suck, finger and grope each other. The men in the videos did things to each other Zak would never have thought of. Now he had seen for himself what possibilities lay before him, all he could think of was Sam. He realized he did want to do those things with Sam. For the first time since his transformation, he wanted to learn about his human body and explore Sam's as well, every square inch of it, including the inside of Sam's mouth. He wanted to kiss Sam and discover what it felt like.

He hoped he hadn't ruined things forever with his rejection of Sam's kiss.

* * * *

As tempting as it was to go down the road to Sam's house, the hour was late and Zak knew there was no possibility of talking to him tonight. Instead he retreated to his room where he locked the door and stripped out of his clothes as quickly as he could.

Even after the shower episode, Zak had taken very little time to study his human body, only doing what he had to in order to rid himself of unwanted erections when the need arose. Now he stood in front of the full-length mirror and took a long, hard look at himself.

The pale skin still took some getting used to, as did the lack of fur, but all in all humans weren't so very different from many of the other races out there. Two legs, two arms, walking upright—all these were pretty standard.

He thought back over the years to the other forms he had taken. He couldn't recall ever being in a body that felt as out of his control as this one did. In every other incarnation, his limbs did exactly what he wanted them to. Even the chimp-like body with the long tail to assist in swinging through the trees hadn't been as difficult to get used to as this human form.

None of his previous forms had had anything resembling sex organs. Like his own people, they had been produced in laboratories. Some of his older siblings had taken the forms of beings who still reproduced through sexual intercourse, but Zak had taken little notice of their stories, something he now regretted.

He ran his hand over his chest, brushing over the light dusting of hair, following the trail down over his abdomen and lower. He hadn't even reached his penis when it started to twitch in anticipation of his touch. Already hard from spending most of the afternoon and all evening watching porn, Zak stroked his length, watching it grow with an almost clinical curiosity.

The experience in the showers had been hurried. This time Zak went slower, keeping his touch light and noting the most sensitive spots, returning to them again and again. His breath quickened and his knees began to buckle. He moved over to the bed and stretched out on the mattress. He wondered if Sam had ever touched himself while thinking of Zak.

The thought of Sam caused a shiver to run through his body and he gripped his cock tighter, groaning loudly.

"Sam," he whispered as he quickened his strokes. "Oh, Sam."

He needed more than this. With his free hand he took hold of his balls, squeezing them gently, rolling them in his hand as he tried to catch his breath.

Semen—no, cum was the common term, he recalled from the Internet—leaked from the tip of his dick. He gathered some of the liquid onto his fingers and brought them to his lips, licking them clean, savoring the bitter taste. It reminded him of a dish he'd eaten on another world, the one of his third transformation, and he laughed at the thought that he might only have taken that particular form in order to get used to the taste of another man's cum.

With his hand clean once more, he decided to do a little more exploration, taking tips from what he had seen online. With his legs spread wide he reached between them, searching and finding his anus. His attempts at inserting his index finger were met with resistance and he growled in frustration. His erection vanished as Zak tried to figure out what he was doing wrong.

Annoyed at his body's lack of cooperation yet again, Zak went into the bathroom across the hall to clean up. When he opened the bathroom cabinet to get the toothpaste he saw something he had never noticed before. He pulled out the box and looked at it curiously. Darren and Eleanor had their own bathroom and never came into this one. Had Darren slipped this in here or had he simply failed to spot it before now? Whatever the truth, Zak felt foolish when he read the instructions for the lubricant.

Zak practically ran back to the bedroom and dove onto his bed. He tore open the box and fumbled with the contents, eager to pick up where he had left off a short while ago.

With the lube coating his digits, Zak reached between his legs and this time when he pushed against his pucker his finger slipped inside with relative ease. He wriggled his arse, fingering himself with surprising eagerness.

Moaning loudly, Zak hoped Darren and Eleanor were fast asleep and unable to hear him. He tried to stifle his noises, but each new discovery only increased his excitement and the volume of his cries.

When he found his prostate his hips bucked and he began to come, despite the lack of attention his dick had been getting the last few minutes. Semen sprayed over his stomach and chest and he screamed out his release. Spots danced in front of his eyes as he struggled to regain control of his body.

"Sam," he murmured as he pictured the dark-haired young man being the one to bring him such pleasure.

Later, before he fell asleep, Zak wondered if he would ever be able to persuade Sam to give him a second chance.

* * * *

Sam tried to ignore Zak as he attempted to make amends for what had happened. It wasn't an easy task at all. Zak moved seats in class so he could sit beside him and made sure to save a place for him at lunch. When he'd had another dizzy spell between classes, resulting in dropping all his books, Zak had carried them for him as he had escorted him to the nurse. He'd even typed up all his notes from the classes Sam had missed while he was off sick, providing him with a copy so he didn't fall behind in his work.

Slowly but surely Zak was wearing him down and getting right back under his skin.

"I'm screwed," Sam complained to Lucy as she drove him to college one morning nearly a month after his discussion with Zak at his house.

"Not yet," Lucy replied with a wink.

"That's not funny. If he doesn't stop being so nice I'm never going to get over him."

"Maybe you should give him a chance."

"A chance to do what? Break my heart?" Sam suspected it was already too late for that, but Lucy didn't need to know.

"Or make you happy."

"It'd never work."

"Why not?"

"We want different things."

"Such as?"

Sam shrugged and restrained himself from saying he wanted a sane boyfriend and Zak wanted a guy whom he never had to touch.

"Sam," Lucy nudged. "You know I'll get it out of you eventually, so you might as well spill now."

"I want a physical relationship with a guy and he doesn't."

"Are you sure about that?" Lucy asked.

"Yes."

"Then why does he keep checking out your arse?"

Sam gaped at his oldest friend. "He does not!"

"He does so. I've caught him doing it twice this week already, and it's only Tuesday morning."

Sam couldn't tell if she was making it up or not, and even if she was telling the truth, she could have been imagining things. "What should I do?" he asked.

"Invite him over this evening and see what happens." Lucy waggled her eyebrows suggestively.

"What if he knocks me back again?"

"If I'm right, he'll be the one making the first move and it won't be an issue."

"What makes you so sure?"

Lucy grinned. "Because you deserve a great guy after all you've been through."

"Deserving doesn't always mean getting."

"No, but it should. Invite him over and let him make a move. I bet he will."

Sam wasn't so sure, but he certainly wasn't getting over Zak by keeping him at arm's length. Every time he saw him, he seemed to be right back at square one, falling head over heels for him all over again.

* * * *

Despite his reservations, Sam invited Zak over after college as Lucy had suggested. Lucy gave the two of them a delighted smile as they climbed out of her car. Sam knew she had missed Zak's company almost as much as he had. If things worked out, Zak would be traveling to and from college with them just as he had before. The longer they spent time together, the more Sam's hopes rose. All the indications said Zak was attracted to him, but Sam had mistaken the signs before. There was definitely *something* there, though.

Zak kept looking at his lips. Sam caught him doing it several times, though he quickly averted his eyes each time he spotted him.

Sam smiled to himself and licked his lips deliberately. For someone who didn't like even the idea of kissing, Zak seemed to be rather obsessive about Sam's mouth. He wondered when Zak would make a move. He hoped it would be soon—otherwise he would be unable to stop himself from pouncing on him, despite his resolve to keep his distance.

"Would you like something to drink?" Sam asked. "I'm parched."

Zak nodded as Sam stood up and went through to the kitchen. He glanced back over his shoulder once and caught Zak blatantly staring at his arse. "Coke okay?" he called.

"Huh?"

Sam chuckled at Zak's distraction and disappeared into the kitchen. He knew he was rather wicked to keep tormenting Zak in this way, yet he couldn't seem to help himself. Zak might not like the idea of most of the stuff gay men got up to with each other, but that didn't mean Sam couldn't try to change his mind.

There was a bottle of wine chilling in the fridge and he was sorely tempted to grab it for the two of them. He sighed when he remembered it wasn't wise for him to drink and picked up two bottles of Coke instead. Perhaps it was for the best. He didn't want Zak to do something he'd regret in the morning and blame it on the alcohol. From what he'd seen of Zak and alcohol at the club, his friend seemed to have very little tolerance as it was.

When he returned to the living room, he found Zak fidgeting in his seat. Sam quickly realized what the problem was and stifled a smile. He suspected it wasn't his History homework that had Zak adjusting his package as soon as Sam's back was turned.

Sam held out the bottle. "Here you go."

Zak took the drink from his hand and took a long swallow.

"Did you find the reference you need?" Sam asked as he sat back down on the sofa.

"Reference?"

Sam gestured to the books scattered across the coffee table.

"Oh, no. I got distracted."

"By what?" Sam asked. He looked innocently around the room as though searching for the distraction in question.

"Nothing," Zak muttered. From the corner of his eye, Sam saw him try to make himself more comfortable again.

"Need a hand with that?" Sam finally asked. So much for subtlety.

Zak flushed a bright shade of red and his hand froze in place.

"Well?" Sam prompted. "Do you?"

Zak gulped down half his bottle of Coke. Sam waited while he composed himself. He couldn't believe he was actually hitting on Zak again, after he'd promised himself he'd keep his distance. But he wanted him. They wanted each other. Zak couldn't hide his growing arousal as Sam moved closer any more than Sam could.

Sam gave his own groin a pointed look and waited for Zak to realize they were both hard right now.

"What sort of hand?" Zak finally whispered.

Sam chuckled and waggled his fingers. "This sort. I'll give you a hand job if you want."

Zak nodded enthusiastically.

Sam put aside his own drink and slid closer to Zak. "You can tell me to stop whenever you want, just..."

"Just what?"

Sam drew in a sharp breath. "Just don't push me away and say you're disgusted, okay?"

"I'm really sorry about that," Zak apologized.

"Just promise me you won't do it again. We're both adults here. If you don't like what I'm doing, ask me to stop."

"Okay."

Satisfied that Zak wouldn't push him away like he had done on New Year's Eve, Sam reached out and slowly lowered the zipper of Zak's trousers. Zak sighed as Sam eased his hand into Zak's briefs, touching the hot, hard flesh of another man's cock for the first time.

Zak groaned as Sam slowly traced his fingers along the length. Sam licked his lips, but he didn't dare to lean down and lap at the flesh he wanted to taste. He'd promised Zak a hand job and that's what he would get. There was no way Sam was going to scare him off by introducing him to blow jobs just yet.

Zak's penis jumped as Sam traced a thick vein. He wasn't circumcised, not that Sam had really expected him to be. It wasn't exactly common in England and Sam knew that few of the young men his age were.

Sam watched Zak's reaction as he played with the foreskin and ran his thumb across the slit. Zak's breath came quickly and his jaw was slack. Sam had to stop himself from leaning forward and kissing the full pink lips. He wanted to do it so badly and only Zak's reaction at New Year stopped him. He shook his head. No, he had to stop thinking about that. Zak was sitting next to him, letting him fondle his dick, and this was exactly the wrong time to be thinking about the past rejection.

Zak made soft noises of contentment until Sam pulled his hand away. The whine of dismay sounded more animal than human.

"Why did you stop?" Zak asked. His voice was husky and his breath came rapidly.

Sam didn't answer with words. He tugged at Zak's belt and pulled down his trousers and briefs so he could see everything he wished to.

Zak kicked off the garments as Sam unbuttoned his shirt, pushing the material aside, though not removing it completely.

Sam ran his hands along Zak's thighs, easing his fingers between his legs. Zak quickly caught his intention and spread his limbs wider, enabling Sam to sit between his limbs.

The clock on the mantle chimed five o'clock and Sam realized his parents would be home in under an hour.

"We'd better go upstairs," he suggested. "I don't want my parents walking in on us."

"Would they be angry with you?"

"No, but I'd be embarrassed. Grab your clothes and we'll go up to my bedroom."

Zak gathered together his clothes and followed after Sam.

"Are we going to have sex?" Zak asked when they were part way up the stairs. Sam stumbled in surprise.

"Not today, no."

"Oh. I thought maybe we were."

"I don't think you're ready for anything more than a hand job right now," Sam explained. "I'm trying really hard not to scare you off."

"Do I look scared?" Zak replied.

Sam turned to face him. Did Zak look afraid? No, he didn't. He looked gorgeous and delightfully aroused. "I guess not."

Zak nodded firmly. "Good, because I'm not. I want you to pick up where we left off downstairs and forget about what happened at New Year."

"I can't forget quite so easily as all that."

"You wanted to kiss me downstairs, didn't you?"

Sam shrugged and carried on up the stairs. "Don't worry. I won't, no matter how much I might want to."

"What if I told you I wanted you to?"

"You don't."

"You can't know that."

"Disgusting was the word you used last time I tried to kiss you."

"I've been doing some research since then."

That got Sam's attention. "What sort of research?"

"Online porn, like you suggested."

"You can't learn about what it means to kiss someone you have feelings for by watching porn."

"Maybe not, but I learnt about a lot of other stuff I want to try."

"Such as?"

Zak grinned. "How about you lead the way to your room and we'll start with the kissing?"

Sam wasn't sure what to make of Zak's about-face. Did he really want to try the stuff he'd seemed so opposed to just a short while ago?

"You don't believe me," Zak said as they walked down the hallway. "But maybe this will convince you."

"Maybe what will convince me?" Sam asked as he turned round to face Zak.

Zak caught him by surprise and pushed him up against the wall. "This," he whispered as he pressed his lips to Sam's.

At first Sam was too stunned to do anything other than stand there stupidly frozen, then he realized Zak was trying to kiss him and he wasn't doing a thing to encourage him. Zak's tongue brushed along his lower lip and Sam opened his mouth with a moan of need.

Although Sam was still fully clothed, he could feel the heat of Zak's arousal through the thin material of his trousers. He gripped Zak's arse and pulled him up against him.

Zak pulled away and sucked in a ragged breath.

"I thought you didn't like kissing," Sam whispered. He raised his fingers to his swollen lips.

"I'm starting to see the appeal," Zak replied, his voice as shaky as Sam's. Sam clung to Zak's shoulders as he tried to regain his composure.

"I need to sit down," Sam said. This current wave of dizziness had nothing to do with his condition and everything to do with the man before him. He nudged Zak toward the door of his bedroom.

They fumbled their way into the room, Sam kicking the door closed behind him. They fell onto the bed and Sam let Zak tear at his clothes. A few frantic minutes later they were both naked on the covers of Sam's narrow single bed.

At first they didn't do much more than look at each other, studying each other's body and anticipating what was to come.

"Are you sure you want to do this?" Sam asked nervously.

Zak's reply was to kiss him again, pushing him onto his back and straddling his hips. Zak's cock rubbed against his own as they shifted positions, trying to find the most comfortable way to fit together. Sam felt as though he might come right then and there.

They rocked together, grinding and groaning, their movements mimicking the act Sam knew they weren't quite ready for yet.

Sam was sure he was going to burst any second and he pushed Zak away as he struggled to regain control.

"Are you okay?" Zak asked with concern.

"Yeah, just give me a minute," Sam gasped out between ragged breaths. "Thought I was going to come."

Zak laughed loudly. "Is that all? Why didn't you say so?" He rocked his hips deliberately and Sam hissed.

"I'll come if you keep doing that," he warned.

"I want you to," Zak replied. "I want to taste you when you do."

Sam's mouth fell open and he thought for a moment lust had caused him to suffer some kind of audio hallucination. "You do?"

Zak sat back on his heels and scooted back down the length of the bed. Sam's dick rose from the nest of dark curls, already leaking pre-cum.

"You don't have to do this," Sam told him. "Not all gay men like to suck cock. They don't all like the taste of cum."

"I know."

"You do?"

"I told you, I've been doing some research. The taste of my own wasn't so bad. I think I'll like yours even more."

The thought of Zak coming and licking up his own semen nearly pushed Sam over the edge all on its own.

Zak smiled at him as he ducked his head and licked along the length of Sam's erection, swiping his tongue over the tip and gathering up every drop of cum he could.

"I'm definitely going to enjoy this," Zak said as Sam tried to calm himself down by gripping the base of his penis.

Sam closed his eyes as Zak sucked the head into his mouth, his teeth carefully covered. Someone had definitely been doing his homework.

Zak alternated between licking and sucking at Sam's throbbing shaft. "Why do they call it a blow job when you're sucking and not blowing?"

"Damned if I know," Sam muttered. "Did you stop just to ask me that?"

"No," Zak replied. "I stopped because I wanted to look at you, all hot and horny because of me."

Sam laughed. "How much porn have you been watching this last month?"

Zak blushed, this time with embarrassment rather than arousal. "A bit."

"How much is a bit?"

"An hour or two."

Sam didn't believe him and made it clear with one dubious glance.

"Every night," Zak amended.

"No wonder your grades have been slipping."

Zak grinned as though he didn't care at all for the decline of his college work. "I think it's been time well spent. Though my dad wasn't too happy when he found out I'd signed up at one of the sites with his credit card."

Sam laughed before he could stop himself. "I'll bet he wasn't. How much did you spend?"

"Enough to get me grounded and doing dozens of chores round the house for a month."

"You're grounded?"

"Yeah, why?"

"Aren't you going to get in trouble for being round here?"

"Why would I? My dad likes you now."

"But you're grounded."

"So?"

"So, it means you aren't allowed to go out except for stuff like college. Grounded means you have to go straight home."

"Does it?"

"Well, yeah. Didn't your dad explain this to you?"

"Not really. He just said I was grounded. I never thought to ask what it meant. I just figured I wasn't allowed to go flying in one of those planes, but since I didn't have any plans to do that... It really means I'm not supposed to be here?"

Sam nodded. "You'd better go home or you'll be in even worse trouble."

Zak shook his head and chuckled. "If I'm going to get confined to the house for even longer, I intend to make the most of this evening."

Sam considered trying to convince Zak to go home. "He might ground you for even longer if you don't do as you're told."

Zak's breath, warm and delightful on the tip of his cock, sent shivers throughout Sam's body.

"You really shouldn't be here."

Zak ignored him as he circled the head with his tongue. The touch sent every sensible thought flying from Sam's mind. "Fuck, do that again!"

Now Zak did exactly as he was told, obeying Sam's cried command immediately.

The hot, wet suction was almost unbearable. Sam moved his hips, slowly at first, then faster, thrusting up into Zak's mouth, straining to reach a pinnacle that until now had always been self-induced.

"Zak," he pleaded. He was so close, so very near to coming.

Zak hummed his answer and Sam shuddered as his balls drew up. "Zak, you'd better pull back, I'm gonna—"

But Zak didn't pull away. He carried on sucking, right through Sam's orgasm, drinking down everything Sam gave him until Sam was a quivering mass of nerves, unable to do anything except gaze at the ceiling above him and wonder what the hell had just happened.

* * * *

At eight o'clock, Zak's phone rang. He contemplated ignoring it since the only people who ever called him were Sam and Darren. Since he was currently in Sam's arms it had to be Darren on the phone, no doubt wondering where he was.

"Aren't you going to answer it?" Sam asked.

"It's only my dad," Zak replied as he pulled Sam toward him for another kiss. Why had he ever thought kissing was disgusting? It was amazing how good he felt when Sam's lips were on his. It was almost as though there was a direct link between his mouth and his penis.

Sam groaned as Zak's phone stopped ringing, then started again immediately. "Maybe you should answer it."

Zak reluctantly picked up the mobile and took the call. "Hello?"

"Where the hell are you?" Darren asked.

"With Sam."

"At his house?"

"Yes."

"Good. I want you walking through the front door in five minutes or I'm going to come over there and fetch you."

"Can I bring Sam back with me?" Zak asked, even though he suspected he would be pushing his luck even asking.

"No. You've got five minutes."

The phone went dead and Zak groaned.

"You have to go home?" Sam guessed.

"Yes. I've got five minutes to get back or he's coming to get me."

Sam chuckled and the rumbling of his chest against Zak's own sent another wave of shivers through him. "Never mind. We can always pick this up again another time. If you want to?"

Sam sat back so Zak could get up, but he didn't intend to let him get away so easily. "I want to," Zak said as he kissed Sam again, pushing his tongue into the other man's mouth and stealing his breath away.

"You should get dressed," Sam whispered as Zak continued to plant kisses on his face, neck and chest.

"Don't want to."

"You can't exactly wander down the street as you are," Sam pointed out. "You might get arrested."

Zak's phone bleeped with a text message. He picked up the phone and saw it was from Darren. It read *Two minutes.*

"You'd better hurry," Sam said as he tore himself away from Zak and helped him gather together his clothes.

"I hate being bossed about," Zak complained. "What gives my dad the right to place me under some kind of house arrest?"

"You're living under his roof, so it's his rules," Sam said. "Besides, if you really used his credit card without his permission he could have called the police on you."

"He wouldn't do that."

"Of course he wouldn't. But some parents would. I think you've got it pretty easy with your folks."

"I guess."

Sam merely laughed at him. "Come here, baby," he teased. It seemed he was as addicted to kissing as Zak was becoming and he put his mouth to much better use.

"Something to remember me by until your grounding is over," he explained.

Zak had no intention of waiting that long for another kiss. "Tomorrow," he promised as he hurried down the stairs, his phone bleeping again as he ran.

* * * *

Darren stood waiting at the front door for Zak and barked at him as soon as he reached the end of their path.

"What part of grounded didn't you understand?" he asked.

"Any of it, apparently," Zak replied. "Sam explained what it was to me. I thought you meant I wasn't to go flying in one of those planes."

Darren's temper receded for only a moment. "And when exactly did Sam explain this to you?"

Zak could tell what he was getting at. "This evening," he hedged.

"What time?"

"A couple of hours ago."

"And you decided to stay out anyway?"

"Yes."

"It didn't occur to you to come straight home after Sam explained things to you?"

Zak shrugged as he walked past Darren and into the house. "I thought about it, but I figured since I was already going to be in trouble, I might as well make the most of my freedom."

"Did you think I'd punish you when you genuinely didn't understand what I meant by grounding you?"

"Would you?"

"Of course not," Darren replied. "But since you've admitted you deliberately stayed out after you knew I didn't want you to, you can consider yourself additionally punished for that."

"How long am I grounded for now then?"

Darren shook his head. "No Internet for a week."

"But I need it for research."

"You can do your homework from your textbooks."

"What about my other research?"

"Online porn, free or otherwise, is *not* research."

"But—"

"No arguments."

Zak stomped toward the stairs. "According to Earth laws, I'm a legal adult, so you can't tell me what to do all the time."

"Not according to your attitude. While you're living here you'll do as I tell you. If you don't like it then I'm afraid it's your bad luck."

There was no point in arguing with Darren, and Zak started up the stairs to his room.

"Zak?" Darren called after him.

"What?"

"You do know I'm not deliberately trying to make life more difficult for you than it already is, right?"

Zak sighed and looked back down to Darren. "I know."

"Would you like to invite Sam round for dinner tomorrow?"

"Can I?"

"Of course."

Zak grabbed his phone and called Sam. "I'll call him and ask him right away."

"Make it quick," Darren warned. "Dinner will be ready in a few minutes and the rule about no calls at the table will be enforced."

Sam answered on the first ring, eager to find out whether Zak was in a lot of trouble for being at his house all evening. They were still chatting away when Zak walked into the dining room.

Darren's frown and a quiet warning of additional punishments were the only way to get Zak off the phone.

Zak didn't mind. He had every intention of calling him straight back as soon as they were done with the evening meal. He had a feeling they would be talking long into the night.

It was well after midnight when Darren knocked on his bedroom door and warned Zak he'd take the mobile phone off him if he didn't end the call right now.

Sam, who had heard the threat clearly over the phone, reminded Zak that they both had college in the morning and perhaps they might do well to get some sleep. Sam's whispered advice went down far better than Darren's threats and they said their goodnights at last.

Even after the call had ended, Zak couldn't sleep. All he could think about was Sam and what they had done in his bed earlier that evening. Did Darren and Eleanor have any suspicions about what he had done? Did he appear different to them now?

Zak grinned in the dark as he recalled the sensation of Sam's hands on his body, touching him intimately. His cock reacted instantly to his thoughts, lengthening and hardening at the mere memory. How was he ever going to sit beside Sam in class without wanting to grab him and hold him close?

He chuckled at the idea of taking hold of Sam in the middle of class and kissing him senseless. That would raise a few eyebrows and no doubt result in an extension of his grounding if Darren found out about it. Nevertheless, the idea was definitely appealing.

Grabbing his phone, Zak sent a quick text to Sam.

Are you my boyfriend?

Sam's reply was a long time coming, so long that Zak began to dread the answer.

Only so long as you don't wake me up at two every night.

Zak cringed as he looked at the bedside clock. Sure enough it was nearly two o'clock. He had completely lost track of time while reliving their time together.

Sorry.

Go to sleep, Zak.

Zak put his phone in the drawer of the bedside cabinet, removing the temptation to carry on texting — and annoying — Sam all through the night.

Finally, he fell asleep, dreaming about what else he and Sam might do together in the days and nights to come.

Chapter Eleven

Zak couldn't stop glancing out of the window during History class. Sam hadn't shown up to Maths this morning. Where was he? Was he avoiding him again? Had he done something wrong?

He thought back to the previous evening when Sam had come over to his house. They had given each other blow jobs and Sam had fallen asleep in his arms. When he'd woken, Sam hadn't given Zak any indication that he was angry with him. He'd been tired, telling Zak he'd been studying until late at night the last few evenings. Zak had scolded him affectionately, but had Sam taken his words to heart?

"Zak, are you listening?"

Zak jumped and turned to see Darren scowling at him from the front of the classroom. The History class had held even less of his attention than usual. He hadn't opened his textbook or taken a single note of the lecture.

"Sorry," he muttered.

"You need to be writing down the homework," Darren prompted with a nod to the board behind him.

Zak dutifully started to scribble down the essay topic, even though his mind wasn't on the task. The fates of people who had died hundreds of years before were of no concern to him, not when he was worried about Sam's disappearance.

After the bell had gone, Zak approached Darren. "Where's Sam?" he asked.

"I don't know," Darren replied. "Didn't he come here with you and Lucy this morning?"

"Lucy's car is in the garage. I had to get the bus, but Sam wasn't at the bus stop with me."

"Was he in class this morning?"

"If he had been, I'd hardly need to ask, would I?"

Darren gave him a hard look.

Zak waited impatiently until he realized he wasn't going to get an answer to his question. "I know, I know, I need to lose the attitude."

"You need to go to English."

"It won't hurt to miss one lesson. What if he's ill?" As soon as the thought entered his head, Zak sensed it was the truth. Sam had been looking pale and drawn the last few days, even more so than usual. He'd had another nosebleed and dizzy spell as well, and maybe there had been more. Sam had clearly contracted some horrible Earth illness, and Zak needed to check he was okay before he did anything else.

"Even if he is unwell, you still need to go to class."

"I'm not going to argue with you. I need to know where Sam is."

Darren rolled his eyes. "Very well, have it your own way."

Zak swung his rucksack over his shoulder and grinned, his decision made. "I'll see you later."

Darren didn't bother to argue with him, not that Zak had any intention of listening. Sam was ill and Zak intended to make sure it wasn't anything too serious. It wasn't like he'd be able to concentrate on his lessons without knowing anyway.

He caught the bus and made his way over to Sam's house, expecting to find him there, being fussed over by his mother.

The house appeared empty and when Zak rang the bell no one came to answer the door.

Pulling out his mobile phone, he hurriedly fumbled his way through the process of calling Sam, only to be frustrated when he was diverted to the voicemail. He sent Lucy a text, but her reply didn't tell him anything he didn't already know. She didn't appear to know where Sam was.

With no more ideas for what to do next, Zak sat down on the front step and settled in to wait for someone to return.

It was dark by the time a car finally pulled up to the house and Zak was disappointed to see it was Darren's Land Rover.

"Do you have any idea what time it is?" Darren called.

Zak looked at his watch. "Nearly eight."

"Get in the car."

"I'm waiting for Sam."

"You need to come with me."

"I *need* to wait here."

Darren sighed. "Zak, you keep telling me that you're not a real teenager — that you're an adult and you're capable of making your own decisions."

"I am!"

"Well, for someone who isn't a real teenager, you're doing a bloody good impression of a moody teenage boy right now."

"I'm not moody. I'm worried about Sam."

Darren sat patiently behind the wheel of the car. "Yes, I know. Do you think I'd drive the few yards up the road just to bring you home? Get in and I'll take you to him."

Zak practically ran to the car and jumped into the passenger seat. "You know where he is?"

"Yes, though I warn you, they'll probably not let you see him. He's in hospital and visiting hours are over for the day."

"Did you know he was in hospital when we spoke this morning?" Zak couldn't believe he'd wasted all this time waiting for Sam when Darren could have known where he was all along.

"No. After you left college I made a few discreet enquiries of my own. A brief outline of Sam's medical history is on his college file in case of an emergency."

"Are you going to get in trouble for telling me what's on his file?"

"I doubt anyone will ever find out I've told you. You and Sam are good friends and you'll find out sooner or later from what I read in his file."

"What do you mean?"

"I'll let Sam explain," Darren said as he pulled into the hospital car park.

"I thought you said they wouldn't let me see him."

"They probably won't tonight, but he has the right to tell you himself."

Zak got out of the vehicle and hurried toward the entrance. Darren was close at his heels. "Let me do the talking," Darren suggested as they entered the building. "Losing your temper won't help you see Sam."

For once Zak did as he was told straight away and followed Darren to the reception. The woman at the desk was pleasant and friendly, but also strict and immovable when it came to the rules, and there was no way she was letting them past her to see Sam tonight.

"We'll come back for visiting hours tomorrow," Darren assured Zak.

Zak grumbled under his breath, but with no idea how to find Sam in the sprawling building he had no choice.

Looking around the waiting area, Zak shivered with horror. One man had a head injury, with blood running down his face, while another held his arm tightly to his chest, clearly in agonizing pain. Zak's heart raced as his worry for Sam increased tenfold. What had happened to Sam that he had to be brought to this terrible place?

* * * *

Sam felt a lot better today than he had the previous morning. He suspected that had a great deal to do with the new drugs the doctor had given him. The pain at least was manageable.

"Mr Johnson phoned us this morning," Sam's mother said as she tidied up the covers. "Zak's going to come to see you."

"What? He can't!"

Mrs Palmer raised an eyebrow. "I thought you'd be pleased to see him."

"I don't want him seeing me like this. I look a mess."

"I'm sure Zak will understand if you appear a little less neat and tailored than usual."

Sam ignored her reassurances. "Can you stop him coming in here?"

"He's very worried about you."

"Just tell him I'll be fine and I'll see him when I'm back home."

Sam cringed under his mother's knowing gaze. "Sam, have you told Zak about your condition?"

"Of course not."

"Why not? I'm sure he'd understand. Is there a reason you don't want him to know about your illness?"

"I just don't."

"I'm sure he won't see you any differently once he knows."

Sam wasn't so certain. When he'd been in school and first diagnosed, other people he'd considered his friends had started to avoid him when they found out. He didn't like to think of Zak deserting him, but in some ways Zak wasn't very mature and Sam had done his utmost to avoid the subject of his illness, brushing off the concerns of his friends whenever they noticed he wasn't quite himself.

"He's going to find out before too much longer," his mother continued. She rested a hand on his arm and Sam turned his head away rather than face the truth in her eyes.

"Not if I get out of here and back to college soon."

"You know that's unlikely. The longer you're in here, the more likely it is someone else will let slip to Zak the reason why. Don't you think you should be the one to tell him?"

"I don't want him to look at me differently. I get that from you and Dad and everyone else, even Lucy. I don't need it from him too."

Sam's mother took his hand in a light grip. "Zak sees you as a clever, handsome young man. He adores you."

Sam snorted and gave his mother a skeptical look.

"He does. And when you tell him about your illness, he'll see you as brave and strong as well."

Sam turned to look out of the window, even though all he could see were the dark gray clouds, promising heavy rain before too much longer.

"Zak should be here soon. I'll give you some time alone to talk to him."

"Mum?"

"Yes?"

"Do you really think he'll still feel the same way about me after he knows the truth?"

"I'm sure he will."

Sam sighed heavily. He wished he had his mother's confidence.

* * * *

Zak arrived right at the start of visiting time. Sam's mother greeted him with a smile and quickly departed from the room, leaving Sam with no other option except to talk to Zak.

"Hi, Zak."

"Hi."

Sam faltered. He knew what Zak wanted to know, even though he hadn't asked any questions. Maybe if Zak didn't actually ask him, he could avoid talking about it.

"You didn't have to come all this way," Sam said. "I'm sure I'll be home again in a couple of days."

"Really?" Zak didn't sound convinced and since Sam had seen his face in the mirror today, he couldn't say he blamed him.

"Maybe a little longer," Sam amended. He couldn't meet Zak's eyes as he lied through his teeth. "What have I missed while I've been stuck in here?"

Zak ignored his question completely. "My dad says your college records say you've been ill before."

Sam swore under his breath. So much for total avoidance. "He shouldn't have been snooping in my files. They're supposed to be confidential."

"He's a teacher. He can look through the files of any of the students."

"It doesn't give him the right to talk to you about what's in them."

"Maybe not, but you should have told me yourself." Zak sat down on the chair Sam's mother had previously been sitting in. "You got better before, right?"

"Yeah, for a while, but now it's back again."

"What is?"

Sam opened his mouth to speak, only to find that his voice had deserted him. In all the time since he had first been diagnosed he had never once said the word out loud. The doctors and nurses had said it. Even his parents had whispered the dreadful 'c' word when they thought he was asleep and unable to hear them. It was a word everyone knew and feared.

"Sam, what is it?" Zak asked with concern. "Are you in pain? Do you want me to call one of those doctor people?"

"No, I'm okay."

Zak sat back, visibly relieved. "What's this illness you have then?"

Sam closed his eyes. "It's the reason I failed my exams last year. I missed too many days while I was stuck in this place. I tried to keep up with my schoolwork at first, but it was too much, too tiring, and I couldn't seem to manage both the assignments and the whole getting well thing."

"And now you're back in here again."

"Yeah. It sucks. I'm going to be missing classes and failing all over again."

"How long do you think you'll be in here?" Zak asked.

"I don't know. The doctors are whispering to my parents again like they did last time, so I guess it could be a while."

"Haven't you asked them yourself? You're an adult, right? Don't they have to tell you?"

"Yes, I've asked them."

"And?"

He wouldn't say it. Zak didn't need to know. If he didn't say it, he could still believe it wasn't really happening.

"Zak," he whispered, clutching at his boyfriend's hand. "I'm scared."

Sam tugged Zak closer, unwilling to let him go.

"What are you scared of?" asked Zak, his tone hushed.

"That this time I'm not going to get out of here," Sam admitted. "Last time I didn't know what to expect. Every day was a struggle to get through. When they finally told me it was in remission I was so sure it was gone for good. I don't know if I can do this again."

Zak didn't say anything as the words tumbled from Sam's lips.

"I want to be at university, getting on with my life, not stuck in here. I want a normal life. Is that too much to ask for?"

"What's normal?" Zak teased weakly. "Me?"

"You know what I mean. It's bad enough when I have to take the course of drugs at home. Being stuck in here is a hundred times worse."

"Can't you do that this time?" Zak asked.

Sam shook his head. "No. The last one didn't do any good and I had a bit of a bad reaction to the new one. The doctors want to keep an eye on me, especially since it's getting worse."

"I don't understand why they can't just give you the right drugs in the first place."

Sam could tell Zak wasn't getting the big picture, and that he would actually have to spell it out for him.

"It's cancer, Zak. I have cancer. There isn't a single drug that'll just cure me. It's more complicated than that."

Zak looked at him blankly. *Was he in shock?*

"What's cancer?" Zak finally asked.

Sam looked at him silently for several long minutes. "How can you not know what cancer is?" he finally replied.

"We don't have it where I come from," Zak said with a shrug.

"You can get it anywhere," Sam snapped. "It's everywhere, in every country in the world."

Zak shifted in his seat. He looked uncomfortable. "I've never heard of it."

Sam didn't know whether to believe him or not. Although Zak was pretty clear that English was his ninth language, Sam had no idea what the first eight were. Maybe he just knew it by another name.

"It's a disease that can kill you," Sam finally said quietly. "It nearly took me out last year, and this time could be it for me."

"But humans can live to be a hundred years old. You're not even twenty."

"Do you think I don't know that? I'm only nineteen years old and I feel like I'm ninety."

"You can't die yet."

"It's cancer, Zak. It can take anyone of any age and it can take me too."

Zak shook his head. "No, it can't."

"Zak, don't."

Zak pulled his hand free of Sam's and began to pace. "This is unacceptable. I'm not going to lose you."

"You may not have a choice."

Zak marched toward the door. "We'll see about that."

"Zak!" Sam called after his boyfriend, but he didn't return. "Terrific," he muttered. "One boyfriend in denial to deal with on top of everything else."

When Zak didn't come back, Sam closed his eyes. When his parents came into the room a short while later he kept his eyes closed and pretended to be asleep.

* * * *

As soon as Zak got home he jumped on the computer and began to search for cancer. The more he read, the sicker he felt.

Darren stuck his head round the door a couple of times before he interrupted Zak's research.

"Did you know?" Zak asked without looking up from the computer.

At least Darren didn't try to pretend he didn't know what Zak was talking about. "Yes. I spoke with his parents last night."

"You could have told me."

"No, I couldn't. Sam had the right to tell you himself, in his own way."

"Why didn't he?"

"You'd have to ask him that, though if I wanted to hazard a guess, I'd say it was because he doesn't like talking about it."

Zak huffed and continued to scroll down the page he had been reading before Darren's interruption. "This cancer thing is stupid. Why don't they have a cure for it?"

"They're working on one, but these things take time. You have to remember that this world isn't as advanced medically as our own. They don't have our technology or our physiology." Darren took a seat beside him. "Sam's a fighter. He beat this once before and he can do it again."

"You sound more sure than he does about that."

Darren shrugged. "You need to stay positive for him. It won't do him any good to have to waste his energy worrying about you. If you care for him as much as you say you do, you'll stand by him and help him get through this."

Zak glared at Darren. "Of course I'm going to help him, but I'm going to do more than just stand at his side."

"I'm afraid there's not much else you can do."

"I can take him to Trimmeron," Zak replied. "The decontamination process will cure him."

"You know you can't return home until the end of your time here. It's strictly forbidden."

"I don't care."

Darren shook his head. "That's one hell of a big risk to take. If you get caught, the punishment will be severe."

"I won't lose him."

"You may not have a choice."

"*This* is my choice. I'll take him home with me, he'll be cured and he'll get to live a long life instead of dying before he's twenty."

"And what about Sam? Don't you think you should talk this through with him?"

"I'll have to convince him I was telling the truth about where I'm from. He didn't believe me last time I tried to tell him."

"If you really intend to take him home with you, I imagine the spaceship landing in front of him will convince him."

Zak chuckled. Yeah, a spaceship would convince almost anybody.

"If it's what you really want, I won't try to talk you out of it."

"Will you send out a signal for the ship to come pick us up?" Zak held his breath as he waited for Darren's reply. He couldn't summon the ship himself. If Darren refused, it didn't matter what Zak and Sam wanted. They would be stuck on Earth until Zak's fostering was over and all he could do was hope Sam lasted that long.

"Not yet," Darren said.

"Why not?"

"I think you should talk to Sam about this, and also his parents."

"What have his parents got to do with anything?"

"They'll have spoken with the doctors about Sam's condition. They'll know what the prognosis is and whether Sam is likely to recover without you stepping in. It may be you're worrying for nothing, and all he needs from you is a bit of support and simply being there for him."

Zak nodded his agreement. Maybe he had jumped to conclusions and Sam was going to be back on his feet again and things would return to normal in no time at all.

Still, he knew what he had to do if he was wrong. He recalled Sam's face when he'd told him how scared he was. Zak could not and would not sit by without doing everything he could to help him. There was a choice and even if Sam didn't believe Zak was from another planet, he'd prove it to him, even if he had to kidnap him to do so.

Chapter Twelve

It had been a long and tiring two months. Sam had been kept in hospital while the doctors — from what Zak could see — poked and prodded him until his poor boyfriend was completely drained of energy and hope. Knowing his own people had the technology to cure him in a matter of minutes made it especially frustrating for Zak to watch Sam quietly suffering.

Lucy had chauffeured Zak to the hospital every single evening. Sometimes she visited Sam too, but other times she just dropped Zak off before hurrying home to look after her siblings. Zak could tell it was hard on her to be torn between her duties to her family and worry over her friend. Zak and Sam scraped together as much time alone as they could, which wasn't much with the doctors, nurses and Sam's parents hovering nearby.

When Sam had told him the doctors were sending him home the next day, Zak had been rather surprised. From what he could see, Sam was still as ill as ever. Sam had told him the previous day that the latest drug hadn't done anything to help him. Were they now putting him on another and sending him home right away? Surely they wouldn't do such a thing when Sam had suffered bad reactions to treatments in the past. Or maybe the doctors knew something he didn't and thought Sam's condition would improve when he was back home, sleeping in his own bed, and out of the hospital environment.

The day at college dragged and Zak had been sorely tempted to sneak out of class to go wait for Sam to arrive home. Only knowing Sam wouldn't be arriving home until the afternoon kept him in his seat, though he couldn't have told anyone what his lessons had been about that day.

Lucy drove Zak over to Sam's house after class, though she declined to come in with him.

"Why not?" Zak asked as he climbed out of the car.

"I'm under orders," Lucy replied with a grin.

"Huh?"

Lucy brandished her phone. "Sam sent me a text about half an hour ago."

"He did? What did he say? He is home, isn't he?"

"Yes, he's back."

"But why doesn't he want you to come in to see him? You haven't seen him in three days."

Lucy laughed and shook her head. "Blimey, you're dense sometimes, Zak."

"What's that supposed to mean?"

"Sam wants to be alone with you."

"He does?"

"Of course he does, you idiot. You're his boyfriend and this will be the first time the two of you have been alone together in two months."

"But you're his best friend. I'm sure he wouldn't mind you visiting him too."

"I'm pretty sure he *would* mind. Tell him I'll stop by on Saturday to check up on him."

"Are you sure?"

Lucy grinned and waved as she pulled away from the curb. "Have fun!"

Zak watched her go before he jogged down the path and rang the doorbell. He hopped from one foot to the other as he waited for someone to come and open the door. Finally Mrs Palmer appeared in the doorway. Sam's mother looked as though she hadn't slept in a week. Even so she ushered him inside with a smile.

"Sam's upstairs in his room," she said. "He's very tired, the journey took a lot out of him, so if he's asleep please let him be."

Zak promised he'd leave Sam to sleep and hurried up the stairs. He eased open the door to Sam's room, quietly peeking round the corner.

"Hey," Sam greeted him from his bed. "Come in and lock the door behind you."

Zak entered the room and flipped the lock as Sam had requested. "Your mum thought you might have been asleep."

Sam patted the mattress beside him, urging Zak to join him. "I had a nap earlier. I wanted to be wide awake when you arrived."

Zak climbed onto the bed and looked Sam over carefully. There were dark circles under his eyes and his color was far too pale. "Are you sure they should have let you home so soon?" he asked. "You don't look any better than you did yesterday. In fact you look worse."

"Huh, thanks," Sam muttered. "That's just what I want to hear from my boyfriend. I'm just a bit tired from the car trip. Now, lie down with me so I can hold you."

Sam pulled him down with a strength that surprised Zak. Zak chuckled as Sam wrapped Zak's arms around him and snuggled closer.

"I missed this in the hospital," Sam said. "Too many nosy doctors and nurses around in that place."

Zak nodded as he hugged Sam tightly. "I'm glad you're home. I don't mind telling you, you had me worried for a while."

Sam remained quiet and Zak nudged him gently in the shoulder.

"In a few weeks' time things will be back to normal and you'll be back on your feet again."

Still Sam stayed silent, so much so that Zak wondered whether he had fallen back to sleep. When he tried to pull away to see, Sam clung to him like a limpet.

"What is it?" Zak asked. "What's wrong?"

Sam sighed. "The same thing that's been wrong since I took sick."

"But you're better now."

"No I'm not."

"But you will be soon, won't you? The doctors must have found the right drugs for you this time."

"They haven't given me a new course of drugs."

"Then why did they let you come home? They wouldn't send you away from the hospital if you were still ill."

"They would if I told them I wanted to spend what's left of my time at home."

"What do you mean?"

Sam buried his face in Zak's shoulder. "Don't make me say it, please."

Zak shivered and his heart began to race. Sam couldn't mean what he thought he meant, could he?

They stayed on Sam's bed for several minutes, neither saying a word, simply holding onto each other. Finally, Sam broke the silence.

"There's another reason I wanted to come home now," he whispered. "One I didn't tell the doctors or my parents."

"What's that?"

Sam pulled away and looked Zak in the eye. "Can't you guess?" he asked.

Zak didn't need to guess. Sam slid his hand down Zak's chest to the zip of his jeans, answering the question for him.

"We can't do this in the hospital," Sam said.

"I don't think your parents would approve of us doing anything too strenuous," Zak reminded him. "Maybe when you're a little stronger we could consider it."

Sam gripped him tightly through the denim. "I'm not going to get any stronger than I am right now. I want us to do this."

Zak couldn't believe he was even considering turning down the opportunity Sam presented to him, but he looked so drained and weak, despite the firm grasp he had on his dick. "Maybe tomorrow."

Sam swore under his breath, although loud enough for Zak to hear the expletive. He pulled his hand away and turned over so his back was to Zak. "If you don't want me now you know, just say so."

"It's not that," Zak hastened to assure him. "But you've just come out of hospital. You aren't well. I don't want to hurt you."

Sam ignored him for several minutes before sighing deeply. "I'm not going to get any better."

Zak ran a hand along Sam's arm. "I couldn't bear to hurt you."

"You won't."

"You don't know that."

"I know I want this," Sam replied firmly. "I've been ill for so long I can hardly remember what it's like to be healthy. I don't have much time left and I don't want the end to come and still be wondering what it's like to feel a lover buried deep within me. I want to know what the connection feels like."

"You might feel differently tomorrow," Zak pointed out. "You could wake up in the morning and feel a hundred times better than you do right now."

"Or I could feel a million times worse," Sam countered. "Please, Zak. I want this so badly."

Zak nodded even though Sam couldn't see him. "Okay."

Sam wriggled back against him and gave a murmur of contentment. "Do you have lube and condoms?"

"Shit, no."

"There's some lube in the top drawer of the dresser."

"What about condoms?"

Sam looked over his shoulder and bit his lip. "I'm clean," he whispered. "We could do it without."

"My dad said I should always use them."

Sam snorted. "You can't get what I've got from sex and even if you're carrying every STD known to man, it won't make any difference since the cancer's going to kill me before they ever get the chance."

"That's not the point," Zak argued. "He said —"

"Your father doesn't know everything," Sam interrupted and he twisted back round so he faced Zak. "He doesn't know I've never been with anyone before, and no matter how many men or women you've slept with, you can't pass anything on to me."

"I've never had sex with anyone else either," Zak said. "It's different where I come from."

"So you keep saying," Sam replied with a roll of his eyes. "So we're both virgins, right?"

"I guess."

"Then it doesn't get much safer than that."

"But—"

Sam cut him off again with an annoyed look. "I'm clean and I trust you are too. I don't care what your dad says about being safe. When he gave you your standard safe sex lecture, he probably didn't have this scenario in mind. Now are you going to fuck me or not?"

Zak nodded, even though he wasn't entirely sure Sam was well enough for any sexual activity right now. It seemed stalling because of lack of supplies wasn't going to work. Sam was determined to do this and Zak could deny him nothing.

Slowly and carefully, Zak eased Sam out of his baggy T-shirt and tossed the garment to the floor. He had lost so much weight while he'd been in hospital. His ribs were far more prominent than they had been the last time Zak had seen him without his shirt. Next to go were the pajama bottoms, which revealed no matter how tired Sam appeared that there was one part of his body wide awake and raring to go.

Sam closed his eyes as Zak looked at his soon-to-be lover, tenderly caressing the pale skin.

"So beautiful," Zak murmured.

"You don't have to lie," Sam whispered back. "I know I look like shit. Hospitals do that to a person. I still say a holiday on the beach would do most patients far more good than being stuck inside those places."

"Maybe we could go to the beach in the summer," Zak suggested.

Sam didn't answer, though Zak could hear the unspoken words. Sam probably wouldn't live to see the summer.

"Are you going to undress?" Sam asked. He flicked at one of the buttons on Zak's shirt, popping it from the buttonhole, before moving on to the next. "I want to feel your skin next to mine."

Zak let Sam undo his shirt buttons one by one. When Sam reached the belt of his trousers, he drew in a sharp breath. The sound of footsteps outside in the hall halted Sam's progression.

"Is everything okay in there?" Mrs Palmer called. The handle rattled as she tried to open the door. "Why's the door locked?"

"We're fine," Sam replied. "We just want some time alone."

"Sam, what's going on in there?" she persisted.

"Nothing," Sam called. He grimaced at Zak. "Chance would be a fine thing."

"Sam, open this door."

"Mum, please!"

"I won't ask you again."

Sam groaned in annoyance. "And you think your parents treat you like a child? Try living with mine fussing over you twenty-four hours a day."

Zak kissed him swiftly on the lips. "Get under the covers," he whispered.

Sam looked at him questioningly as he got up from the bed and re-did the bottom few buttons of his shirt.

"Do I look presentable?" Zak asked in a hushed tone.

"Apart from the raging hard-on," Sam replied, in a voice a little too loud not to have carried outside the room.

Zak went to the door and opened it.

"What's going on in here?" Mrs Palmer asked.

"Nothing," Sam replied. "I just wanted some time alone with my boyfriend. Is that too much to ask for?"

"You've only just come home," Mrs Palmer reminded him. "You aren't well enough for whatever it is the two of you have in mind."

"Sex, Mum," Sam said. "And I think I'm the best judge of what I'm capable of."

Mrs Palmer turned to Zak. "I thought you'd have more sense. Surely you can see Sam's not up to this."

Zak looked at Sam, his gaze drawn to the tented sheet where Sam's erection made it clear he was definitely up for something. "I'd never do anything to hurt Sam," he assured her.

Mrs Palmer shook her head and glared at Zak. "I could insist you go home right now."

"Mum!" Sam exclaimed.

Zak gestured for Sam to stay quiet. "I'll take care of him," he said.

"That's beside the point. You don't understand how poorly he still is."

"I understand well enough. But Sam's an adult and if he thinks he's well enough to do this, surely that's his choice to make."

"Mum, let me have this with Zak. Don't send him away when I need him the most."

Mrs Palmer hovered in the doorway for what seemed like forever. Finally she gave a curt nod and turned to leave.

"Be careful with him," she whispered in Zak's ear before leaving the room and closing the door behind her. This time Zak didn't bother with the lock. He knew Sam's parents would stay downstairs and give them the privacy they needed.

"What did she say to you?" Sam asked as Zak made his way back to the side of the bed.

"Nothing I wasn't already planning on doing," Zak replied.

Sam pushed back the covers and patted the mattress. "Come back to bed," he suggested in a voice that practically purred.

Zak quickly shucked off his clothes and slipped in beside Sam.

"No more excuses," Sam whispered. "I need to feel you inside me."

There would be no talking Sam into waiting until he was stronger. In his heart Zak suspected there wouldn't be a time when he was. He twisted round and grabbed the lube from the nightstand.

His hands shook as he fumbled with the lid. Sam placed a hand over Zak's and stroked the quivering flesh.

"You don't have to do this," Sam said. "If you're not ready, we can wait."

Zak looked into Sam's earnest eyes. "I'm okay. This is just new to me."

"Me too."

Sam's lips brushed against Zak's, tentatively at first, then with more force. Zak groaned into the kiss. How had he ever thought this anything except wonderful?

They clung to each other, they bodies sliding together. Sam's erection pressed hard against Zak's thigh and he pulled back far enough so he could reach down between them and take him in hand.

Sam pulled away and gasped. "Stop!"

Zak stilled his hand immediately. "What is it? Are you hurt?"

Sam shook his head. "It's too soon. I can't come yet. Need you inside me."

Zak scrambled for the lube he had dropped during their groping. "How are we going to do this?" he asked.

"How about on our sides?" Sam suggested. "I don't think I could stay on my hands and knees for long, and I know I'm not strong enough to ride you, much as I wish I could."

The fresh reminder of Sam's poor health made Zak cringe, but he helped Sam roll over so his back was to Zak's front.

He ran his hands down Sam's back, tracing his spine, before sliding his fingers between the cheeks of his arse.

"Lube," Sam reminded him as he explored.

Zak hurriedly undid the lube and poured a generous amount onto his hand. He swiftly returned to his exploration, finding Sam's pucker and rubbing against it.

Sam keened at his touch, pushing back against his fingers with eager anticipation. "Inside," he moaned. "Need you inside."

Zak pushed his index finger into the tight opening and Sam clenched around it.

Sam whimpered as Zak eased the digit inside as far as it would go. "So tight," Zak whispered. "How will I ever fit in there?"

"You will," Sam said. "Try another. Stretch me."

Zak did as Sam asked, still unsure as to how they would manage this. Sam wouldn't be satisfied with being fingered forever, though. He wanted everything Zak had to give, even if Zak privately thought it would be too much for him to take.

Eventually Sam pulled away from Zak's fingers and looked back over his shoulder. "Now," he said, the one word, spoken firmly, telling Zak the time had finally come.

Zak pushed one of his legs between Sam's, opening him wider. Neither of them seemed to be entirely sure about what limb to put where, but they eventually settled into a comfortable position. After applying the lube to his thick shaft, Zak slowly eased his way inside.

Sam tensed around him and Zak tried to pull away. He knew this was a bad idea. How could Sam possibly enjoy being used in such a manner?

"Don't," Sam hissed, reaching behind him and gripping Zak's arm. "Stay right there."

"But you're hurting."

"No, it's just a question of adjusting."

"Maybe we should have done this the other way round," Zak suggested.

"Next time," Sam replied. "Needed to know what this feels like."

Zak snorted. "Well, now you know, so can we stop?"

"Hell no," Sam said. "This is just the start. If you stop now it'll be like going to the cinema and only seeing the commercials. You have to go through with the main event or it isn't worth it."

"But—"

"Stop worrying, Zak," Sam snapped. "Push the rest of the way in before I fall asleep here waiting for you."

Zak chuckled at Sam's words. It seemed he had his orders. "You'll tell me to stop if it gets too much for you?"

"Damn it, Zak," Sam groaned. "Just fuck me already."

Taking him at his word, Zak pushed the rest of the way inside until he was completely buried in the tight heat of Sam's arse.

"Oh, God," Sam moaned. "I've never felt anything like it."

"Are you still doing okay?"

Sam tilted his head. "I'm doing great. Now move."

"I don't think I can," Zak admitted.

"Sure you can. Do the whole pump in and out thing and before you know it you'll be coming."

Zak rolled his eyes. "I know what I'm supposed to do, but I think if I move so much as an inch I'm going to lose what little control I have left."

Sam laughed and the movement of his inner muscles caused Zak to gasp.

"Can't stop it," Zak cried as he felt his balls tighten.

"Then don't," Sam replied.

Zak closed his eyes as Sam grabbed his hand and pulled it in front of him. He wrapped his fingers round Sam's cock, hot and thick.

"Feel how close I am," Sam said. "Just a few strokes and I'm going to come."

Sam didn't wait for Zak to reply, merely moving their hands in tandem until a few moments later Sam cried out as he shot his load over their entwined fingers.

The feel of Sam coming while he was still inside was too much for Zak and he choked out a gasp as he too came in powerful spurts, buried deep within his lover's arse.

Chapter Thirteen

Sam slept for a long time after Zak had finished making love to him. He was exhausted, more so than he could ever remember being in his life. When he woke, Zak was still at his side.

"I thought you might have gone home," Sam said.

"I called my dad while you were sleeping and told him I'm staying with you for a while."

Sam gave a small chuckle. "Did my parents agree to that?"

"I didn't ask them."

"What time is it?"

Zak checked his watch. "Just after eleven. How do you feel?"

"Tired and a bit sick."

"Do you want me to get you anything?"

"Could you get me some water?"

"Of course." Zak went to the bathroom across the hall and returned with a glass of water. Sam struggled to sit up and Zak had to help him so he could take a drink.

"You should probably go back to sleep."

"Will you stay the night with me?"

Zak put aside the glass and crawled under the covers with his lover. He kissed Sam softly on the lips. "I'll be right here when you wake up."

Sam closed his eyes and went back to sleep. Sure enough, when he woke just after dawn the following day, Zak was right beside him.

"Are you going to college today?" Sam asked.

"No."

"You'll fall behind."

"I don't care. I'd rather stay here with you."

Sam didn't have the heart to argue with him. He preferred to have Zak with him today as well. For one reason, they needed to have a long-overdue talk.

"I suppose you want to know why I didn't confide in you about my illness," Sam said.

"Not if you don't want to tell me."

"It's okay—I don't mind you knowing now. It's because, for the first time in a long time, someone— you—saw me as something other than the kid who had cancer."

"I never thought of you as a kid at all."

"I know, but that's how everyone else here sees me. I became ill the year before I sat my GCSEs. When the doctors told me and my family it was cancer, I was terrified. I didn't want to be ill. I wanted to be at school with my friends. I tried to keep up with my lessons, but the worse I got, the harder it became to focus. I barely scraped through my exams."

"It wasn't your fault."

"I know, but it was hard and when I started my A Levels it was even tougher. My parents wanted me to take some time out of education to get well, but I refused. I couldn't just sit in a hospital bed, or at home, staring at the four walls. I had to do something to keep myself occupied and I wanted to go to university with my friends. I thought if I kept up with my classes I'd be able to go, though in reality there's no way my parents will let me leave home while I'm still ill. As it happened, the choice was taken out of my hands since I didn't get all the grades I needed for the course I wanted to do."

"You'll get them this time round," Zak assured him. "You work harder than anyone in class."

"I hope so," Sam said. "Anyway, when you arrived you didn't know anything about my illness. Lucy knew because we used to go to the same school before she and her family moved across town after her parents got divorced. Everyone at my school knew about me. I hated it. I felt like everyone was staring at me and talking about me behind my back. The kid with cancer. I didn't want that to happen again, so I didn't tell anyone at college and the only one who knew was Lucy."

"You could have told me. You can tell me anything."

"I know, but I didn't want anyone to know. I didn't want to talk about it. I made Lucy promise not to tell you, even though she disagreed with my decision. Last year the doctors said it had gone into remission. I thought I was well again and for a few months I nearly was. Then I started to recognize the symptoms coming back and I knew it wasn't over. I thought it would go into remission again before you had to find out. Only this time the chemo didn't work. The doctor said it was too soon since the last time I had the treatment and the cancer wasn't responding to it this time."

"Is there really nothing else they can try?"

"They've tried so many different drugs I've lost count. The side effects from the last treatment made me feel worse than the cancer ever did. I told the doctors I wanted to stop taking them. My parents are kind of pissed off about my decision."

"Why?"

"Because they don't want me to give up."

"Is that what you're doing?"

"Maybe, but I'm an adult and it's my choice. If you're going to bitch at me about my decision then don't bother."

"I wouldn't do that. I can see how hard this is for you."

"My parents want me to try a different drug, but the side effects sound awful. I can't face taking another course of drugs that'll make me feel even worse than the cancer does. Not right now, anyway."

"Your parents think you'll change your mind later, don't they?"

"My mum thinks nagging me will work. She doesn't understand. I want to enjoy the life I've got left. I know now I won't make it to university, but I still want to pass those exams. I hate that I've missed so many classes again this year while I was going in for blood tests and check-ups."

Zak pulled Sam close and held him tight against his chest. "What would you say if I told you I could help you?"

"You already are helping me," Sam whispered round a yawn. "Being here and not turning your back on me helps more than you'll ever know."

Zak stroked his back until Sam drifted off to sleep again. He was right on the edge of slumber when he thought he heard Zak speak.

"I won't lose you, Sam. I won't."

Zak couldn't lose Sam, not now he had found him. Finally, he knew why he had turned into a human instead of one of the many other life forms out there. He loved Sam with a passion that frightened him when he considered how close he was to losing him forever.

Zak's phone rang the next morning and he reluctantly answered it. "Hi, Darren."

"Are you planning on coming home any time this week?" Darren asked.

Zak looked at Sam who was gazing at him with sleepy eyes.

"Is that your dad?" Sam asked.

"Yeah."

"You should probably be heading home soon."

"I'd rather stay here with you."

"I can hear you," Darren interrupted, reminding Zak that he was still on the other end of the phone. "I want you back this afternoon when I get back from college."

"Aren't you going to tell me to go to class?" Zak asked.

"No."

Zak couldn't cover up his surprise. "Why not?"

"I've been talking to Sam's parents."

"You know he…" Zak didn't want to complete the sentence in front of Sam. He didn't have to.

"I know he doesn't have much time left," Darren said.

"Then you know why I can't come home," Zak said.

"No, I know why you have to. We need to talk about your options."

And there was the one reason why Zak had to leave Sam's side. "I'll be home for dinner," he promised.

Zak ended the call and turned back to Sam.

"You dad knows about me, doesn't he?" Sam asked quietly.

"Yes, and we're going to find a way to help you."

"There isn't anything you can do apart from be here with me while I need you."

Zak kissed Sam lightly on the lips. "I won't be gone for long. Besides, we have all day together, with no interruptions."

A knock on the door sounded just before Sam's mother called to them. "Zak, Sam, I'm making breakfast, are you awake yet?"

Sam sighed. "So much for no interruptions."

"You need to eat," Sam's mother insisted.

Zak climbed out of bed and pulled on enough clothes to makes himself respectable. Sam stayed in the bed and nodded that Zak could open the door. Mrs Palmer stood on the threshold looking at them both with open curiosity.

"Yes, Mum," Sam said. "We did it, and I'm perfectly fine, as you can see."

"Do you need anything?" she asked. "Help in the shower perhaps?"

Sam flushed and ducked his head. Zak was well aware that the room reeked of sex.

"I'm going to stay with him today," Zak stated firmly. "I'll help him."

"That isn't your place."

Zak faced down Sam's mother. "You need some rest."

"You should be going to class today."

"I'm staying with Sam."

Mrs Palmer folded her arms and gave him a smug look. "I could call your father and see what he has to say about that."

Zak shrugged and returned her look with a smirk of his own. "He knows where I am and he's expecting me home for dinner. Until then, I'm staying with Sam."

Sam's mother looked as though she wanted to argue with him, but surprisingly she backed down. "I'll bring you some breakfast up. There are clean sheets in the hall closet."

"Mum!"

Zak ignored Sam's embarrassed exclamation as he nodded and shut the door behind his boyfriend's mother as she returned downstairs. "I thought she was going to throw me out."

"I wouldn't let her," Sam said. "I'm not going to be without you for even a minute longer than I have to."

* * * *

Sam's strength waned as the day wore on. "This sucks," he complained.

"My skills in bed suck?" Zak asked with a teasing smile.

Sam smacked him on the chest, though Zak barely felt it.

"I want to have the energy to enjoy your body," Sam explained. "Instead I feel even more drained each time we make love. Even when we've barely done more than bring each other off with a couple of strokes, I feel exhausted."

"I should have let you sleep longer," Zak said as guilt settled in his stomach.

"No," Sam replied. "I wanted this. I still want it."

"It isn't fair," Zak said as he looked at the clock. Darren would be driving back from the college right about now and he expected Zak to be home when he returned, which meant he had to leave his boyfriend — lover — very soon.

"Life seldom is fair," Sam whispered as he snuggled close to Zak. "All we can do is play the hand we're dealt."

"I don't like this hand at all."

Sam smiled. "I don't mind it so much."

"But you're dying!"

"I know, but right now I have you in my arms. That doesn't seem so bad."

"What if I told you I could save you?"

"There's nothing you can do. You can't fight destiny."

Zak wanted to tell him he didn't believe in destiny, only he did, the same as the rest of his people. Whatever power caused his people to change forms during their years of puberty knew his destiny. Each of his forms served a purpose, his human one more than any of the others. Without this form he'd never have met Sam and he'd not have fallen in love with him.

Oblivious to Zak's inner turmoil, Sam continued to talk quietly. "I believe everyone dies at the exactly moment in time they are meant to. Even if the cancer was gone, if it's my time to die I will. I'd be in a car crash or get food poisoning or something else. You can't fight your destiny and mine is to die young. At least this way I get to make the most of my time with you. I know to treasure every moment as if it's my last."

Zak held Sam close, feeling a dampness on his chest. Sam's brave words were a stark contrast to the tears he couldn't quite hide.

When Mrs Palmer put her head round the door, Zak waved her away, knowing her son wouldn't want his mother to witness his breakdown. She retreated silently, leaving them alone once more.

Zak left Sam, albeit reluctantly, and went home to talk to Darren. Time was running out for Sam and if Zak was going to save him he needed Darren to summon the nearest spaceship right away. He wasn't going to take no for an answer. He wanted Sam for the rest of his life, not just the short span of time his lover had left.

"Have you thought this through?" Darren asked once Zak had told him of his plans to share his life with Sam in the way of his people.

"Yes, and you're not going to get me to change my mind."

"But sharing your life with Sam is a huge step to take. Have you discussed this with him?"

"Not yet."

"You can't make this decision without talking it through with Sam. He may not want to live for thousands of years."

"I'm sure he'd find that preferable to dying in a matter of weeks."

"He probably would, but what about your own life? I'm sure you realize joining your life force with Sam's will halve your own lifespan."

"Yes, and I'm happy with that, if it means I keep him with me."

"Are you sure this is what you want? You've known Sam less than a year. You're still young, far younger than most of our people are when they take that step. The joining of life forces is irreversible and will bind the two of you together until the end of your lives."

"You joined with Eleanor," Zak pointed out.

"Yes, but we were married for several years before we made the decision to return to Trimmeron to be joined. It isn't something we decided to do on the spur of the moment."

"The elders said you've not been back to Trimmeron since you reached maturity?"

"They probably don't know. We were only there for a few days and it was a long time ago."

"Then you managed to sneak on and off the planet without anyone noticing?"

"We were hardly sneaking. No one keeps tabs on those who have reached maturity. We can come and go as we please. That doesn't mean you'll be able to do the same. You'll be taking a huge risk if you go back now."

"You aren't going to talk me out of this."

"I don't think you've really thought this through," Darren argued. "You said yourself, Sam didn't believe you when you tried to tell him where you're from and who you are. Until he knows the truth, he can't make a proper and informed decision about this."

"He can make a proper decision when he *does* believe me."

"When the craft lands for the pickup? That's hardly fair now, is it? How can Sam be expected to make a decision about the rest of his life in a matter of minutes?"

"He doesn't have to. He can come with me and decide on the journey. If he doesn't want to go through with it, we'll come back here and he can live whatever life he has left. At least the decontamination process will cure him of the cancer."

"Do you expect me to believe you won't try to push him into the joining?"

"I'll leave the choice to him."

"I know how much you care for him. I can see it in your eyes every time you look at him. He's the reason you became human, just like Eleanor was the reason I did."

Zak looked at Eleanor, who had remained quiet through the conversation. "I love him."

"I know you do, but you can't force him to join with you without him knowing what it means."

"I wouldn't let him go into this blind."

"You'll regret it if you do. Once you're joined it will be impossible to keep secrets from him. He'll be bound to you completely for thousands of years."

"Better that than dead," Zak countered. "Are you going to call the ship to pick us up or not?"

With a reluctant sigh, Darren pulled open an ancient chest and revealed the beacon. With a few turns of dials and the flick of a switch it was done. The nearest passing cruiser would divert to pick Zak up in a few days' time.

"What are you going to do if you get caught?" Darren asked. "You know you aren't allowed to leave Earth until your fostering is over."

"Sam doesn't have that long. I won't risk his life for anything."

"You're avoiding my question."

Zak huffed. "I don't know what I'll do. It depends what punishment the elders decide on. As long as Sam's safe, I don't care."

Darren didn't press him any further and all Zak could do now was wait.

* * * *

Getting Sam to the hillside proved to be rather more challenging than Zak had intended. His health was failing, leaving him so tired he could barely get out of bed, let alone go gallivanting over the countryside.

His parents, his mother in particular, watched over him like hawks and although they hadn't tried to curtail Zak's visits, they drew the line at anything that would cause their son more pain than he already suffered.

Zak finally managed to convince Sam and his parents there would be a meteor shower on the night the ship was due to arrive, which could only be viewed from this particular spot. Sam wasn't convinced at all—Zak hadn't expected him to be—but his parents weren't into astronomy and didn't question his story. They knew Sam loved watching the stars and they couldn't deny him the chance to see this once in a lifetime event. They did insist on coming with them. Zak didn't mind. In fact he was grateful, because at least this way they would know the truth and not be worrying about where their only son had vanished to.

Sam curled into Zak's side as Darren drove them out of the town and into the countryside.

"Tired?" Zak asked.

"A little," Sam replied, although the yawn punctuating his words suggested a lot might have been a more accurate reply.

"You can sleep a while if you want. We've got a little way to go yet."

Sam nodded and snuggled closer. Zak tilted Sam's face toward him and kissed him softly on the lips. Eleanor, sitting in the front with Darren, caught Zak's eye in the mirror and smiled.

"Shut up," Zak told her after he had ended the kiss.

"I didn't say anything," Eleanor replied. "Just thinking about how cute you two look back there."

Zak grimaced at being called cute, even though privately he thought it was a very accurate word to describe Sam.

Sam smiled and closed his eyes. Within a few minutes he was fast asleep.

"So, you seem to have got over your aversion to kissing," Darren commented from behind the wheel.

Zak grinned and licked his lips. "You don't know what you're missing."

It was Darren's turn to frown. He shook his head and gave an exaggerated shiver.

"This is what I keep telling him," Eleanor said to Zak. "But try as I might, I can't convince him that kissing is good. You'd think after so many centuries he'd have seen the appeal, but no." Eleanor twisted round in her seat to face him. "Every time he sees me swooping in for a kiss, he screws up his face, like this."

Zak chuckled as Eleanor pulled a face that was reminiscent of someone who had just caught the scent of something foul.

"That's it, just gang up on me," Darren said.

Zak and Eleanor laughed at Darren's feigned sulkiness and Sam began to stir. Zak got his giggles back under control and raised his finger to his lips. Sam needed his sleep and Zak intended to make sure he got it.

Sam's parents drove behind them and Zak glanced through the rear window every ten minutes or so to make sure they hadn't lost them. The last thing he needed was for them to get held up on the car journey and miss the craft. Not that he could explain this to Sam or his parents.

"Is he asleep?" Darren asked as they approached the vaguely familiar hillside where Zak had been dropped off all those months ago.

"No," Sam murmured in response.

Zak smiled and hugged him close. "We're nearly here. I recognize the road we're on now."

"Why are we really here?" Sam asked. "And don't give me that rubbish story about a meteor shower. I know there isn't one tonight and even if there was, I could watch it just as well from my bedroom. I can't believe my parents fell for your story."

"There's something I need you to see," Zak replied. "It'll be here soon."

Darren looked at the clock on the dashboard before adding. "It should arrive in about half an hour. Looks like we've judged our arrival quite nicely this time."

Darren steered the car into a small car park and turned off the engine. "We'll have to walk from here," he said.

"Walk?" Sam asked. "Can't I see whatever it is from the car?"

"It's not far," Zak assured him. "I'll help you."

Sam didn't look very enthusiastic, but eventually he agreed to walking up the hill. "It better be close," he warned. "I don't think I can make it very far at all. I'm so tired."

They were just locking up the vehicle when Sam's parents pulled in behind them.

"What's going on?" Mrs Palmer asked. "Are you okay, Sam?"

Sam nodded as he clung to Zak. "I'm fine. We're just going to head up the hillside to get the best view."

"No one said anything about walking anywhere," Mr Palmer said. "Sam's not fit enough to be traipsing around in the middle of the night. He could barely manage to get into the car. I knew this was a bad idea."

"I'm fine," Sam insisted. "I'll be okay for a little while. I want to see this while I still can. I don't want to spend the rest of my life in bed, waiting for the end to come."

"We don't want you to stop living, but you have to understand there are limitations to what you can do, especially if you insist on refusing to try another treatment."

"Don't start, Mum," Sam snapped. "Do you think I don't know my own limits? It's just a short walk and if I start to struggle we'll come straight back to the car. Zak will be with me every step of the way. He won't let anything happen to me."

Darren stepped over to Mr and Mrs Palmer and gave them a reassuring nod. "It really isn't far. We would never do anything to hurt Sam. I promise."

Somewhat reluctantly the Palmers agreed and they all made their way up the rocky path.

Eleanor had thoughtfully brought a couple of deckchairs with them and she set up one for Sam to sit in to wait.

"It's a bit cloudy," Mr Palmer said as he looked up at the night sky. "I hope, after all this trouble, Sam gets to see these bloody meteorites."

Zak grinned at Sam's father. "Believe me, I wouldn't bring you all up here if I didn't think you'd get to see the event of a lifetime."

Mrs Palmer gave him a doubtful look. "You can't control the weather, though."

Zak chuckled. It was on the tip of his tongue to say that actually he had some experience in controlling the weather on his home world, but he didn't want to tell Sam and his family the truth until the craft was here and they couldn't deny the evidence of their own eyes. The last thing he wanted was to risk Sam disbelieving him again and insisting on returning home before the proof arrived.

They sat companionably for a while, Zak silently counting down the minutes as he scanned the sky for the cruiser. They wouldn't miss the ship now they were here. Darren's transmitter, hidden in his jacket, would give a signal to let them know when the ship was about to arrive.

Zak heard the soft bleep of the transmitter and he looked over to Darren who gave him a small nod. The cruiser was entering into the atmosphere of the Earth and would be here in a matter of minutes.

"Sam," Zak began. His boyfriend's name was as far as he got before his entire prepared speech flew from his mind.

Sam's eyes widened and when Zak followed his gaze he saw the three purple lights of the ship in the distance.

"Is that a plane?" Sam asked.

"It has purple lights," Sam's father said. "I don't recall seeing one of those before."

"It's not a plane," Zak replied for Sam's ears alone. "It's a spaceship."

"Very funny," Sam said.

"I'm not joking." Zak took hold of Sam's hand and held it tightly. "Do you remember the day I tried to convince you I come from another planet?"

Sam nodded mutely, his eyes never leaving the lights of the incoming cruiser.

"You didn't believe me, and I don't blame you, but the proof you wanted is heading right here."

"What was that you said?" Sam's father asked.

Zak glanced at Mr Palmer before turning back to Sam. "Please believe me, Sam."

The ship drew closer and closer until they could all see exactly what it was. Sam and his family looked as though they couldn't quite believe their eyes.

Sam finally turned away from the ship and looked at Zak. Zak kept a hold of his hand, determined not to let it go.

"You're leaving, aren't you?" Sam whispered.

"Not without you," Zak replied with a smile.

"You're really from another planet." It wasn't a question and Zak didn't answer it. "Bloody hell, you really *are* an alien, aren't you?"

"Would you like to come with me?" Zak asked.

Sam's eyes watered and a single tear ran down his cheek. "I wish I could."

"You can." Zak looked over his shoulder and saw that the craft was nearly upon them. There was no longer any mistaking what it was. No one on Earth, save for his family, had ever seen anything like it before.

"Maybe if I were healthy it'd be different, but we both know I'm not going to get better. I'd only be a burden if I came with you."

Zak cupped Sam's cheek with his right hand. "You could never be a burden to me. Come with me, Sam."

Sam's father had moved into earshot and caught the last of his words. He glared at Zak. "Get away from my son, right now."

Zak scowled up at him and made it clear with one quelling look that he had no intention of leaving Sam's side. He turned back to his boyfriend. "If you come with me, we can cure you."

Sam's eyes widened even more than they had at the first approach of the ship. "What do you mean?"

"Stand back from my son!" Mr Palmer shouted as he tried to pull Zak away from Sam.

"Take your hands off him!" Darren yelled as he ran at Sam's father just as he was about to take a swing at Zak. His caught his arm just in time. "Zak, hurry up and explain what you need to."

Zak took a deep breath and turned back to Sam. "No diseases are allowed on my world. As soon as any visitor arrives, you go through a decontamination process that removes any form of illness. It's a precaution since my people are fostered to lots of different worlds during their puberty and they want to make sure none of us brings back something that could cause an epidemic."

"Cancer isn't contagious."

"It doesn't matter, it'll still cure you."

"You'd never heard of cancer before," Sam reminded him. "How do you know it will cure me?"

"It will," Darren said from behind Zak, where he was still keeping a secure hold on Sam's father.

"You're really serious, aren't you?" Sam said to Zak.

"Yes. There's something else I'd like to do while you're there too."

"What's that?"

"I'd like to join our life forces together."

"What do you mean, like a marriage or something?"

"Not exactly. It means you'll live a long and healthy life, the same as me."

Darren coughed behind him.

Zak glared over his shoulder before turning back to Sam, who raised an eyebrow in question at the silent exchange.

"Darren thought I'd forgotten to tell you something," Zak explained. "I just hadn't got to it yet."

"Got to what?"

"My people live a lot longer than humans. If you join with me you'll live to be thousands of years old."

Sam's jaw dropped.

"Eleanor was born human until she joined with Darren when he came here to Earth. They met in the late thirteenth century. Those paintings in their house of people who look like Darren and Eleanor aren't look-a-likes. They're paintings of them, done in different years over the centuries. Eleanor actually painted many of them herself."

Sam opened and closed his mouth several times.

The ship was right overhead now and slowly descending in response to Darren's signal.

"You don't have to decide right now," Zak said. "If you get there and change your mind we can just come back here. You'll still be cured of cancer. The joining has nothing to do with the decontamination process."

"My boyfriend's an alien," Sam said. He gave a small, almost hysterical laugh and shook his head.

"Are you okay with this?" Zak asked. He rubbed his thumb over Sam's knuckles. He thought Sam might have taken the news a little better than this. Maybe he was in some sort of shock.

"Sam, we're going home," Mr Palmer shouted as he finally twisted out of Darren's grasp.

Zak could hear the fear in his voice and regretted his decision to let them come along tonight. Perhaps he should have insisted they remain behind, though he doubted any request of that nature would have been well received. Before Zak could say anything, it became clear that Sam's mother had other ideas.

"What a minute, what if he's telling the truth?" she asked. "There's an honest to God spaceship right over our heads. Perhaps we should listen to what they have to say."

"Don't be ridiculous. Sam, we're leaving right now."

"You can't deny the evidence of your own eyes," Zak said. "Look right above you and tell me you've ever seen anything like it before."

"Yeah, I can see it," Mr Palmer said. "And I'm not going to let some alien kidnap my son."

"Dad, Zak wouldn't take me against my will," Sam said as he finally seemed to get a handle on what was happening around him. "But this could be my only chance."

"Chance of what?"

Eleanor stepped toward Sam's parents and placed a calming hand on Mr Palmer's shoulder. "It's okay. Sam's not in any danger."

"You're all crazy," Mr Palmer shouted. "Sam, I insist you come back to the car at once."

"Dad, it's all right," Sam said. "Zak wouldn't do anything to hurt me. I'm at least going to hear him out."

Zak gave a sigh of relief. "There's not much more to say. If you come with me, you'll be cured, and if you join your life force to mine, you'll get to live a long, long time."

"Can I come back here again?" Sam asked.

"Of course, though when you aren't visibly aging it's wise to move around a bit. It'll mean a lot of traveling."

Darren gave a guilty cough. "It'll mean new identities now and again too. I can help you with those. Eleanor and I have had a lot of practice in that regard."

"See," Zak said. "It'll be great. We can travel the universe as well if you want to. Whatever you want. At least you'll have the options."

"Sam, get in the car right now!" his father shouted.

They tried again to calm down Mr Palmer, but Sam's father was beyond listening to any of them.

"Our people can save him," Zak said, addressing his words to Sam's mother, who he could see was taking the arrival of the ship far better than her husband. At least she wasn't getting hysterical or trying to separate him from Sam.

"You're talking about aliens and spaceships," Mrs Palmer said. "It's a lot to take in."

Eleanor stepped forward to face the other woman. "We're talking about saving your son's life. I know what it's like to bury a child. I was born human and even though I have lived hundreds of years, my children have all had human lifespans. Although I don't regret my decision to be with Darren, watching my children die is the hardest thing I've ever had to do. I feel the loss of every single one, even those who lived to become parents and grandparents themselves. But the sharpest pain is to lose those who were taken too young. We can spare you that pain by making sure Sam lives a good long life."

"What if it doesn't work?" Sam's mother asked. "To give him this hope and then tear it away will kill him."

"It will work," Darren said. "I promise you, if you let Sam go with Zak, he'll return here healthy and well."

"I'm dying, Mum," Sam added sadly. "We all know it. If Zak's right it means I don't have to."

"Or he could just be kidnapping you to do some kind of experiments on!" Mr Palmer interrupted.

Zak laughed. "There are many things I want to do to and with Sam, but experimenting on him—in the way you mean—isn't one of them."

Eleanor gave him a sharp look. "That isn't helping, Zak."

"You need to make a decision now," Darren said as the ship came to a halt several feet above the ground. "The pilot won't want to hang around for long."

Zak clung to Sam as he watched his boyfriend's reaction to the landing. The purple lights on the bottom of the craft caused the ground below it to glow dark lilac. Part of the side of the craft extended down to the floor, making a ramp that could be walked up. Despite being such a huge vehicle it made not a sound as it opened to let on passengers. Swift and silent was the motto of the cruisers—they needed to be considering how many of them there were on Alliance worlds at any given time.

"Zak?" Sam whispered.

"Come with me," Zak begged.

Sam nodded and threw his arms round Zak's neck.

"Sam, you can't do this!" his father shouted. "I insist you come back to the car with us right now."

"I'm nineteen years old," Sam reminded him with a smile. "I'm an adult and old enough to make my own decisions."

Zak helped Sam to his feet and guided him toward the ramp. "I'll bring him home safely, I promise."

"No!" Mr Palmer ran forward and grabbed Sam by the arm. "You're not going."

"Let him go," Zak shouted. "It's his choice, not yours."

"I won't let you take my son away."

Zak struggled to keep hold of his boyfriend as his father began a tug-of-war with Sam in the middle. "Darren, help me."

Darren stepped up to Sam's father and pulled him away from them. "Get him on the ship, Zak. Quickly."

Zak helped Sam toward the ramp. They hurried as fast as they could, which wasn't very speedily, considering Sam's condition.

"Zak will bring him home safely," Eleanor said.

"You're damn right he will," Sam's mother said as she looked toward the spaceship. "I'll make sure of it."

"What do you mean?" Sam asked.

"I'm coming with you, of course."

"What?" Sam's father shouted as his wife stepped toward the ramp. "You aren't seriously considering getting on that thing. Have you lost your mind?"

Sam's mother crossed her arms and Zak recognized who Sam had inherited his stubbornness from. "I'm not letting my baby go on that thing alone."

"I'll be with Zak," Sam pointed out.

"And me," his mother replied.

"What if it doesn't work? What if you go to wherever it is Zak comes from and you don't get cured? What if you don't make it back?"

"I'll bring him home again, no matter what," Zak assured her.

"I'm coming with you, so you might as well get used to the idea." With those words Sam's mother marched toward the spaceship and climbed the ramp.

Sam turned to his father. "I'll be okay with Zak. He won't let anything happen to me."

Mr Palmer continued to struggle in Darren's grip. He glared at Zak. "If you don't bring them back I'll track you down wherever you are."

He didn't need to say it, but Zak knew he meant across space as well if he had to. Zak nodded. Sam's father didn't need to worry. Sam would be safe with him. He just hoped Darren and Eleanor would be safe with Sam's father. The man was furious and Darren was barely holding him back from charging up the ramp and dragging Sam back.

"Take care," Eleanor called out.

Zak gave her a quick wave and slowly walked the rest of the way up the ramp. Sam leaned heavily on Zak, his breath coming short after the exertions of the last hour.

"My dad's really pissed off."

"I know."

"I hope your folks will be okay with him in such a temper."

"Darren was a warrior in medieval times. I think he'll be able to handle him."

"Should I worry about my husband?" Sam's mother said as they caught up with her at the top of the ramp.

"He'll be fine," Zak assured her. "We all will. Now let's go find some seats before Sam collapses.

Zak spared one last glance for his foster parents and Sam's father as the ramp rose once more, sealing them securely inside. Sam's father still looked murderous, but Darren had him well in hand. Eleanor waved them goodbye. "Hurry home," she yelled. Zak knew she was referring to Earth and not Trimmeron, and he realized that Earth had become his home after all.

Chapter Fourteen

Sam clung to Zak's side as they boarded the spaceship. Bloody hell, he was on an actual spaceship. His boyfriend was an alien and the planet Earth would soon be a tiny speck in the distance. What had he gotten himself into?

Zak led them down an empty corridor. There was no one in sight in any direction.

"Who worked the ramp?" he asked.

"The pilot and crew in the main navigation room control the outer doors and the ramp," Zak explained.

"How could they see when we were on board?" Sam's mother asked. "I can't see any cameras or anything."

"There are cameras on all the corridors, but they don't look like the ones on Earth. There are also sensors on the ramp to prevent it being operated while anyone is standing on it." Zak pointed out one of the cameras as they passed it, but Sam didn't take much notice of it. He just wanted to sit down somewhere and sleep until they arrived on Zak's planet.

They carried on down the corridor that seemed to be never-ending. Every step was sapping more and more of his energy. Finally they reached a door that Zak opened by pressing his palm to the panel on the wall.

On the other side of the door were so many strange creatures, Sam didn't know where to stare first. Tall and short, bipeds and quadrupeds, furry and scaly, there was an incredibly wide range of beings on the craft and not one of them was even remotely familiar. Sam inched even closer to Zak, wondering if any of them were dangerous.

The noise of the dozens of passengers chattering away in a babble of strange languages temporarily chased away Sam's lethargy, though he knew it would return soon.

"It's okay to be a bit scared," Zak said. "I was terrified the first time I went off world."

"You were?"

"Yes. I was leaving my parents for the first time and I had no idea what to expect. I'll have to introduce you to them when we get there."

"You mean your real parents?"

"Yes. Darren and Eleanor are my foster parents while I'm on Earth. Every word I told you before was true."

"I'm sorry I didn't believe you."

"It's all right. I don't blame you for disbelieving me. Most people would."

Sam still felt guilty for doubting him and sought a change of subject. "Are your real parents like Darren and Eleanor?"

"No. Darren is a better father to me than my real dad ever was."

"Tell me about your real parents."

"What do you want to know?"

"Well, why do you say Darren is a better father?"

"Maybe better is the wrong word. I just haven't seen much of my real parents since I hit puberty."

"That must have been very hard for you," Sam's mother commented as Zak led them to a relatively quiet corner of the cabin. They found some comfortable seats near a large floor-to-ceiling window showing the dark expanse of space and settled down for the journey. Sam curled up against Zak, resting his head on his shoulder. He was really struggling to keep his eyes open. The other passengers didn't seem to take much notice of them and gave them a wide berth. Once Sam was sure that no one was going to approach them, he closed his eyes and relaxed for the first time since the spaceship had descended to Earth.

Sam cast his mind back to his previous conversation with Zak. "You're fostered to other planets when you take other forms, right?" His voice sounded sleepy even to his own ears.

"Yes."

"How does that work?" Mrs Palmer asked.

Zak gave her his attention as he explained. "When we reach puberty we change forms. We never know what we'll become until the transition happens. We feel instinctively when the time has come to return to our natural state. At that point, we return to Trimmeron for the next change. We can be in an alien form for anywhere from a couple of months to a couple of years. During that time we're fostered to the worlds where the forms we have are native. We spend time learning the ways of the other species until the time comes to return home and take a new one. We have a few days with our parents between changes, but we're shipped off pretty quickly. I've barely seen my real parents in the last twenty years."

Sam twisted round and opened his eyes to look at him. "Twenty? I thought you were nineteen."

"I'm nineteen in Earth years, or at least I look it. In the terms of my own world I'm nearly forty."

Sam snickered. "Guess I got myself an older man, huh?"

"Maybe it's the other way round," Zak teased. "I never bothered to calculate the actual conversion from Trimmeron years to Earth years. It could be you who's the older one."

"What's your world like?"

Zak sighed. "It's beautiful. Do you remember the painting of the mountains Eleanor showed us?"

"Yes. Are they really from your world?"

"Yes."

"What are they called?"

"The Sacred Peaks."

"Why are they sacred?"

"Because that's where my people go to join their life forces."

"And your planet is called Trimmeron?" Mrs Palmer asked.

"Yes."

"That's a rather strange name."

Zak visibly bristled. "So is Earth, from my point of view."

"I'm sorry. I didn't mean to insult you."

"You didn't. I know it sounds a little strange."

Sam struggled to stay awake and he yawned loudly. "It sounds nice to me. I just hope I get to see it."

"You will, I promise. You should try to get some sleep."

Sam smiled and rested his head on Zak's shoulder again. "How long will it take to get there?"

"It'll be a while yet. I'm afraid we haven't quite mastered instant travel."

Sam closed his eyes. "Keep talking to me. Tell me about the mountains and what else you have on your planet."

Zak obliged him by quietly talking to him as the ship made its way through the stars. Sam listened as long as he could before eventually falling asleep.

Zak looked down at Sam, snoring peacefully, nestled against him. "He's asleep," he commented needlessly.

"Good," Mrs Palmer said. "I think it's about time we had a little chat."

Zak tried not to fidget in his seat. He didn't want to disturb Sam. "Okay."

"Do your people really have the ability to cure Sam, or was that just a lie to give him some sort of trip of a lifetime?"

"The decontamination will cure both of you."

"There's nothing wrong with me."

"You've been trying to shake off that cough since Christmas. The process will get rid of that for you as well as Sam's cancer."

"They're hardly the same thing."

"No, but that's how it works. No disease is allowed on my planet."

Sam's mother still looked skeptical, but she would simply have to wait and see. In the meantime she had other questions for him.

"You said you take new forms until you become an adult."

"Yes."

"What happens then?"

"I revert to my true form, but can take the shape of any of my previous incarnations whenever I wish. Until I'm mature, I can't control the changes."

Mrs Palmer looked around the passenger room. "There are so many...er..."

"Strange creatures?" Zak guessed.

She replied with a nod. "I didn't like to say it out loud in case I insulted someone."

"They wouldn't be able to understand you anyway."

"Why not?"

"Earth and the languages spoken on it aren't taught across the universe."

"You speak it well enough, though sometimes I have wondered whether English wasn't your first language."

"It's my ninth and I still struggle with it at times. I'm only the second of my kind to turn human. Darren was the first."

"What do you look like when you're not human?"

Zak gestured discreetly across the room. "Do you see the man standing near the far window?"

Mrs Palmer turned in her seat. "The big blue one?"

"Yes. He is from my world and in his true form."

"You have blue fur and skin?"

"Yes."

"Oh." The movement was subtle, but Zak caught her edging away from him slightly.

"Is there a problem?" Zak asked. "I'm the same person I always was."

"No, no problem." She halted her fidgeting and looked him in the eye. "It's just a surprise, that's all. If I ever think about life on other planets, which I admit isn't that often, I guess I always assumed the people would have evolved in the same way we have."

"We aren't so different," Zak replied with a smile. "We might look different, but we have the same feelings as humans do."

"Do you?" Sam's mother looked at her son. "How do you know that you feel as strongly as he does?"

"How do you know you love Sam's father as much as he loves you?"

"I just do."

Zak smiled triumphantly. "And there's my answer, too."

"And what happens to the two of you when you become an adult?"

"Like I said, I can choose any of my forms to take. Since Sam seems to like my human appearance, I suspect I'll keep this one."

"That's not what I meant. Where will you go? You have a whole universe out there to explore, why would you stay on Earth?"

"You're worried I'm going to take Sam away from you." It wasn't a question. Zak could tell what was worrying his boyfriend's mother.

"He's my only child."

"He's a grown man now."

"That's not the point. He'll always be my baby, no matter how old he gets."

"Like I said back on Earth, if Sam chooses to share his life with me he'll live a lot longer than a normal human lifespan. He could live on Earth for a hundred years and still have plenty of time to travel the rest of the universe."

"What if he wants to do the traveling with you right away?"

"He won't."

"You don't know that."

"I know Sam, and I know he wouldn't want to do anything to hurt anyone, least of all you. He'll wait until you're ready to let him go before he leaves Earth. You could even come with us for the occasional holiday."

"His father and I wouldn't want to impose on the two of you. Well, that's assuming his father has calmed down by the time we get home. Unlike me and Sam, his father has always been eminently sensible and isn't given to flights of fancy of any sort."

"You seem to have your feet firmly on the ground to me," Zak said with a wry grin when he remembered where they were right now. "Anyway, I wouldn't see your presence as an imposition, and I'm sure Sam wouldn't either."

"I can't lose him."

Zak tightened his arm round his lover. "Me neither."

"You won't," Sam murmured sleepily before drifting off once again.

* * * *

Sam was once again snoring away at his side when the craft began the approach toward Trimmeron.

Zak was loath to disturb him, but eventually he had to nudge him awake.

"Wha—?" Sam muttered incoherently as he sat up and rubbed at his eyes.

"We're nearly there," Zak told him, nodding toward the front of the craft where the planet was clearly visible. Sam's mother stood at the window, where she had been for the last half hour, watching the planet grow larger as they approached.

"It looks green and blue, like Earth." Sam looked at him questioningly, clearly surprised at what he saw.

"Yeah, the land masses are different and our climates are more temperate than some of the extremes you have, but you'll find many of the inhabitable worlds are composed of sea and land. Some are more golden and blue, like the desert worlds, but for the most part, this is what you'll find."

"I guess that was a bit of a stupid thing to say," Sam said.

"Not really. Most people would probably think the same thing. You can't see my sector from here yet—it's round the other side—but I'll point it out to you as soon as it comes into view."

Sam joined his mother at the window in eager anticipation. Zak stood at his side, watchful in case the excitement was too much for him.

"We should get there in about half an hour."

"How long have I been sleeping for?" Sam asked. "I thought it'd take weeks to get here, if not months."

"We might not be able to manage instant travel across space, but we can manage to get around a lot quicker than humans," Zak replied with barely concealed smugness. "We can travel across galaxies faster than you can travel around your planet by plane."

Sam poked him in the chest. "There's no need to sound so pleased with yourself," he teased. "It's not like you personally invented the spacecraft."

Zak chucked.

"How long *has* it taken to get here?" Sam asked again. "The last thing I remember is getting up to go to the bathroom."

"The journey has taken about sixteen hours."

"Bloody hell!"

Zak stretched across and pointed out of the window. "There it is. See the white caps of the mountains?"

"Yes."

"Those are the Sacred Peaks. I grew up at the base of the largest."

Sam leaned against Zak and sighed. "Do you think they'll like me?"

"Who?"

"Your parents."

"They'll adore you," Zak assured him. "And even if they don't, it'll make no difference to us."

"You don't think it'd be hard having your parents disapprove of me?"

"They rarely leave this planet these days. If they hated you we'd never have to come back here. There's a whole universe to explore, you and me, together."

"Maybe after I've finished university," Sam amended with a quick glance at his mother, who nodded approvingly.

"You'll learn far more traveling with me than you'll ever learn in university on Earth."

Sam twisted round to give Zak an annoyed look. "I realize now why you don't rate Earth and what it has to offer, but I've put so much work into furthering my education the last few years, and I don't want it all to have been for nothing."

"What makes you think I don't believe Earth has anything to offer?"

"Your whole attitude about college when you first arrived was a pretty big clue."

"I've been doing the homework and going to class."

"Yeah, I know. You've been getting through the work in half the time it takes me."

"Only in Maths. I'm still struggling in English and History is just a confusing mess of battles and dates I can't remember."

"That's because you can't be bothered with trying," Sam said. "If you put your mind toward studying you'd fly through the lessons in no time."

Zak sighed. "If you really want to go to university then I'll come with you."

Sam's face lit up with a bright smile. "You will?"

"I'm never going to leave your side."

Sam gave a humorous snort. "Sounds like I have my very own stalker."

* * * *

Sam couldn't seem to stop staring at everything he saw as Zak led them off the ship. They followed after several other passengers who were also disembarking, though most of the travelers were apparently staying on board for the next leg of the craft's journey.

"Strange, huh?" Zak whispered in his ear when he caught Sam goggling at a large woman with tentacles who, according to Zak, had taken it upon herself to get into an argument with the stewardess about just how far she could go with her ticket. They gave her a wide berth as they headed toward the ramp.

"Is that what you look like?" Sam asked. "All scales and tentacles?"

"No, my natural form is much worse than that."

Sam couldn't keep the horror from his face. Only when Zak began to laugh did he realize he'd been teasing him.

"You'll have a fair idea of what I look like soon enough," Zak said. "Come on. Unless you want to stay on for the next stop, we need to hurry up."

Sam quickened his pace as best he could. Even though he had just slept for most of the long journey, he still felt exhausted. He wondered how long it would be before they reached the decontamination place that Zak was sure would cure him of his illness.

It was dark outside and Sam wondered whether it was always like that or whether they had simply arrived in the middle of the night. When he turned to look back at the spaceship he caught sight of three familiar moons in an arc in the sky.

"The view is even better from the mountains," Zak said. "I'll have to show you them before we return home."

"How far is the place where I can get cured?" Sam asked. He didn't like sounding so impatient, but his strength was failing again and he wasn't sure how much longer he could remain on his feet.

"It's just inside the reception building," Zak replied with a nod toward the large glass structure about twenty meters ahead of them.

Sam looked ahead with relief that the place was close by. The building wasn't particularly large, although it appeared quite tall thanks to the domed roof. The entire structure, including the curved roof, appeared to be made of clouded glass. The door to the reception seemed to shimmer and vanish as people approached it, then reappear again after they went through.

"Just hang in there a few minutes longer and it'll all be worth it," Zak promised

Sam remained skeptical but he kept his opinion to himself. With what he had already seen in the last day, he could keep going on faith for just a little longer.

When they reached the door, Sam looked back over his shoulder one time and to his surprise the spaceship they had arrived on had vanished.

Zak chuckled as he caught Sam's surprised expression. "They don't hang around when they're on a schedule."

"I didn't even hear it leave."

"They're silent because some worlds, like this one, have many ships arriving throughout the day. By the time we've gone through decontamination another ship will have been and gone, maybe two if there's a queue. Imagine how noisy this place would be if every ship sounded as loud as your rockets."

Sam cringed at the thought. Zak's mode of transport seemed to be better all round.

As they entered the building, Sam became aware of a strange floral-like smell.

"It reminds me of my grandmother's garden in here," his mother said. "You never knew her, but she grew a lot of herbs and this smell reminds me of the days I used to help her with the gathering."

His mother's memory comforted Sam in the strange environment. The only beings in the room were those who had come off the ship. At first glance there didn't appear to be any workers in the place at all. Then he caught a glimpse of blue above them. A balcony ran around the whole of the room and blue, furry bipeds scurried back and forth as they went about their business.

"What are they?" he whispered to Zak.

"My people," Zak replied cautiously.

Sam took another look up at them at Zak's quiet response. "Oh."

"Yeah, I'm actually blue and furry," Zak said.

"I bet you're really cute," Sam teased.

"I hope you think that when you see me in my true form. Now here we are." Zak nodded toward a pool of water directly ahead of them.

Sam, who had been expecting something more like a laboratory or hospital, looked at the pool with doubt.

"You can both swim, can't you?" Zak suddenly asked.

"Not very well, but yes," Sam said and his mother confirmed she could too. The pool was quite small and stretched across to the far wall. There didn't appear to be any way out of the room they had entered. There were no stairs up to the balcony and the only door was the one they had entered through.

There were a couple of scaled beings ahead of them and Sam watched them climb into the pool, swim to the far side of the room and dive below the surface as though they were perfectly at home in the water.

"Are they your people too?" Sam whispered.

Zak shook his head. "They're our nearest neighbors. Their world is far more water-based than this or Earth. Their planet is three times the size of Earth, but they only have one land continent, which is about the size of North America. They have evolved to survive in the water rather than on land. They often come here to buy supplies as their own world can't sustain their current population."

Sam turned to Zak curiously when the couple didn't reappear.

Zak pointed to the far side of the pool. "The exit is down there. We have to go under the water, through the doorway and emerge on the other side. You'll only have to hold your breath for a few seconds. Do you think you can manage it?"

Sam's breath had been coming shorter and shorter in recent months, his strength sapped by his ill health.

"You don't have to do this, Sam," his mother said. "Surely there's another ship that can take us home again, right, Zak?"

"Yes, but if Sam doesn't go through the pool, what is there for him to go home to?"

"I can do this," Sam interrupted. "It's just a few seconds."

"Come on then," Zak said as he steered Sam to the short queue. "There aren't too many people here today, so we should be through to the other side in a couple of minutes."

Zak jumped into the pool first and turned round to help Sam down the steps to one side.

As soon as he put one foot into the water Sam felt a strange tingling on the skin that touched the liquid.

"What's in the water?" asked Sam, peering down into the pool, trying to see what caused the sensation.

"I don't know," Zak admitted with a shrug. "But whatever it is, it works."

Sam wasn't entirely convinced, but the deeper he went into the pool, the more energized he felt. The tingling moved from his feet, up his legs, over his abdomen and chest until it reached his neck.

Zak tugged him toward the far side of the pool. Below the water, Sam could see the doorway leading through the wall.

"You ready?" Zak asked. "You have to go under the water for it to work. Otherwise the cancer could linger in your body, hiding out in the untouched part until it strikes again."

Sam nodded and drew in a deep breath before ducking under the surface. He followed Zak to the other side of the barrier and when he came out the other side he felt like a new man. His mother was close behind him and she looked at him expectantly.

"Your doctor will be able to confirm the cancer has gone," Zak said. "It won't come back either, it's gone for good."

"I don't need a doctor to tell me it's gone," Sam said. "I can tell just by how I feel. It's like a huge weight has been lifted from my shoulders. I don't feel tired any longer and the feeling of sickness and dizziness has vanished. I've felt so weak and so ill for so long I'd forgotten what it feels like to be healthy."

"And now?"

Sam laughed loudly. "I feel like I could take on the world."

Zak staggered back as Sam threw his arms around him and inadvertently ducked him back under the water.

"There's something else I'm feeling as well," Sam whispered in Zak's ear when they came up for air.

Zak chuckled as Sam rubbed up against him, making his meaning more than clear. "Later," he promised.

Sam intended to hold him to that.

Zak climbed out of the pool and Sam and his mother followed close behind. "Was it really bad?" Zak asked.

Sam nodded, too choked up for words as thoughts of the last few years invaded his mind.

Zak pulled him back into his arms. "You never complained about the pain."

All of a sudden it was too much and Sam wrapped himself round Zak, heedless of the other arriving visitors passing them by. His eyes welled up and he sobbed quietly.

"Thank you," he finally whispered. "Thank you for giving me back my life."

Zak stroked his hair and held him while he pulled himself together.

Finally, Sam drew back and saw that there were two of Zak's people apparently waiting to speak to them. Taller than even Darren, they looked male although

Sam wasn't entirely sure of their gender. With all that fur it was rather difficult to tell, at least until they spoke.

"Zakrynious," the first one said after he'd gotten their attention.

"Yes?"

The second stepped forward and placed a hand on Zak's shoulder. Sam didn't understand what he said, but from the look on Zak's face the news wasn't good.

"What is it?" he whispered as they followed after the two strangers.

"I've just been arrested," Zak murmured back.

"What for?" Mrs Palmer asked as Sam stumbled at Zak's words. What the hell sort of trouble had Zak got himself into?

Chapter Fifteen

"What do you mean by arrested?" Sam asked.

"Pretty much the same meaning as on Earth," Zak muttered. "I thought we could slip in here and get back off world without anyone noticing."

"You mean you weren't supposed to bring me here?"

"I'm not supposed to come back here yet," Zak explained.

"Why not?"

Zak didn't see the point of avoiding telling Sam the truth. Even though Sam wouldn't be able to understand the language his people used, he would probably be better off with the facts. It wasn't as though it made any difference now. Now they were here and Sam had been cured, he didn't need to worry about Sam refusing to come with him on the basis that it might get Zak into trouble.

"When we're fostered off world, we're sent until our next transformation. It's forbidden for us to return before the signs appear that another transition is upon us."

"Can you pretend you're about to change?" Sam suggested.

"Unfortunately not. I know instinctively when the change is due to happen, but the elders will know I'm lying because they know in advance how long each form will last for each youngster."

"How can they tell?"

"I don't know. Their methods are shrouded in secrecy."

"So, what you're saying is, you're in trouble because you've brought me here?"

"Pretty much."

"You should have said something. I'd never have agreed to come if I'd known you weren't allowed to."

Zak snorted. "Which is exactly why I didn't tell you," he replied. "Don't worry—once I explain the situation everything will be fine."

"I can't believe you got arrested because of me."

Zak stopped in his tracks and turned to face Sam. "I have no idea when my time as a human will be over. We don't become an adult on a certain date and time, it depends on the individual. I could have a few more weeks as a human or another year or more. I couldn't risk losing you by waiting and it's not as though I could just wave you off from Earth and send you here on your own."

"Why not?"

"Because you wouldn't know where you were going and you'd probably have slept through the stopover here."

"I'd have made sure he woke up," Sam's mother said.

"And how would you have known when the ship arrived here?" Zak asked. She didn't reply, because of course she wouldn't have known where they were and had no way of communicating with the other travelers or the crew. Zak continued walking after the two officials, leaving the others to follow him.

Sam wasn't going to let things go so easily. "You could have asked Darren to bring me."

"You aren't Darren's responsibility."

"I'm not yours either."

"Yes, you are."

"Since when?"

"From the moment I fell in love with you," Zak snapped.

Sam stopped walking and tugged Zak round to face him again. "You're in love with me?"

"Shit!"

"You're *not* in love with me?"

"Yes, but I didn't mean to tell you like this. I wouldn't even consider sharing my life with you if I weren't in love with you."

One of the officials coughed pointedly, urging them to continue on their way.

Zak cursed the rotten timing as they followed the officers to the chamber where the elders would be waiting to deliver their punishment.

The elders were all present when Zak and Sam were brought before them. This time they didn't look at Zak with curiosity—they turned their furious gazes on him, making it clear they were far from happy to see him back before them so soon. He knelt on one knee directly before the leader.

"You know the rules of fostering?" the leader barked.

"Yes."

"And yet you returned here before your time. Why?"

Zak glanced over to Sam. "My lover needed to visit this world."

The elder's argument was the same one Sam had offered a few minutes before. "You could have made other arrangements for him to journey here. Either after your fostering is over or by sending him here without you."

"He was dying from an Earth disease. He could not travel alone." Zak didn't add his thoughts that he had been terrified of losing Sam and couldn't bear to leave his side. His people had little use for emotions and wouldn't understand what he meant. They had no experience of the intensity of human feelings and dealt with cold, hard facts.

"It would appear he had company in the form of another human, so was not alone."

Zak tried to keep his voice steady and even as he pointed out the obvious. "His mother would not know where to disembark the craft any more than he would."

"You could have made alternative arrangements."

"He's *my* responsibility."

"Your responsibility is to learn the ways of humans. How do you expect to do that if you leave their world?"

"I couldn't let him die!" Zak's outburst took the elders by surprise and he tried to bring his temper back under control.

The elder looked over toward Sam. "He does not say anything in your defense."

"He does not understand our language," Zak reminded him. "Another reason why I had to escort him."

"You did not *have* to bring him. There were other options had you chosen to look for them."

Zak bowed his head. Of course there had been other choices. He had chosen to ignore them because he had wanted to be the one to introduce Sam to his world. He hadn't wanted Darren to bring him here. His selfish desire to keep Sam to himself was the only reason he found himself in the position he now was.

"You know the punishment for returning early."

Zak shook his head. He actually had no idea what the penalty was, since he could not recall any of his people ever doing such a thing.

"Banishment is the only recourse."

Zak looked from one elder to the other. All nodded in agreement.

"By not staying on Earth for the duration of your fostering, you will be exiled to Earth for the rest of your life."

If Zak hadn't already been on his knees he'd have fallen to them at the elder's words.

"Do you understand?"

"What of my transformations?" Zak asked. "Will I have to return here again for another potion?"

The elders conferred amongst themselves for several minutes. Finally one of the women turned to him.

"This is your last transformation before you reach maturity. You do not need to return here for another potion."

Zak breathed a sigh of relief, but they hadn't finished.

"We will send someone to Earth to meet with you shortly before you come of age to extract the knowledge you have acquired for our database. There will be no reason for you to return here at all."

Zak nodded his understanding. "May I see my parents, to say goodbye?"

The elders again whispered to each other before agreeing that he could. The next ship going in the direction of Earth would leave the following evening. He was to be on it, but until then he could spend his time as he wished.

Zak stood up shakily as relief flooded through him. His only real fear had been the possibility of separation from Sam. Although he was sure that the elders had not intended it as such, banishment to Earth was hardly a punishment at all.

As soon as they had left the chamber, Sam bombarded him with questions.

"What happened? What did they say? Are we free to go?"

Zak stopped his barrage of questions with a kiss. "My punishment is banishment to Earth for the rest of my life."

"But you live thousands of years!"

"Yes. I'm afraid it means if you want to travel the universe, you'll have to go without me."

Sam shook his head. "I go where you go. If Earth is where you have to live from now on, so be it."

* * * *

Sam wasn't sure that Zak was quite as content about his punishment as he made out to be. He suspected Zak was merely putting on a brave face for his sake. Unfortunately, Sam could do nothing except stay with Zak and help him through the coming months, when the shock had worn off, and he found himself trapped on Earth.

"Let's get changed into some dry clothes and go meet my parents," Zak suggested. "I'm sure you'll like them, and you'll get to see how I look when I'm not human."

"Are you stuck in your human body forever now?" Sam asked.

"Only until I reach full maturity. The transformation back to my true form happens no matter where I am when the time comes."

"What if you're in public when you change?"

Zak laughed. "Can you imagine the look on everyone's faces if I did?"

"I'd rather not." Sam grimaced, still concerned about the prospect.

"Don't worry," Zak assured him. "I have plenty of advance warning before I turn all blue and furry."

"What sort of warning?"

"You'll see," Zak replied with a wink.

"Why don't I like the sound of that?"

"Don't worry, I'm only teasing. The warning won't out me as an alien to the general population. I'll simply know a few days before the time, just as I've known before each of my other transformations was due. In the past this usually meant calling the nearest spacecraft and heading home where I'd revert to my natural form. Though the last time I expected it to be the last transformation and didn't come home right away. It wasn't until I found myself permanently blue and furry I realized I had another form coming and had to rush back here to get my next potion."

"What does the potion do?"

"It's a revolting concoction that triggers the change to another species and makes it pain free. If I hadn't gotten back here in time I'd have changed without it and from what I've heard it isn't exactly a pleasant experience."

"What about when you change back again?" Sam asked. "Will it hurt if you can't come back here?"

"No. The change to my own form never hurts, it just happens."

"Are you sure? You're not just saying that?"

"I'm sure. I'll know a few days in advance that I'm due to change back, which will be plenty of time to make sure no one sees me. I'll transform just like before, but this time I won't have to come back here to drink a potion to trigger another change. This human body is my last new one and once I've switched back to my natural one again I'll have complete control over my body. I'll get to pick and choose what form I want to be in whenever I like, though most of the species I've turned into would be rather out of place on your planet."

"How do you know it'll be the last one? What happens if you get stuck in your alien body like you did last time?"

"I won't. This is definitely the last transformation. The elders just told me."

"And you're sure you won't suddenly change into another body in the middle of class and wind up in a government laboratory somewhere?"

"Yes, I'm positive."

A little less worried now than he had been, Sam hooked his arm through Zak's and they strolled along what appeared to be the main street of a bustling town.

Like the reception building at the spaceport, the town consisted of domed structures made of clouded glass. The shops, however, also had clear glass fronts, much like those on Earth, so shoppers could see the wares on display. There was also much more variety as to the color of the buildings and Sam soon realized they were color-coded. The green glass indicated food stores, blue for clothing, yellow for furniture and many more. The sky had lightened during their time with the elders and the sunlight lit up the street in a kaleidoscope of color. Sam expected the sun to cause blinding reflections as it hit the glass, but something in their structure seemed to stop that from happening.

The main street felt strange beneath Sam's feet. The ground had the appearance of tarmac but was soft as sponge. When Sam looked down he saw most people were barefoot as they went about their business.

"Your people start their days very early," Sam commented.

"Not really," Zak replied. "The shops are open all the time. The owners just work in shifts. The morning workers will be arriving soon and the ones you see now will go home."

A vehicle, as silent as the spaceship, passed them as it sped along the main thoroughfare.

"That seems kind of dangerous," Sam's mother said. "What if you didn't hear it coming?"

"The pool cures all forms of deafness," Zak replied.

"That's not the point. Going at that speed, when you can't hear it coming, is lethal."

Zak laughed and stepped into the road. "Watch."

"Zak!" Sam cried as another vehicle, hovering half a foot off the ground, sped toward him. He stepped forward to pull Zak clear, but his mother's hand on his arm held him back. The craft was nearly upon them when it swerved gracefully to the left and passed Zak by.

"See," Zak said. "Nothing to worry about. The sensors won't allow them to hit anyone or anything. They're all totally automated. You just put in the location you are at and where you want to go and you're on your way."

Sam glared at him. "You could have just said that instead of giving the practical demonstration."

Zak laughed as he walked back to Sam's side. "Sorry," he offered, though he certainly didn't sound it.

They continued on their way at a leisurely pace. A few people looked at them curiously, smiling as they passed by. Sam guessed it was because they had never seen humans before.

It wasn't long before they left the shops and town and arrived in what appeared to be the residential area. Unlike the shops, the houses appeared to be carved into the earth itself. Sam tried not to goggle at dwellings that wouldn't look out of place on a *Lord of the Rings* set. He half expected to see a hobbit popping out of one of the buildings that appeared more organic than built.

The gardens were well tended and even the flowers were in orderly lines. Insects more than twice as large as those on Earth hovered over the plants. Other animals looked at them curiously as they approached. One rather friendly creature bounded up to Sam's mother on six legs and ran around her at a speed to rival a spaceship.

"Is it friendly?" Mrs Palmer asked as she hesitated to pet it.

Zak looked back over his shoulder. "Sure, he's just looking to see if you have any treats. They're kind of like our version of dogs." He reached into one of the gardens and broke something off one of the plants.

"Isn't that stealing?" Sam asked.

"No, the crops in the front gardens are for anyone to help themselves. The ones in the back are for the residents alone."

"That's very generous."

"It's easy to be so when we have more than enough for everyone." He crouched down and held out the yellow berries to the animal. Sensing the food, the animal came to him immediately and slowed down enough for Sam and his mother to see it properly. With long fur all over its body, it bore more resemblance to a mop than a dog. Sitting on its back two legs, it used the front two to take the berries from Zak and the middle two to beg for more.

Sam picked a couple of berries for himself and his mother to feed to the animal, but before they could give them to it, a second one arrived to beg too.

"That's the only problem with snuppets," Zak said. "They're greedy as hell and can sense a soft touch a mile away."

"They're so cute. Where are their owners?"

"They don't have them. They hate being indoors so generally run wild. We'd better give them the berries and get moving or we'll end up here all day."

Sam passed a couple of berries to his mother and they fed and petted the snuppets. The animals followed after them for several minutes, clearly hoping for more treats, until they realized there was nothing else on offer and scurried off to beg from the next passer-by.

"The air's so clean here," Sam commented, breathing in deeply, savoring the freshness.

"No pollution."

"So I see. And I don't see anyone glaring at us either."

"Why would they?" Zak asked.

"Haven't you noticed? On Earth, people tend to stare at two men together like they're some sort of freak show."

"Homophobia is very much confined to Earth."

"You don't find it anywhere else in the universe?" Sam's mother asked. Sam hadn't realized she was listening to their conversation. She walked several paces behind them, stopping occasionally to look at one thing or another.

"No. And hopefully one day it won't be found on Earth either. I hope Sam and I both live to see that day arrive."

"I doubt it'd be in my lifetime." Sam spoke without thinking. Of course, if he joined his life force with Zak's, it could be, and more than likely would.

"If we joined, you'd see it," Zak said, almost as though he'd read Sam's thoughts. "No pressure, of course."

"Is it possible we can do this back on Earth?" Sam asked.

Zak shook his head. "I'm afraid it has to be done here, in the pool on the Sacred Peaks."

"I guess I'd better make my mind up quickly then."

"Perhaps there might be a little pressure," Zak amended.

Sam stopped walking and turned Zak to face him. "I already know what my answer will be."

Zak looked crestfallen and Sam could tell immediately he thought his answer would be no.

"Maybe you should take a little more time to think things over," his mother suggested.

Sam shook his head. They didn't have very much time for him to consider his options, and even if they had years ahead of them for him to consider his choice, the decision was an easy one to make. He wanted Zak by his side and the thought of leaving Zak to live countless centuries after he had died didn't sit well with him, not when they had the opportunity of spending many years together. "I don't need any more time. Zak, you've given me my life back. I would love to share it with you, for as long as you'll have me."

Zak's face lit up and he swept Sam up into a tight hug, spinning him round in a circle.

"Put me down, you maniac," Sam cried between gasps of choked laughter.

"Never," Zak replied. "I'm not letting you go, now or ever again."

Eventually Zak had to put Sam down so that they could continue on their way. Sam glanced at his mother and saw the worry in her eyes. "I know what I'm doing, Mum," he said.

"Are you really sure about this?"

Sam nodded and took hold of Zak's hand once more. "You don't need to worry about me. Zak wouldn't let anything happen to me."

"I'll always worry about you," his mother replied. "And this is such a huge step to take. You're talking about living for thousands of years."

"I know, but if I'm spending them with Zak I can't see it as being a bad thing at all. Look at his foster parents — they manage all right."

"I just wish you'd think things through a little more."

Sam sighed as he recognized the stubborn tone in his mother's voice. He had always known he had inherited that trait from her. "Mum, I've had several years to think about my mortality, when other kids my age were thinking about video games, first dates and whether they'll get the grades they want for uni.

You can't know what it's like to be doing your exams, while knowing that even if you pass it won't make any difference to what lies ahead for you. To be listening to everyone making plans for their futures, knowing you don't have one."

Sam's voice broke as he realized his mother was trying to hide her tears. "Mum, it's going to be okay. Really."

Mrs Palmer nodded and wiped her eyes. "I won't stop you if this is what you really want."

"It is." He let go of Zak's hand to hug his mother tightly. "You'll see."

Zak waited patiently until Sam let go of his mother and returned to his side. They carried on up the gradual incline toward the mountains.

"What do your real parents do?" Sam asked as they strolled hand in hand along the path.

"My father is training to become one of the elders."

"If he becomes one, can he reverse your punishment?"

"I'm afraid not. Our penalties are harsh, but because of them we have very little crime on this world. I knew the risk I took when I made my decision to bring you here. My banishment is just."

"What about your mother? What does she do?"

"She and her partner are healers. We don't have diseases or sickness here, but people, particularly youngsters, are quite prone to accidents. When they happen, the healers are summoned. They also monitor disease on other worlds, to insure our healing waters continue to protect us from any new viruses or ailments."

"Your parents are divorced?"

Zak laughed. "They were never married. There's no such thing here, just the joining of life forces, which is completely irreversible."

Sam's confusion must have shown on his face because Zak immediately elaborated to alleviate his confusion.

"Reproduction by Camyl'ons—that's what my people are called—isn't done by sex. We don't have sex here at all."

"What?"

"Sex isn't something my people do. It's common on other planets, such as Earth, but not on this one. We are produced in laboratories, our parents chosen on the basis of compatible genetics."

"That sounds really...er..."

"Weird?" Zak suggested with a wink. "So does sex from our point of view."

"Oh." Sam looked down at his feet rather than meet Zak's eye. He had foolishly thought Zak enjoyed making love with him. "I didn't realize."

Zak gave Sam's mother a look that she understood immediately, stepping away to give the two of them some privacy. Once she had moved out of earshot Zak tipped up Sam's chin with his finger. "Hey, it doesn't mean I don't enjoy it."

Sam remained skeptical.

"When I first found myself with a penis, I had no idea what it was for. Now I know *just* what to do with it and I love the feeling of being joined with you in that way. I can't wait until we're joined in the way of my people as well."

"How do your people show their love for each other if they don't have sex or even kissing?" At least now he understood why Zak had been so shocked when

Sam had thrust his tongue in his mouth on New Year's Eve.

Zak frowned as though he didn't know how to answer the question. "We take care of each other and put our partner's needs before our own. I've never doubted my mother and her partner love each other. They're almost always together."

"Is your mother's partner another woman?"

"No, why do you ask?"

Sam shrugged. "You use the word partner, which often gets used for a member of the same sex on Earth."

"It's the closest word I know in English for what they are. We don't have marriages here and husband and wife aren't words we use either."

"I'm just wondering what to expect when I meet your mother."

"You'll see soon enough," Zak said as they continued to walk. The road began a steep incline and Sam found himself gasping for breath even though he was now in perfect health. Zak was barely even winded and Sam struggled to keep up with him. To his surprise, Sam's mother was rather spritely and kept up with Zak's fast pace with ease.

Zak looked over his shoulder to where Sam lagged behind. "Need me to carry you?" he called out teasingly.

Sam flipped him the bird and picked up the pace a little to prove he could do just as well. All too soon, though, he was falling behind again. He wondered how far it was to Zak's mother's house. They hadn't seen any other residences in quite a while.

"How do you keep up this pace?" Sam panted after he had caught up with Zak and his mother again.

Zak hopped up from the rock with a wide grin. "We draw our strength from the world around us. I can only do it when I'm either in my true form or on my home world. When we're back on Earth I'll be just as much a weakling as you until I reach maturity."

"Weakling, huh?" Sam punched Zak in the arm as hard as he could. Zak didn't even flinch.

"On this world in my true form I'm even stronger."

"Show-off."

Zak laughed and started to walk up the hill again, this time at a slower pace than before.

"I thought you said you grew up at the base of the mountains, not halfway up one of the things," Sam complained.

"I did," Zak agreed. "I lived with my father, but he'll be at work until later. My mother works from home, though, and she won't mind us showing up out of the blue."

"I'd have thought she would be kind of pissed off about your breaking the rules," Sam pointed out.

"She probably is, but she won't turn us away, not when she knows this may be her only chance to see her son and his partner for a long time."

"Can't she visit Earth?"

"Yes, but she has no human form, so she'll find it difficult to blend in and go unnoticed. Hopefully, in time, Earth will become part of the Alliance of Worlds and humans will become fully aware of the other species out there. When such a time comes, she and my father can visit without any fear of exposure."

"Do you see that happening any time soon?"

"Honestly, no. Maybe in a thousand years or so."

"I guess the people of Earth have a long way to go before they're ready for all of this," Sam said. "If aliens arrived openly on Earth right now, the army would probably open fire on them."

Zak nodded his agreement. "Yes, but one day things will get better and it'll be safe for us in our own forms. In the meantime we'll have to be very careful if my parents ever want to visit us."

Sam felt a pang of regret at the thought of Zak losing his family because of what he had done for him.

"No regrets," Zak scolded when he turned to face him. "I have you, and that's all I need. If I need parental advice, I'm sure Darren and Eleanor will be happy to oblige."

"You have Sam's father and me as well," Sam's mother said.

"How did you know what I was thinking?" Sam asked. "Are you reading my mind or something? Is this another super power you forgot to tell me about?"

"No mind-reading, just your face. Now, are you ready to meet my mother?"

Sam looked around him in confusion. He couldn't see any form of abode at all. "Are we here?"

Zak pointed upwards and when Sam looked above their heads he saw an elaborate home built into the trees above them.

"And how do we get up there?" Sam asked. He couldn't see a ladder or even a rope leading up into the trees and it had been a number of years since he'd been climbing trees like a monkey.

"We climb," Zak replied, as though this was obvious.

Sam looked at him doubtfully and Zak burst out laughing. "You git!"

"Did you think with all the technology we have, we'd have to scramble up the tree trunks like a bunch of overgrown squirrels?" Zak asked.

Sam flushed in mild embarrassment at his ignorance. "You're enjoying this way too much."

"Oh yes. I've felt like a complete imbecile most of the time I've been on Earth. I'm enjoying being back in familiar surroundings again."

"Your mother lives in a tree?" Sam's mother asked dubiously.

"My mum has a bit of a problem with heights," Sam explained.

"I don't have a problem with them. I'm happy at any height, just so long as I can't see down."

"It's perfectly stable and secure," Zak explained. "The rooms are all enclosed, though you have to go down a few walkways in the trees to get between different areas of the house. Once you're inside you can hardly tell you're above ground at all. We don't get high winds here so there isn't much movement of the trees. You'll be fine once you're up there."

"So, how do we get up to your tree house?" Sam asked.

Zak led them over to the largest of the trees and pulled aside a piece of bark. Inside was a lever and when Zak tugged it into the lower position, the platform above them started to move down. Zak pulled them all to the side so they were standing in one of several gaps and the platform slowly lowered around them, until it rested flat on the ground. They stepped onto the floor, which looked like wood but sounded more like metal underfoot. Zak hit the lever a second time and they began their rise up into the trees.

"What, no teleportation?" Sam teased.

"Oh, dear," Mrs Palmer cried as she held the wooden railing with a grip that turned her knuckles white.

"Just close your eyes and we'll be up there in no time," Zak assured her.

"They're already closed," Sam's mother replied. "It's not helping."

"Just a few minutes longer," Zak said. "It has to rise slowly for safety."

"That's not the only thing rising," Sam muttered. Zak stood dangerously close to him, and his newly healthy body was very much aware of the fact.

"Later," Zak promised with a quick, yet heated kiss. It wasn't enough for Sam, who clung to him desperately, but, with his mother standing just a few feet away and Zak's mother no doubt close by awaiting their arrival, it would have to do.

They broke apart when the platform came to a halt. Both were breathing quite heavily now. It seemed there was one way to cause Zak to lose his breath while he was on his home world.

"Is it over?" Sam's mother asked in a shaky voice.

"Yes, we're here," Zak replied while Sam turned away to try to hide his arousal.

"For someone who had never heard of kissing before coming to Earth, you're getting really good at it," Sam whispered.

Zak practically glowed under his praise and leaned down to kiss him again.

"Ahem," a voice said, distracting them from each other.

They all turned to face the newcomer.

Zak greeted her with a nod of respect. He said something in his own language before turning back to Sam. "This is my mother, Aristania."

Sam wasn't sure whether to stick out his hand for her to shake or what. He had no idea what the correct protocol was for meeting your alien boyfriend's mother. He had never seen anything or anyone quite like her. She was tall and willowy, with long dark green hair. Her skin was a lighter shade of green and there were tattoo-like patterns over her arms, upper chest and the sides of her face. Her eyes were yellow and slanted upwards at the sides.

Aristania smiled at him, revealing white teeth with fanglike incisors. For a moment Sam wondered if he had gotten himself mixed up with a race of vampires, before he swiftly dismissed the idea as being completely ridiculous. Then again, he reconsidered as he looked at Zak, so was the idea of a boyfriend who was really an alien from another planet.

Zak chattered to his mother for several minutes, although Sam didn't have a clue what they were saying.

From the expression on Aristania's face, she didn't seem overly angry with her son. In fact she seemed quite calm, which made Sam wonder whether Zak was giving her the whole truth or an edited version.

Zak did most of the talking in a language that sounded almost musical in quality. His mother's responses were short and quietly spoken.

When Zak turned to him at a pause in the conversation, Sam raised an eyebrow in question.

"My mother suggests that if we're going to be joined, we do so right away."

"That's all she had to say? What does she think of you joining with a human? Is she angry about you coming back here?"

"She understands why I did it, and she has no problem with my choice of partner."

"But is she angry?"

"No. My people don't feel emotions as much as humans do. Even if she were furious you'd probably get the same reaction."

"You seem to have emotions the same as everyone else I've met."

"That's because I'm in a human body. It came with a whole range of human emotions that I wasn't expecting at all. In my natural form my feelings are muted."

"Your mother doesn't even look like the same species as the blue furry beings we saw when we arrived."

Zak chuckled. "In her natural form she is, but this is the body she likes to live in day to day. It isn't native to this planet, but is one she took during her own years of puberty. As a healer she needs to keep calm and level-headed at all times. This form helps her with that."

"Will you lose your feelings when you transform again?" Sam asked.

Zak tipped his chin up and kissed him softly. "I'll be able to revert to my human body right after my last transformation. I might not like all the array of human emotions, but there is one I can't imagine living without now I've felt it."

He didn't need to say which one it was. It was right there in his eyes for Sam to see. "I love you too."

Sam still had a feeling a lot more had been said in the exchange than Zak was telling him, but Zak was already leading him away from his mother toward a long walkway through the trees.

"What about my mum?" Sam asked.

"She can't come with us for the joining. No one can."

Zak said something to his own mother, which again Sam didn't understand, and Aristania turned to Sam's mother with a smile. Through gestures and smiles she guided her toward a nearby doorway.

"It's okay, Mum," Sam assured her. "Zak's mother will take care of you."

Mrs Palmer didn't look too sure, but when she saw the narrow pathway through the trees that Sam and Zak were about to take, she swiftly made her choice.

"We'll be back soon," Zak promised before leading the way for Sam to follow him.

"Where are we going?" Sam asked.

"To the Sacred Pool."

"To be joined?"

Zak stopped and turned to him. "You do still want to?"

"Of course."

"I just want to make sure you don't feel as though you're being pressured into this."

"I'm not. I know what it is you're asking, and I'm fine with it. How could I not be okay with the idea of spending thousands of years with the man I love?"

"Thousands of years is a long time if you aren't sure."

"I've never been more certain of anything in my life."

"Then come on and let's do it."

The walk through the treetops was at least shorter than the one up the side of the mountain. The trees seemed similar to the ones on Earth although far larger than any Sam had seen before. They were more like those found in the deepest parts of the jungle and forests, where only the occasional documentary team ventured. Immense in both height and width, they had been allowed to grow without human interference to stunt their progress.

"I don't see any animals up here," Sam commented.

"They tend to avoid the Sacred Pool."

Sam came to a halt. "Are the waters of this pool poisonous or something?"

"No, but the wildlife can sense there is something strange about it and stay away."

Sam kept up with Zak easily as they made their way along the winding pathway. It eventually opened out onto another platform, this one in a half moon shape that fanned out over an expanse of water at least four times the size of an Olympic swimming pool. Sam could see cascading falls on the opposite side, though the river feeding them was hidden in the trees on the side of the mountain. Below, the waters were dark and murky. From what Zak had said about the wildlife avoiding the pool, Sam was sure there were no fish or other creatures living in the waters. The only movement was from the waterfalls. Everything else was still, almost frozen in time.

Sam expected Zak to reveal another lever and lower them down to the ground again, but instead Zak stepped toward the edge of the platform.

"Be careful," Sam warned. The platform had no railing and Zak was precariously close to the edge. It was a long drop to the water below, probably around a hundred meters.

Zak turned round and beckoned him closer.

"No way," Sam replied, stubbornly crossing his arms and shaking his head.

"Did you inherit your mother's fear of heights?"

"No, but I'm quite happy right where I am, away from the edge."

Zak held out his hand and waggled his fingers. "Sorry, but you're going to have to come over here."

"Why? Can't we just go down to this Sacred Pool of yours?"

"The pool is right below us. We need to dive in from here."

Sam laughed and shook his head. "Do you think I'm going to fall for that again? Where's the lever hidden?"

Zak took a step back toward Sam, his arm still extended. "I'm not joking this time. Come, let me show you."

Even though he wasn't entirely sure Zak wasn't pulling his leg, Sam took hold of Zak's hand and let him guide him to the edge of the platform.

"Do you trust me?" Zak whispered.

Sam nodded slowly, casting a cautious glance toward the pool. It was a hell of a long way down.

Zak undid Sam's robe and pushed the fabric back off his shoulders, kissing the bared skin and doing more to help Sam relax with his tender touch than any words could have managed.

"We really have to jump in there?" Sam asked. "How deep is it?"

"Deep enough that the dive won't kill us."

"Are you sure?"

"Trust me, Sam. I'd never do anything to hurt you."

Zak pulled Sam into his arms and kissed him thoroughly. Sam could feel himself being turned around and he tried not to think about how close they were to falling.

"Ready?" Zak asked breathlessly.

Sam looked behind him. Open air was just a half step away. He shook a little and clung to Zak tightly.

Zak sighed heavily. "We don't have to do this. We can go back the way we came if you want. You're still cured and I'll be with you the rest of your life, no matter how long or short it is."

"I don't like to think of you being stuck on Earth without me after I'm gone."

"That day is a long way off. We'll have many years together before then. Come on, let's go back and see how our mothers are getting along."

Sam's eyes widened. "No!"

"I think you need more time to prepare," Zak suggested, guiding Sam back toward the walkway. "We can always come back in the morning if you change your mind."

"I've not changed my mind now. I want to do this. I'm just scared."

"It's okay. I can't say I like the idea of jumping off the platform either, but it's the only way to do this."

"You're nervous too?"

"Yes. I don't mind you knowing I plan on keeping hold of your hand the whole time."

Sam gripped Zak's hand tightly. "Let's do it."

"You're sure?"

Sam turned back to the edge and took a few steady breaths. "I love you, Zak."

"I love you, too."

Together they leaped from the platform, aiming for the pool below.

Chapter Sixteen

The first surprise Sam got was when he didn't hit the water. Instead he found himself suspended in mid-air, just a dozen feet below the platform.

Zak still held his hand and he gave it a tight squeeze. "Is this supposed to happen?" Sam asked him.

"You ask me like I know. I've never joined with anyone before."

"Didn't you ask your mother what would happen?"

"No."

"Then how did you know we had to jump from the bloody platform?"

"That's the one thing everyone knows."

"And how long are we going to be stuck here like this?" Sam asked.

"Until our life forces are joined," Zak replied easily.

Sam wasn't exactly reassured. Below them the waters of the pool began to churn as a spontaneous whirlpool appeared in the center. The idea of falling into the pool became even more daunting, not that Sam could see they had any choice in the matter.

Suspended and helpless, Sam watched as the waters began to rise in a circular column surrounding them on all sides. The almost deafening rush of water echoed around him, becoming louder and louder as the waters closed in.

The spray of the water was warm on his skin and Sam held tightly to Zak as the rushing waters crashed over them, enclosing them completely before finally sucking them into the torrents.

Sam held onto Zak's hand for as long as he could, but it was an impossible task and he felt the fingers slip from his grasp as he struggled against the flow of the water. Was he going to drown here on this strange planet?

Choking and gasping, Sam tried to see which way was up, even though he wasn't sure that would even help at this point. He couldn't hold his breath for much longer and eventually the need to open his mouth to try to draw in air was too much and he gave in to the urge, swallowing the liquid he now realized wasn't water at all, but something strange and sweet he had never tasted before.

Just like water, though, he couldn't breathe with his lungs full of the liquid and he had no choice except to let the blackness take him over.

* * * *

Sam opened his eyes and looked up at the sky above him. "Am I dead?" he asked.

Zak replied from somewhere to his right. "Not for a long time yet."

"Are we joined now?"

"I think so."

"How can you tell for sure?"

"I'm not sure. I thought I'd feel different, but I feel the same as I always did. Bollocks."

Sam eased himself onto his side so he could face Zak. "Say that again."

"Huh?"

"You said bollocks. I've never heard you use that word before."

Zak looked at Sam and repeated the expletive. "I know what it means as well," he said with obvious surprise. "Can you understand what I'm saying?"

"Yes, of course," Sam replied.

"But I spoke in my own language."

"Are you sure?"

"Of course I'm sure. You understand my language and I seem to have a better grasp of English and... Sam, did you learn French in school?"

"Yes, why?"

"I understand a bit of that language too, or at least I think I do." Zak pulled his hearing aid from his ear. "Say something else."

"Like what? Can you even hear me without that in?"

"I can hear you just fine. I always could. This is a translator Darren invented to help me on Earth. Use a word that I won't have heard of, one I'd need the translator for."

"Like what?"

"I don't know. If it's something I'd have heard of the translator wouldn't do anything."

"Er, how about Pokémon?"

"Yes!" Zak punched the air triumphantly. "It's a game you used to play when you were laid up while you were ill, right?"

Sam nodded. "Yeah, I had way too much spare time on my hands. What would the translator have said about it?"

"Probably nothing. It's sort of a work in progress and I doubt Darren's spent much time playing Nintendo. It'd probably just ignore the word and make me look like a dunce for the gazillionth time."

Sam leaned forward to kiss Zak quickly. "You never looked like a dunce to me. So, does this mean you don't need the translator anymore?"

"It means it's not only our life forces that have joined, our knowledge is pooled as well. You know what I know and vice versa. Hopefully it works with the written word too, since I appear to have lost my glasses in the pool." Zak paused as something else appeared to occur to him. "That's how Eleanor always knew when I swore at her in my language."

"Why did you swear at her at all? She seems nice enough to me."

Zak looked rather ashamed of himself. "She is. I was just being a brat, as you would say."

"I guess you owe her an apology when we get back," Sam said.

Zak nodded in agreement and sat up. "We should get back to my mother. She'll be worried about us."

Sam opened his mouth to ask whether the joining could have hurt or even killed them. Before the question had even formed on his lips, he realized he already knew the answer. The reason Zak's mother, a healer, lived so close to the pool was because it took lives as frequently as it joined them. If a couple weren't meant to be together, they wouldn't be joined and would be lucky to survive the ordeal.

"How did you know?"

"That we were destined to be together?"

"Yes."

Zak kissed him softly before he answered. "When I thought I was going to lose you, I knew I would never love anyone else. The idea of living without you terrified me more than anything I've never known."

"And ten thousand years is a long time to—" Sam stalled mid-sentence as another tiny piece of new knowledge popped into his mind.

"Sam?"

"You should have told me!" Sam shouted. "Why didn't you tell me how this worked?"

"It makes no difference."

"Your life has been cut in half and you think it makes no difference?"

"It doesn't!"

Sam shook his head. "How did you think it would make me feel to discover the only reason I'll get to live so long is because I'm sharing your years? That every year extra of my life after the normal span is over is at the expense of my lover?"

"I didn't think you'd ever find out," Zak muttered half under his breath.

"How can you possibly be okay with this?"

Zak looked at Sam, his eyes shiny with tears. "When Darren told me he'd joined with Eleanor, a human like you, I didn't understand how he could do such a thing. He told me that five thousand years at the side of the one he loves was far better than ten thousand years on his own. When I knew I loved you, I finally realized what he meant. Ten thousand years without you at my side would be torture. When my people ask another to share their life with them, we mean it literally."

Sam felt ashamed of his harsh words and he threw himself into Zak's arms, hugging him and kissing him until they were interrupted once again by Zak's mother, who had clearly come to find them.

"I see you are once again enjoying the more physical aspects of your human body," she said with a teasing smile.

Zak and Sam pulled apart and got to their feet. Aristania passed them both fresh robes so they could change out of their second set of wet clothes for the day.

"Welcome to the family, Sam," Aristania said. "I'm pleased to be able to speak to you properly now. We have a small feast prepared in celebration of your joining."

"Mother..." Zak's tone held a note of warning.

"It's tradition," Aristania said, waving away his concerns. "It'll be a long time before we can all be together again in such a way. You wouldn't deprive your family of the chance to get to know your partner, would you?"

"I guess not. Just don't invite the *whole* family, please."

"Your father is probably here now. I believe he might have been coming with some of the members of his side of the family."

"Mother!"

Sam chuckled and linked his arm with Zak's. "Come on, it'll be fun. They can tell me all the embarrassing stories about you as a child, and I'll get to see your baby photos."

"We don't have photographs."

"None at all?"

"It's worse than that," Zak whispered. "We use holographic recording devices."

"I can't wait!" Sam teased.

Zak grimaced and Sam once again used his new-found knowledge to ascertain the problem.

"I don't care what you look like in your true form. I love you no matter what."

Zak breathed a sigh of barely concealed relief. "I know. I'm just very different in my native form."

"I know. I have your knowledge and know you look like some kind of overgrown Care Bear."

"I do *not* look like a cartoon bear!"

"Oh yes you do. Just like a giant Care Bear without the pretty picture on your tummy, but with fangs."

Zak laughed. "You don't sound very happy about my teeth. Are you afraid I'm going to suck your blood?"

"No."

"Don't worry—I've no taste for your blood, only your cock."

"I'm not sure I want those incisors near my dick."

Aristania turned to look at them. The expression on her face was one of confusion, but Sam didn't want to be the one to go through with her the finer points of the human male anatomy.

"What language are we speaking right now?" Sam asked.

"We're each speaking our own, though you can speak mine if you think about it first. Instinctively, you'll probably always speak in English first. Why do you ask?"

"Just wondering how much of the conversation your mother understands."

"Enough that we should probably change the subject."

Deciding it would be a good idea to take Zak's advice, Sam asked Zak about his family, and was somewhat surprised to discover that Zak was one of numerous half-siblings, his parents having produced many children with various different people.

"I grew up with my father and two of my half-brothers and a half-sister," Zak explained. "There wasn't really room for any more than that. My mother was raising six of my other half-siblings here, where there's quite a bit more space. Then there were others raised by other mothers and fathers too. I don't think I've even met all of them."

"That seems a strange set-up."

"Not to me. That's what happens here. To me it's strange for two people to raise a child together, like your parents did."

"And for the woman to actually carry the child," Sam said as he realized Zak had not seen a pregnant woman in close enough quarters to realize that is what she was.

Sam's comment seemed to send Zak's thoughts in a similar direction and he stumbled mid-step. "The fat woman in the line at the cinema was carrying a baby!" he exclaimed with sudden realization.

"Yeah, which is why she wasn't too happy with your loudly whispered comment to me about her getting so much food to eat during the film."

"Maybe I should track her down and apologize too."

Sam smiled. "I'm sure she's probably forgotten about your insult by now, and chances are you'll never see her again anyway."

"But if I do see her, I'll apologize."

"You do that," Sam said as they finally arrived at another platform, this one already lowered ready to take them up into the treetops once more.

"Are you ready to meet your new family?" Zak asked as the platform rose.

Sam's stomach flipped nervously. "I think so."

"Too late now," Zak whispered in his ear.

Sam turned to look behind him. A crowd of strange looking beings congregated in the entrance to what was, essentially, a tree house, albeit a very elaborate one. His mother was with them and she rushed forward as though they'd been separated for days.

"Are you all right?" she asked, checking Sam's limbs as though she feared he might have lost one. "You've been gone for hours. I was so worried when Aristania disappeared."

"She was just coming to check on us," Zak explained.

"I didn't know. I can't understand a word anyone is saying to me. She made it clear I should stay up here and I think she was trying to say she wouldn't be long, but other than that I was completely clueless."

"It didn't seem like hours to me," Zak said. Sam nodded his agreement.

"Time moves differently when you're in the sacred waters," Aristania explained. "I tried to convey that to Sam's mother, but I'm afraid the language barrier prevented my reassuring her."

"Well, we're back now," Sam said to his mother. "And we can translate for you."

"We?" His mother looked from him to Zak and back again.

"I can understand Zak's language now, and his English is now as fluent as ours."

"Come on," Zak said. "Let me introduce the two of you to some of the rest of the family."

Zak waved the crowd toward him. Sam half expected them to surge forward and sweep him into a dozen hugs. Instead they all hung back, nodding their greetings and giving Sam a wide berth. At first he thought maybe they just didn't like him very much, until he realized this was simply their way.

Thankfully for Sam, Zak had learned a great deal on his time on Earth about how much humans craved the touch of another—Zak remained by his side for the rest of the afternoon and long into the evening. One-armed hugs, light touches to any patch of bare skin he could reach, soft kisses stolen whenever their gazes met. In this alien environment, Sam found comfort from Zak's physical affection.

Sam's mother remained close by as well. She was quite out of her element being the only one there who couldn't speak the language. Nevertheless she kept a smile on her face and eagerly partook of the strange and exotic foods that had been prepared for the party. Zak and Sam took turns in translating for her and between the two of them they managed to insure that she knew what was happening throughout the evening.

"Everyone's so friendly," she said to Sam later in the evening.

"Of course they are," Sam replied with a smile. "These are Zak's people. Did you expect anything else?"

"I think humans are pretty friendly too," Zak said before kissing Sam on the lips. The soft, chaste kisses they shared became longer and harder as the evening progressed and this one was intense enough for Sam to feel it right down to his toes. He tried not to be embarrassed about Zak openly showing him such affection in front of so many strangers, all of whom clearly had no idea what a kiss was.

"What is this thing you keep doing with your mouth?" one of Zak's elderly female relatives asked.

Zak blushed and turned to the woman. "It's called a kiss."

"But why are you doing it? It seems rather odd to me to be putting your mouth on someone else."

Zak winked at Sam. "Seemed strange to me too the first time, but it didn't take me too long to discover how much fun it can be."

A few of the younger members of the family looked as though they might be open to the idea of kissing themselves, although the older generation continued to give them dubious glances. Sam didn't care what they thought about the way humans showed their love for each other, not so long as Zak remained by his side.

Sam did draw the line at Zak openly groping him at the table. Zak's people might not have a clue about cocks and erections, but his mother certainly did and she was sitting right at the other side of him.

"Don't tell me you don't like it," Zak whispered in his ear.

"The problem is I like it a bit too much for polite company," Sam hissed back. "Now stop it before I make a complete spectacle of myself."

"Maybe I want you to."

Sam's mother coughed loudly from his other side. "I think I'm going to retire for the night. It's been a long day and I didn't get any sleep on the journey here. Is there somewhere I can rest?"

Zak nodded and stopped teasing Sam long enough to escort her to a small room away from the noise of the party.

* * * *

Zak returned to the festivities, watching Sam from the doorway for several minutes, delighted to see him healthy and happy, he suspected for the first time since they had met.

Sam caught him staring and waved him over. "Is my mum okay?"

"She's fine, though I suspect she'll be relieved to be down on the ground again tomorrow. How are you doing?"

"Still trying to get used to speaking a new language," Sam admitted. "Is this what it was like for you having to learn English?"

"I had it pretty easy thanks to Darren. You'll get used to it, or actually you probably won't. Once we're back on Earth there won't be a need to speak my language."

"That's a shame."

"Why?"

"I kind of like it. There's a musical quality to it that gives me the shivers."

"Yeah?"

Sam leaned closer and pressed up against Zak. "I want to hear you whispering in my ear in your language while you make love to me."

Zak could feel Sam's erection pressing against his thigh and his own body responded to the heated touch. He was about to suggest slipping away from the party and finding somewhere private when his mother called the room to attention.

"A toast, to my son and his new partner Sam," she said as drinks were passed around to everyone. Once everyone had a glass, they raised them to Zak and Sam, congratulating them on their union and wishing them well for the future.

Zak and Sam clinked their glasses together. "To us."

They remained at the party for as long as they could, but it had been a long day for all of them. When Zak caught Sam yawning for the third time, he pulled him aside. "Let's find somewhere to sleep."

"Sleep?" Sam asked, his speech slightly slurred thanks to a rather odd effect on his human body of drinking the fruit juice they had raised a toast with. Zak, not having realized what would happen, had imbibed quite a bit of it himself. Thankfully his experience with alcohol on Earth had alerted him to what was happening and he had slowed down his drinking. Sam, on the other hand, was already too much under the influence and seemed to have a very low tolerance for the juice compared to Zak.

"You're too tired to do anything else," Zak replied as they said their goodnights to Zak's family and slipped from the room.

Zak led Sam down a walkway leading to one of the many guestrooms and they went inside, closing the door behind them.

"I hate to leave our party so soon," Zak said as he guided Sam toward the bed. "But you're just about dead on your feet here."

Sam fell back onto the bed and giggled loudly. "Fuck me."

"Tomorrow," Zak said. "You're too tired to get it up right now."

"I don't need to get it up, you do," Sam argued as he pulled Zak's robe open. "I like these clothes."

"Yeah, I can see that," Zak mumbled as he batted Sam's hands away.

"So easy to get to what I want with these."

Zak jumped back. "You need to sleep now."

"Need your cock more."

"You're drunk."

"I've only had that fruity thing."

"Yeah, and it's like you've been downing pints in the pub all evening." Zak pushed Sam back onto the mossy bed.

"Wanna go down on you," Sam said as he made another attempt at grabbing beneath Zak's robes.

"Sam..." Zak began to relent. Hell, if it was up to his dick it would already be in Sam's sweet mouth. The treacherous rod was already straining to get to his lover.

"Oh," Sam suddenly stopped his groping and looked at Zak with amusement.

"What?" Zak asked suspiciously.

"I just saw the memory of your first hard-on."

"Great!"

"You didn't even know what to do with it," Sam teased. "Let me show you, right now."

"I know now," Zak pointed out.

"But you don't know everything," Sam replied with another drunken giggle.

"I know everything you know," Zak reminded him.

"Gonna have to learn some new stuff then." Sam's fingers found their target and wrapped around the hot, hard flesh. "Let's start now."

"Urgh," Zak gurgled as he fell forward onto the bed. "Sam, you'll regret this in the morning."

Suddenly the grip on his cock slackened and Zak looked up at Sam. His mouth hung open and he let loose a loud snore. Zak chuckled and maneuvered them both into a comfortable position. He closed his eyes and soon joined Sam in sleep.

Chapter Seventeen

Zak woke to the sound of groaning and swearing. It appeared that Sam had something of a hangover. Thankfully, Zak was clear-headed and knew exactly where to find the cure for Sam. He slipped out of bed and went to track down his mother. She had anticipated their needs and met him halfway to the main house with a tray containing both breakfast and a herbal cure for Sam's headache.

When he got back to the guestroom, Sam was sat on the edge of the bed, clutching his head.

"What happened last night?" Sam asked.

"You had a bit of a reaction to one of our fruit juices," Zak explained. "You got quite drunk and very horny."

"Did I do anything stupid?"

"No, just amusing. At least until you passed out."

Sam crawled back onto the bed and curled up. "Wake me up when we need to leave for the spaceship."

Zak set down the tray and passed Sam the herbal drink. "Here, this should help."

"What is it?"

"An herbal cure for your hangover."

"Are you sure? How do you know I won't react to that in the same way?"

"Because my mother made it for you, and she knows what she's doing."

"But she's never had to make a hangover cure for a human before."

"Well, you can try this or continue to suffer."

Sam opened one eye and reached for the wooden beaker. Zak watched him carefully to make sure he drank the lot before taking the beaker from him and putting it to one side.

"Better?" he asked.

Sam sat up and smiled. "Wow, that's some hangover cure."

"I take it you're feeling more like yourself now?"

"Oh yes. I've never had a hangover before and I don't want one again if that's what they're like."

"Haven't you ever got drunk before?"

"No. I wasn't allowed to have alcohol while I was on the medication and before that I was too young to drink."

"You missed out on a lot of stuff while you were ill, didn't you?"

Sam nodded. "I try not to think about it much."

Zak didn't blame him. "From now on I'll make sure you get to experience all life on Earth has to offer."

"That could be quite expensive."

"Don't worry about that. We'll have plenty of time to save up for the more pricey stuff."

Sam laughed. "We could always take that hangover recipe back to Earth. We'd make a fortune."

"I doubt it would work on alcoholic hangovers," Zak admitted.

"Pity."

Zak sat down beside Sam and grinned. "Maybe now you're sober we can decide what to do today."

"We could stay in bed all day?" Sam suggested.

"Or I could show you what I can of my world, while I have the chance," Zak countered. "I suspect your mother might prefer a tour to hanging around up here waiting for us to finish shagging."

Sam laughed. "Your dad, Darren I mean, is going to freak out when he hears all the new words you've picked up from me."

"He's joined with Eleanor, so I'm sure he knew what would happen when we took the plunge."

"Do we have to…er…consummate our joining?"

"No. We're joined whether we have sex or not."

"Damn."

"There'll be plenty of time for us to be together later."

"But I want to fuck you right now."

Zak looked at Sam to see if he was serious. "You do? Last night you wanted to do it the other way round."

"Last night I was drunk. Now I know *exactly* what I want."

Sam pulled Zak down onto the bed with enough force to take his breath away.

"You seem to be a lot stronger than you were," Zak said. "I'm guessing you have something of my strength now too, at least while we're here on Trimmeron."

Sam climbed on top of Zak, straddling him with ease. "If your tour means as much walking as we did yesterday, it's a good job too."

Zak laughed as he tried to maneuver Sam underneath him without success. "Come on, lazy bones, let's get up and go find your mother."

Sam scowled down at him. "I really don't want to think about my mother when we're naked in bed."

"She'll be wondering where we are."

"I'm sure she knows what we're doing. I just don't want to think about the idea of her knowing we're having sex."

Zak finally moved Sam off him and climbed out of bed. He grabbed a robe for himself and tossed a second one to Sam.

Grumbling under his breath, Sam dressed and after they had eaten he let Zak drag him back to the main house where their mothers were eating a breakfast consisting of something that looked like blue grapefruit.

"I'm thinking of showing Sam around the area today," Zak said as he helped himself to a drink. "Would you like to come with us, Mrs Palmer?"

Sam's mother shook her head. "Call me Helen, please."

"Are you sure you don't want to see this world?" Sam asked. "It's a once in a lifetime opportunity."

She shook her head again. "I've had other amazing experiences, most of which I've shared with your father."

"I'm sorry he didn't want to come with us," Zak said. "He would have been most welcome."

"I know, but he was in shock. A little warning might have been helpful."

Zak smiled sadly. "You know as well as I do, he wouldn't have believed it."

She sighed and nodded in agreement. "I know. Now why don't you two go explore?"

"Are you sure?"

"Quite. If you could just explain to your mother what time I need to be at the spaceport with you, I'm sure she'll get me there before the ship leaves."

Zak did as she asked and a short while later they said a brief goodbye before setting out to explore. "I'm surprised your mother didn't want to spend more time with you," Sam commented after they were back on ground level.

"She has to work. I'd only be underfoot if I hung around here all day."

"But she may not get to see you again for hundreds of years."

"I've barely seen her in years anyway. My people aren't as big on emotional attachments as humans."

"It just seems so strange. She's your mother."

Zak pulled him to a stop and looked Sam in the eyes. "I know you're worrying about this, but please stop it. I'll be perfectly fine with you as well as Darren and Eleanor."

Sam sighed. "I know, but if my kid was going to be leaving—banished—forever I wouldn't be working all day. I'd be savoring every moment I had left."

"I know you would, as would I, now I know what it's like to have human feelings. But you have to understand that to my people these feelings are a waste of time because they don't feel them or understand them."

"And that includes sex, right?" Sam said.

Zak nodded. "I'm afraid so. But I promise I don't see sex as a waste of time. I happen to enjoy it very much indeed. My people don't know what they're missing."

"I enjoy it very much too." Sam turned and started walking backwards down the path. "We have a long trip back to Earth. Can you get us a private cabin on the ship?"

"What about your mum? Are you planning on leaving her behind or having her watch?"

"Idiot! She can have a cabin of her own too, or travel in the main passenger cabin like we did on the way here."

"Charming. I'm sure your mum would love to know she's being shunted down to second class so her son can get laid in first."

"Okay, a private cabin for her as well. Do you think you can get a couple or are they too expensive?"

"They aren't very expensive."

"So you can get them?"

"Maybe."

"Maybe? I'm not sure that's good enough. Perhaps you need some incentive."

Sam eased the soft fabric folds of his robe apart, revealing his bare chest.

"I'm getting convinced," Zak said.

Sam pulled the robe apart, showing Zak he wore nothing underneath. He fondled his cock, casually stroking the flesh. Zak was sorely tempted to forget about the tour and simply take Sam right there and then.

"A private cabin..." Sam whispered. "Just think what we could do during the tediously long trip back to Earth."

"Oh, I'm thinking."

"My cock, buried in your arse," Sam suggested. He fingered the tip and gathered up the cum from the slit, bringing it up to his lips and licking them clean. "Want a taste?"

Zak stepped forward, ready to drop to his knees and drink down everything Sam had to give him. Before he could get there, Sam quickly pulled his robes back into place and tied them closed. "A private cabin," he said firmly.

"You got it," Zak agreed, his voice husky. "Anything you want, Sam. Anything at all."

Sam smiled and turned back to the path. "A private cabin, with a nice big bed."

Zak nodded mutely, even though Sam couldn't see him. He had a feeling it was going to be a very long day, especially if Sam planned on teasing him like this. He was already hard as a rock and ready to blow and it was eighteen long hours until the ship left. He wished the days on Trimmeron weren't so long, though right now even an hour seemed like a lifetime.

* * * *

They explored hidden groves on the mountainside and the freshwater creek where Zak had learned to swim. Zak introduced Sam to the strangest of foods, which seemed exotic to Sam, even though they were actually quite common here. Sam's favorite was a sweet-tasting fruit that looked similar to a peach, yet tasted like the freshest of strawberries with a sprinkling of sugar. When Zak told him they never went bad, no matter how long they were left uneaten, Sam made him promise to bring a large supply back to Earth with them.

They wandered through the quaint little shops, buying clothes and knick-knacks to remind Zak of his home. Sam questioned whether they would be allowed to take the things back to Earth, but Zak assured him there was no such thing as export control and it wasn't like anyone on Earth would be checking their luggage when the spaceship dropped them off.

About an hour before they were due at the ship, Sam noticed they were being followed. Zak nodded that he had seen the security officer too.

"Making sure you don't miss the ship?" Sam asked.

"Yeah. They'll force me on it if I try to stay here."

"You're going to miss this place, aren't you?"

Zak kissed Sam quickly. "Not so long as I have you with me."

"I can't replace your entire world and all the people in it."

"You *are* my entire world," Zak replied, kissing Sam again, more slowly this time. "We should head to the spaceport."

"Is there anyone else you want to say goodbye to? We still have time."

"My parents will be waiting to see us off."

"Don't you have any friends here?"

"Not really. My siblings—the ones I grew up with and other Camyl'ons my age—are mostly off world in their own foster placements at the moment. Those who have finished their fostering were either at the party last night, or have been living off world since they reached maturity."

"You didn't see much of them after you began being fostered, did you?"

"No."

"It sounds very lonely. Did you make many friends on the planets you were fostered on?"

"A few, but no one I've remained in contact with since leaving."

"I'd hate that."

"It isn't so bad. It's what all my people do. Besides, if this wasn't the way we did things, I'd never have come to Earth and met you. As long as I have you, that's all I need."

Sam was sure the loss would hit Zak later, but for now he was just happy to be going home again.

* * * *

Goodbyes were said at the entrance to the craft and Sam was again struck by the stiff way Zak's parents held themselves, even as their son hugged them tightly as he secured their promises to visit him on Earth as soon as they could.

Sam exchanged a glance with his mother. "They love him very much," she said.

"How can you tell when they don't even hug him goodbye?"

"Because I've spent most of the day watching hologram recordings of your Zak. His mother has hours and hours of them, and as she showed me them, I could see the love she has for her son. She gave me one of the recordings and a device to play it on, and I could tell it was hard for her to part with it. But I think she wanted you and Zak to be able to show your children who he was as a child."

"Then why don't they show him they love him?"

"It's not their way, and until he came to Earth I'm sure it wasn't Zak's way either. I remember him being quite a reserved young man when you first brought him home. I'm sure he knows how much they love him."

When Zak pulled away from his parents he gave them one last kiss each — which his parents looked rather bemused over — before he beckoned Sam over.

"I know you will never come back here," Aristania said. "Your place is at Zakrynious' side and the elders have decreed his life is to be spent on Earth. I trust my son to your care and as soon as it is possible we will visit you. This is not a final goodbye."

Sam nodded, tears in his eyes for all that Zak was about to lose. Despite the reservations of Zak's people, Sam pulled Aristania into a hug. "I'll take care of him for you."

"I know you will."

Zak's father, even more reserved than his mother, stepped back when Sam turned his attention to him.

"My father doesn't do hugs," Zak said in English.

Sam understood and didn't try to approach the older man. "You will both be welcome in our home."

Zak's father nodded that he understood, but said nothing. Sam had already discovered Cor'shi was a man of few words.

Then they were being shepherded on board with their luggage and souvenirs, the door was closing behind them and they were being shown to their private rooms.

"Those security men are on board too," Sam whispered to Zak after the door had closed behind them. His mother was safely ensconced in her own room a few doors down the hall and they were alone in their quarters. He wasn't sure where the security men had disappeared to, but he had a feeling they weren't very far away.

"My banishment is to Earth," Zak reminded him. "They have to make sure that's where I go. Don't worry about them. They won't bother us in here."

Sam hoped that they didn't, and also that the metal door was thick enough to prevent them from hearing the two of them, because as soon as the ship was away from Trimmeron Sam intended to take Zak to bed, and he had no intention of letting him out of it until Earth was visible. If his mother knocked on the door he would have to feign deafness, though he suspected she knew full well what would be happening in their room and would keep her distance until they were in sight of Earth.

They sat in the window seat, eating a snack as they waited for the ship to depart.

"Oh shit!" Sam exclaimed as he looked across at their luggage.

"What's wrong?"

"I forgot to get lube." Sam jumped to his feet and bolted for the door. "Have we got time to go buy some before take-off?"

Zak didn't get up from his seat. "I've got it covered. Come back here and calm down."

"I don't remember seeing you buy any."

"I didn't. There's no such thing on Trimmeron. I brought it with me from Earth."

"Oh."

Zak patted his lap. "Come and sit here."

Sam did as Zak asked and straddled his boyfriend's thighs.

"That wasn't quite what I meant," Zak said.

"Wasn't it?" Sam inched closer so that their groins rubbed together. "I'm quite comfortable like this."

Zak pulled Sam down into a hot kiss. He slid one hand into Sam's robes, brushing his erection lightly before reaching around to grip his arse.

Sam continued to wriggle forward as he pushed Zak's robes aside.

Skin to skin, they kissed passionately, not even noticing when they left the atmosphere of Trimmeron. Zak caught a last glimpse of his home world in the window as the ship drew farther away, but he was too wrapped up in Sam to give it much more than a fleeting thought.

Their bodies became slick with sweat as they rocked together.

Sam nipped on Zak's ear. "I want to ride you," he whispered.

Zak was more than open to the suggestion and he pushed Sam off him just long enough to dig out the lube and return to his seat. Sam climbed back onto his lap and grabbed the lube from his hand.

"Let me," he said as he poured a healthy amount of lube into his hand and began to prepare himself first, then Zak.

"Ready?" Sam asked as he rose up on his knees.

Zak nodded. "Are you?"

Sam didn't answer with words. He grabbed Zak's erection and lined it up with his arse, sinking down onto the hot flesh swiftly and completely.

"Holy fuck!" Zak shouted. When they had made love before, he'd been so careful and so afraid of hurting his brave, yet weak Sam. He hadn't even thought it could feel this way. He couldn't imagine anything better. When Sam began to move, Zak was forced to take back that thought.

Sam rose up and sank down, his hands gripping Zak's shoulders tightly as he set a fast, almost desperate pace.

Outside, the stars twinkled as the ship continued its long journey. Sam took one of his hands from Zak's shoulder and placed it on the window. Zak held his gaze as Sam strained to reach the stars.

"Touch me," Sam begged.

Zak did as he asked and took hold of Sam's erection. It only took a single stroke to bring Sam to the brink. The tensing of Sam's arse as he climaxed caused Zak's own orgasm to follow swiftly and he came hot and hard buried inside Sam, holding him close, clinging to his lover and silently promising never to let him go.

* * * *

Sam and Zak moved from the window seat to the bed, where they curled up together to nap.

When they woke, Sam looked around the room and sighed softly.

"What's the matter?" Zak asked.

"Nothing, it's silly."

"What is?"

Sam shook his head and snuggled closer.

"I could torture the information out of you," Zak suggested. "Are you ticklish?"

"No."

"Liar." Zak tapped his temple. "I not only know you're ticklish, I know where too. Now what's bothering you?"

"I just thought being in space would be different. You know with less gravity and stuff like that."

"All our crafts have artificial gravity generated by the rotation."

"So I see. When I looked up at the stars and imagined what might be out there, all I wanted to do was travel into space like the astronauts I'd seen on television."

"You are traveling through space. You've gone farther than any of the Earth astronauts have."

Sam grinned. "I guess I have. I just would have liked to do the whole floating thing too."

"You just want everything, don't you?" Zak teased. He kissed Sam's neck, sucking hard and leaving a red mark. "I bet I can make you fly."

Sam's eyes sparkled with mischief. "And how would you manage that?"

"I have a few ideas."

"Me too," Sam replied.

Zak turned onto his side and ran his hand up Sam's thigh, lingering on the ticklish spot on his hip. There was open lust in his eyes as he gazed at Sam. "I want you to fuck me."

Sam thought for a moment he had misheard. "Really?"

Zak nodded as he caressed Sam's leg and arse. "I want to know what it feels like to have you inside me."

"You might not like it."

"We won't know unless we try."

"Are you sure?"

"You have my memories, the same as I have yours."

"I know, but what does that have to do with you wanting to bottom?"

"I have your memory of how it felt when we first screwed back on Earth."

Sam chuckled.

"What's so funny?"

"You are." Zak didn't seem to know the source of his amusement so Sam elaborated. "You've picked up all these wonderful new phrases for having sex from me, but you're completely avoiding the one I think is most appropriate."

"Oh. Which one is that?"

Sam leaned over and kissed Zak softly. "Making love," he replied.

Zak repeated the words back to him. "So many words for the same thing," he complained. "Even with all your knowledge in my head, I still can't get it right."

"I'll help you, and you can always use your own language as well now."

Zak pulled Sam into his arms and kissed him hard. "I love you," he said in his native tongue. Shivers went down Sam's spine as Zak held him close and whispered words of love in his ear. Sam suspected he would never grow tired of hearing Zak speak in his own language. Zak's voice turned him on like nothing ever had before. His arousal became more obvious and when his erection prodded Zak's stomach, his lover turned to get into position on his hands and knees on the mattress. Sam twisted round and knelt behind him. Zak blew him a kiss over his shoulder. "Go easy on my arse," he teased in English.

"Whose arse?" Sam asked as he stroked the round globes and slipped his fingers between the cheeks, spreading them gently apart. "I believe this is mine."

Zak shivered under his touch and when Sam bent down to lick at the hidden pucker, he only hesitated a moment before diving right in. Any brief worry of Zak freaking out because of where Sam shoved his tongue disappeared from his mind as he licked at the ring of muscle and pushed his tongue inside.

"Oooh," Zak groaned as he pushed back against Sam. His movements told Sam just how much he was enjoying this. Sam reached round and took Zak's cock in his hand. Yes, he was definitely into what Sam was doing to him, so much so that he might not make it to the main event. Sam moved his hand to the base of Zak's erection and squeezed, bringing Zak back down from his high for the moment.

"I never knew," Zak whimpered as Sam sat back on his heels.

Sam grabbed the lube and coated his fingers. He pushed the first one inside with ease, then a second.

"How could I not have known?" Zak asked as Sam carefully stretched him, preparing him to take the full length of his cock.

"It's not your fault," Sam said. "Different cultures and ways. I understand you better now."

"Me too," Zak replied. "The joining gives us that connection. I never want to lose it."

"You won't," Sam assured him. "I'm yours forever, remember."

Sam retrieved the lube once more and slicked himself up. Then he slowly pushed his way home.

"Forever," Zak cried.

Together, the two of them moved in a near perfect rhythm, urging each other to the edge over and over again, until finally they could hold off no longer. They tumbled over the precipice, collapsing onto the mattress in a sticky, sweaty heap.

"I need a shower," Sam grumbled.

"You didn't ask for a shower in here," Zak reminded him. "You wanted private and a bed."

Sam looked up at Zak sleepily. Zak grinned back at him. "It's across the hall."

Closing his eyes, Sam wrapped himself round Zak. "You're such a tease."

Zak's chuckle rumbled in his chest and Sam smiled at the sound. "How long until we arrive home?" he asked.

Zak stroked Sam's hair as he replied. "I'm already home," he said.

Chapter Eighteen

Sam waited in the main passenger cabin, glued to the window, during the approach to Earth. His mother stood at his side, as transfixed as he was.

"It looks so small," Sam said.

"Compared to many inhabited worlds, it is." Zak wrapped his arms around Sam's waist and pulled him close. "Tell me what you're thinking."

"That it's such a tiny planet to have to spend the rest of your long life on."

"*Our* long life," Zak reminded him.

"But—"

"Oh," Zak said. "I didn't think. You do know you can go explore the universe if you want to, right?"

Sam twisted round in Zak's arms. "Do you really think I'd go traveling the galaxy without you?"

"I don't want to tie you to Earth, not if you want to see more of what's out there."

"I'm not going anywhere."

Zak gave an audible sigh of relief. "I don't know what I'd have done if you wanted to leave me."

"That's never going to happen. I just wonder if you'll be happy on one world, when before you had so many open to you."

"It doesn't matter what other planets are out there, Earth is my home now. It's the only world I'll know from this point forward. I'm happy because I know you'll be facing the future with me."

Sam realized that Zak was content with the choice he had made. Secure in the knowledge, he finally made peace with his own guilt. When they reached Earth it would be the start of a new life for both of them.

"Have you decided what you're going to tell Lucy about where you've been?" Sam's mother asked.

"No," Sam replied with a sigh and another wave of guilt. "She's not stupid so the explanation will have to be good. Maybe I could say I've been at some research center where they found a miracle cure for me."

"A research center that sells toys?" his mother reminded him. Sam had purchased a cuddy toy for Lucy. The plush animal was a representation of a greedy, friendly snuppet and had quickly caught his eye. If they hadn't been so averse to living indoors, Sam might have been tempted to ask Zak if he could bring a live one back to Earth.

Sam turned to Zak. "What would she say if I told her the truth?"

"I don't know."

"What if she doesn't believe me? I didn't believe you when you tried to explain where you were from and who you were."

Zak pulled from his pocket the Trimmeron equivalent of a mobile phone. "I haven't sent a message to Darren yet. How about I ask him to bring

Lucy to the drop-off point when he comes with your father?"

Sam hugged Zak tight as he nodded his agreement to the suggestion. "She'll have to believe the evidence of her own eyes, just like I did."

The ship drew closer to Earth, Zak contacted Darren and a short time later the craft finally entered the atmosphere. Sam wondered if anyone was watching through a telescope as he once had, seeing the UFO and speculating about its origin.

Finally the craft arrived on the hillside where Zak's foster parents and Sam's father waited for them. Lucy stood with them, her jaw hanging open in shock. Sam knew there would be a lot of explaining to come over the following days. Not right now, though. First he needed to go to his father.

"Are you mad at me?" he asked.

"Why would I be?" his father replied as he pulled him into a tight hug.

"I know you didn't want me to go."

"I was scared, but I've spent quite a bit of time with Zak's foster parents the last couple of days and I understand better now."

Sam turned to the Johnsons and saw them hugging Zak tightly.

Mrs Palmer ran to meet her husband, who released Sam so that he could sweep her up into his arms and kiss her soundly. "You should have come with us," she said. "It was amazing and our Sam's well again."

"So I see, darling," Sam's father replied with a smile. "I'm sure you'll both have a lot to tell me over the next few days, but the most important thing is our son's health and I'm overjoyed to see him well again after all this time."

The Johnsons joined them and Darren looked to Zak with questions of his own. "What happened?" he asked. "Did you get caught?"

"Yes, as soon as we'd gone through decontamination. I shouldn't have expected to pass under the radar."

"I see you've picked up a new Earth phrase. Does that mean what I think it does?"

Zak nodded. "We're joined and we'll be staying on Earth from now on."

"Exile?"

"Yes."

"How long for?"

"The rest of my life."

Darren cringed. "That's a little harsh in the circumstances."

"As the elders pointed out to me, there were other options that didn't involve my leaving Earth. I chose to ignore those and this is the result."

"And you're going to be okay with spending the next five thousand years here?"

Zak looked at Sam with love. "Yeah, you're all stuck with me from now on." He turned back to Darren and grinned wickedly. "Dad."

Darren smiled back. "I haven't had anyone call me that for a long time."

"Or ever," Eleanor interrupted. "It was always Father or Papa, if I recall correctly."

"Too weird?" Zak asked.

"Not at all. I'd be proud to call you my son."

Eleanor pulled Zak into a hug. "And I'm equally happy to have you as a permanent part of this family."

Zak held her tightly and whispered a thank you in her ear. "Thanks, Mum."

Darren ruffled his hair and waved Sam over. "Welcome to the family, Sam."

Eleanor hugged Sam as well and repeated Darren's welcome.

"How did your parents take the news?" Eleanor asked Zak. "I imagine they'll miss you a lot."

"They'll visit when they can," Zak replied. "It'll be difficult for a while, though. Neither of them has a human form."

"I'm sorry. I know you'll miss them too."

"It's okay. I'll see them again one day, and in the meantime I have you two."

"We know we can't take the place of your real parents," Eleanor said. "We wouldn't even want to try."

Zak wrapped his arms round her again. "My mother and father will visit when they can. You and Darren are my mum and dad, though, and that will never change, not even when I'm a thousand years old, or when my biological parents are able to come to Earth."

Eleanor turned away to dab at her eyes with a handkerchief.

In the joy of the various reunions it then became apparent that someone had been forgotten.

"Sam!" Lucy shouted above the noise of everyone talking at once as she stomped across the hillside. "Have you got something you want to tell me?"

Sam looked at Lucy, who stopped and pointed at the spaceship still hovering a few inches above the ground behind them while the security officers unloaded their luggage.

"Like what?" Sam asked. "I'd have thought everything was pretty obvious."

"Obvious!" Lucy screeched. "You're supposed to be bedridden, dying in fact, then you disappear for three days and return here on a fucking spaceship, looking healthy as a horse."

"See, it *is* obvious," Sam replied with a wide grin.

"Sam!"

"It's like this, you see," Sam said as he pulled Lucy into a one-armed hug. "My boyfriend's an alien."

Lucy looked back at him with wide eyes. "That explains *so* much."

Zak gave her a shove in the shoulder, only realizing too late that he still had some residual strength from his visit home. "Sorry, I forget my own strength sometimes."

"Ouch," Lucy complained as she rubbed her arm.

Behind them the security officers finished removing their luggage and re-boarded the craft.

"How much stuff did you bring back?" Darren asked. "You left with only the clothes you were wearing."

"Speaking of which," Lucy interrupted, "why are you wearing dresses?"

"They're robes," Zak said, smoothing out his own dark blue garment with pride. "And not much, Darren. I just wanted a few reminders of home."

"We bought presents for you all, too," Sam added.

Lucy's eyes lit up as though it were Christmas morning. "Presents?"

Sam dug into one of the bags and pulled out the stuffed toy. "Here you go," he said.

"You bought me a toy?" Lucy asked. "I'm not twelve anymore."

Sam held onto the stuffed animal. "Never mind then. I'm sure I can find someone else who'll like him."

Lucy leaped forward and pulled the toy from his hands. "I didn't say I didn't want him. Does he have a name?"

"You give him one," Sam suggested as he pulled out more gifts for the others, including his mother, even though she had been there with them. By the time he and Zak were done passing them out, the spaceship was ready to depart once more.

They watched it leave the Earth, knowing that Zak would never be able to do so again. Tears slid down his cheeks and Sam brushed them aside, first with his fingers, then kissing them away with his lips.

"We're going to be all right," he assured him quietly.

"I know."

"Let's go home," Darren said. "It's late and you all have college in the morning."

"College?" Sam asked. "Are you joking? We're not even going to get a single day off?"

"Not now you're well," Darren replied. "Come on, there's no point lingering here any longer. You all need to be up bright and early in the morning."

"You too," Eleanor reminded him with a smile. "It wouldn't do for the History teacher to be falling asleep in class."

"Can I stay with Sam tonight?" Zak asked.

"I'm not sure that's a good idea," Sam's mother replied.

"Mum!"

"You need to get some sleep. I'm fairly sure you didn't get much during the journey back to Earth."

"What do you mean?" Sam's father asked.

"Sam insisted on a private cabin with Zak and I'm sure you don't need me to tell you what they were doing in there."

"And you let them?"

"Sam's nineteen years old. It's not like I could stop him."

"But still, you don't have to encourage them. Sam has college in the morning. He needs to rest."

"I know, which is why I said I didn't think it was a good idea for Zak to spend the night."

Sam had heard enough. "Mum, I'll be spending the rest of my life with Zak. I don't want to spend another night apart from him."

Sam's father huffed and shook his head. "You're talking as though you're married."

"We're joined in the way of Zak's people," Sam replied. "It's far more permanent than just a marriage, although I suspect in a few years' time we might do the whole marriage thing as well."

"I don't understand," Sam's father said.

Sam looked at his mother pleadingly. "Mum."

Mrs Palmer sighed and turned to her husband. "You don't need to understand. Perhaps we just have to accept that Sam is a grown man now and capable of making his own choices about his life. Thanks to Zak, he'll have the full life we always wanted for him. We should give him the chance to live it."

She turned to Zak and gave him a warm smile. "You can come and stay with Sam any time you like." She looked up at the sky in the direction the spaceship had gone. "I suspect I couldn't stop you even if I wanted to. Just let Sam get some sleep when he needs to be up early in the morning, please."

"I need sleep just as much as he does," Zak reminded her. "I'm human now and likely to remain so for many years to come."

Sam laughed and slipped his hand into Zak's robes. "My plans for you tonight don't include much sleep," he teased in a voice low enough for only Zak to hear.

Arm in arm, Zak and Sam descended the hill to the waiting cars with Darren and Eleanor and Sam's parents close behind them. . Lucy trailed behind, casting longing glances at the sky.

In the back of the car Sam and Zak kissed and cuddled for the whole journey home.

"The look on Lucy's face when you told her your boyfriend was an alien was priceless," Zak said.

"Well, it's true."

"I guess, though, from my point of view, you're the alien."

"Human or alien, it makes no difference to how much I love you," Sam said.

"Me neither," Zak replied. "I'll love you, my human alien boyfriend, for the rest of our lives."

About the Author

I live in England, in a quaint little village that time doesn't seem to have touched. No, wait a minute—that's the retirement biography. Right now I am in England in a medium sized town that no one has ever heard of, so I won't bore you with the details. Keeping me company are numerous sexy men. I just wish that they weren't all inside my head.

L.M. Brown loves to hear from readers. You can find her contact information, website details and author profile page at http://www.totallybound.com.